Lia Riley writes offbeat New [...] the last [...]
University of Montana-Missoula, she [...]
[...]ckpack, overconfidence and a terrible sense of direction. She counts
shooting vodka with a Ukranian mechanic in Antarctica, sipping yerba
mate with gauchos in Chile and swilling XXXX with station hands in
[...]tback Australia among her accomplishments.

[...] British literature fanatic at heart, Lia considers Mr Darcy and Edward
[...]chester as her fictional boyfriends. Her very patient husband doesn't
r[...]d. Much. When not torturing heroes (because c'mon, who doesn't
l[...]e a good tortured hero?), Lia herds unruly chickens, camps, beach
c[...]bs, daydreams about as-of-yet unwritten books, wades through a
m[...]e-high TBR pile and schemes yet another trip. Right now, Icelandic
h[...] springs and Scottish castles sound mighty fine.

Sh[...] and her family live mostly in Northern California.

Visit Lia Riley online:
www.liariley.com
www.facebook.com/authorliariley
www.twitter.com/LiaRileyWrites

Praise for Lia Riley:

'*Upside Down* gave me all the feels. Romantic and poignant, the journey
[...] love and acceptance lingers long after the book is closed' Jennifer L.
Armentrout/J. Lynn, #1 *New York Times* bestselling author

'*Upside Down* is a refreshing and heartfelt New Adult contemporary
romance' *USA Today*

'Fresh, sexy, and romantic, *Upside Down* will leave you wanting more.
Lia Riley is an incredible new talent and not to be missed!' Kristen
Callihan, award-winning author of the Darkest London series

'This story shows just how frightening it is to let yourself fall in love
and be that vulnerable' *Heroes & Heartbreakers*

'*Upside Down* is one of those books I wish I could read for the first time
again . . . it's beautiful, heart-wrenching and something that everyone
needs to read for themselves' *Books by Migs*

'Lia Riley turned my emotions *Upside Down* with this book! Fast
paced, electric and sweetly emotional!' Tracy Wolff, *New York Times*

The OFF THE MAP series
by Lia Riley:

Upside Down
Sideswiped
Inside Out

inside OUT

AN OFF THE MAP NOVEL
Book Three

LIA RILEY

piatkus

PIATKUS

First published in the US in 2014 by Forever Romance, an imprint of
Grand Central Publishing, a division of Hachette Book Group, Inc.
First published in Great Britain in 2014 by Piatkus
This paperback edition published in 2015 by Piatkus

1 3 5 7 9 10 8 6 4 2

A CIP catalogue record for this book
is available from the British Library.

ISBN 978-0-349-40754-8

Printed and bound in Great Britain by
Clays Ltd, St Ives plc

Papers used by Piatkus are from well-managed forests
and other responsible sources.

MIX
Paper from
responsible sources
FSC
www.fsc.org   FSC® C104740

Piatkus
An imprint of
Little, Brown Book Group
Carmelite House
50 Victoria Embankment
London EC4Y 0DZ

An Hachette UK Company
www.hachette.co.uk

www.piatkus.co.uk

For Nick, because HEA, matey

ACKNOWLEDGMENTS

Where to begin? I am in many people's debts. Emily Sylvan Kim, many thanks for being my agent and friend. I value your insight and perspective more than you'll ever know. Team Forever, all the love! Glitter rocket launch to Lauren Plude and Madeleine Colavita—you worked editorial magic on this book and it's SO MUCH BETTER because of your involvement. Elizabeth Turner, this cover is my hands-down favorite (shhhhh, don't tell the others). Jamie Snider, sorry for burning your eyes with my errors; you are a copyediting dream. Kristine Fuangtharnthip, for being a subsidiary-rights diva. Marissa Sangiacomo, I require a Jurassic Park laboratory to genetically engineer a Thankliasaurous for you and your amazing support.

Piatkus and Hachette Australia, you guys have been fab. In particular, tackle hugs to Grace Menary-Winefield; you're a delightful partner and your e-mails always brighten my day.

Jennifer Blackwood and Jennifer Ryan, ladies, thank you. I need far better words than these poor eight letters, but they are meant from the bottom of my heart. Beyond grateful, my appreciation is a messy thing.

Lots more people to thank:

Don Hood and Gabrielle Covers, cutest cover models in history? Yes, I think so.

Jennifer Armentrout, for a killer cover blurb. Also, Melissa West, Kristen Callihan, and Cindi Madsen for generously reading and giving such nice love notes.

Megan Taddonio, for dishing on the Peace Corps and sharing truly horrific worm stories.

My writing peeps, for keeping me as sane as possible.

To the readers/bloggers who've walked with Talia and Bran for three books: you took a chance, and it means the world. (Sil, Chester the Chinchilla is yours, if you want him, but careful what you wish for.)

My friends and family, for (mostly) putting up with me and (mostly) accepting that I'm often stuck in a plot rabbit hole and unbelievably crappy at returning phone calls. I am alive and do think of you often.

J & B for choosing me as your mama; it's my life's privilege.

Nick, for continuing to teach me what a real HEA means. It's not always easy, but it's so damn worth it. I love you.

inside out

inside
OUT

The world breaks everyone and afterward many are strong at the broken places.

—Ernest Hemingway

I
TALIA

"**M**zungu!" The village kids can't get enough of daring each other to spy through my mud hut's single window. "*Mzuuuuuuuuuuuungu.*" They break into convulsive giggles.

Mzungu means "white person" in Chichewa, Malawi's national language. Since arriving in Africa as a Peace Corps volunteer, the word follows me throughout the day. It's taken the last three months in-country not to cringe at the term and to accept the truth stamped in my pigment. I am an outsider.

"Hey, *mzungu*!"

I uncurl from child's pose, push off the straw mat, and wince. Yoga therapy isn't doing much in the way of curing my abdominal crampage. Still, I manage to make it to the front door. "Boo!"

My barefoot students scream with delight and scamper toward the shoreline. Lake Malawi is one of the largest in Africa. Mozambique is on the other side, the distant hills obscured by a hazy plume, as if the water itself is on fire. Weird. Maybe it's going to rain? The wet season is long over, but this country is nothing if not unpredictable. I swipe my hand over my brow. The noonday sun is pleasant, nowhere near hot enough to justify this much sweat. My mouth fills with saliva.

Great, here we go again.

I shuffle around the side of the hut to the latrine in the back-yard. Eighteen steps. Twenty at most. I enter just in time, thighs quivering from the effort and get quietly sick for the fourth time today. How the hell did I catch a stomach bug? I'm anal-retentive about using a water filter and iodine purification tablets. Still, there was clearly a breach in my defenses. Local families have taken turns hosting me for dinner since my arrival in a sweet, generous gesture of hospitality. It doesn't take an expert in cross-cultural communi-cation to know it's impolite to drill people on their household food preparation methods if you're the guest of honor. No matter how teeth-clenchingly bad you want to do exactly that.

My stomach roils, painful to the point that a moan escapes. I brace my hands on my knees and pant. What if parasitic worms are hatching in my stomach or burrowing through my liver?

I step back outside and linger in the mango shade, resisting the urge to scratch the welts speckling my arms. Mosquitos are eating me alive, so taking antimalaria medication has become an accept-able nightly ritual. The dark cloud over the lake drifts closer. A trio of local women skirt my yard, swinging plastic utility buckets and handwoven baskets. Their lively chatter makes me miss my best friends, Sunny and Beth. I wonder what they're up to? I've avoided their e-mails since Bran and I got back together.

To say my girls aren't Bran's biggest fans is a rather epic under-statement. In December he morphed into a Big Bad Wolf, shredded my heart as easy as a straw house. After a cooling-off period—literally, in his case, as he joined a marine activist organization dedicated to preventing illegal whaling in the Antarctic—he wrote an apology and asked for an opportunity to set things right.

I've seen Bran at his worst, know his best, and somehow reconcile the two. He's broody, unpredictable, and twists my brain like a pretzel, but my love for him isn't a word, it's an involuntary, instinctive act, like breathing. Our connection is the one thing I trust in this far-too-fragile world. Despite his past wounds, he craves heart-peace as much, maybe even more, than I do. When he finally mustered the guts to step up and show courage, there was no way I could say good-bye. I want to believe he has a chance for happiness.

I need to trust we both do.

The women notice my stare and slow their pace, brows knitting. I haven't been at my site for long. The mandatory three-month volunteer training in the capital, Lilongwe, wrapped a few weeks ago and here I am. Home. Sort of. The village is quietly assessing me, and I'm not exactly putting my best foot forward. This is my fifth day out sick from teaching. Hardly a confidence booster.

I raise a hand in forced cheer that the women return with shy waves. Once they're safely out of sight I double over. It takes serious diaphragmatic breathing before I can hobble back toward the refuge of my bed.

The doorway provides a welcome rest stop. Fussy stomach aside, I'm glad I came to Africa, right? I mean, in a great many ways, I've gotten exactly what I wanted—plus a guy who loves me and has come around to accepting that long-distance relationships don't mean doom. I should be happy. Am I happy? Sometimes.

And sometimes not.

When we get what we want, the dream becomes real, and

real life is never perfect. I realize some of my naïveté in joining the Peace Corps. I think deep down inside I believed something would shift in me, in my life, like I'd wake one morning and it would be a whole new world. Instead, I'm still me. Just here, in Africa, teaching English as a Second Language in a rural school.

I adore my students and their sweet enthusiasm, but my assigned project? Not so much. ESL isn't the work I want to ultimately pursue. I'm no grammar whiz and get nervous talking in front of groups. Every morning I wake hoping today is the day where I'll stop second-guessing and start to thrive, and every night I fall asleep uncertain, listening to the mosquitoes' unrelenting hum.

I was having a twentysomething crisis when I applied to the program, running from big decisions on what to do with my life. The Peace Corps was one of many pipe dreams that floated around during my undergrad, and in a desperate Kermit flail I snatched the opportunity with both hands.

My Facebook feed was littered with people from my major squee-ing over cool jobs, internships, or graduate school admittance, and I wanted in on that success. The Peace Corps seemed like the perfect way to have an adventure while advancing my future. But just because an idea is good in theory, doesn't mean it works in practice. Now that I'm actually here, I can't shake the sense that I'm an imposter, a fraud. Am I an intrepid development worker, decked in head-to-toe khaki and ready for anything? Not by a long shot. I should like being here more. And I don't.

God, whatever, Talia. Pack away the tiny violin.

Got to stick it out because ultimately, I like the stigma of failing even less.

I shuffle to the plastic milk crate beside my bed. Inside are seven crinkled pieces of paper. I've printed each of Bran's e-mails. Our communication has been infrequent. He's not able to write much from the ship, and I have to hitch to Lilongwe to source reliable Internet access.

When we met in Australia during my exchange, I tried to convince myself he was a little adventure, some uncomplicated fun. The first time he touched me, my body went, "Ah, okay, *there* we go." Bran revealed himself to be the exact puzzle piece I was missing. I ease onto my bed and peer at the first dog-eared page.

Hey Darling,

Wait a second. My eyelids twitch and vision goes wonky. I blink to refocus.

Hey Darling,

What the hell? Words skitter in every direction. I try to give chase, but my eyes no longer operate in unison. Pain explodes behind my sockets like a hand grenade, radiating through my temples. I've never had a migraine hit with such sudden intensity. Maybe I'm dehydrated from throwing up so much. I fold Bran's note and tuck it inside my shirt, next to my heart as my stomach constricts again, from agony and mounting dread.

At one point or another, most everyone confronts debilitating sickness during their Peace Corps placement—practically a part of the job description. The other volunteers regard parasitic worms as an African red badge of courage. More power to them. Me? I'm content to play the coward.

The doctor blew off my vague symptoms—fatigue and nausea—at the health clinic this morning. He was nice enough, but the halls were filled with villagers suffering from actual diseases like AIDS and hepatitis. Part of me wanted to demand tests, but I've freaked out about so many phantom ailments in my life that a little voice kept whispering, *What if the sensations are all in your head*? Guess I should have rethought the decision to go home and sleep it off, because this feels different. Something is wrong, really amiss. I'm the Boy Who Cried Wolf who's finally in the shit.

Cracks fang over the hut's interior walls like sudden lightning. I hunch forward, dig my elbows into my thighs, and count them off in sets of two. I hate that I keep doing this but it's the only way to ground myself. I never sought appropriate cognitive therapy and stopped taking my medication because mental health issues posed clearance challenges to becoming a Peace Corps volunteer.

Sucking it up and trying harder, my two plans for coping, don't seem very successful.

I miss a crack. Shit. Now I have to go back and begin counting all over.

No! Not again. Stop it. Just…stop.

I wrench my gaze from the wall and push down the dread that if I don't count exactly right something terrible will happen. I breathe deep but the anxiety lingers, debating whether or not to grow into an angry monster or slink into my subconscious.

Better not to give it a choice. I need a mission, something to distract me. A tin pail sits in the corner of my makeshift kitchen, a grandiose title for what amounts to a table, rickety stool, and bowl of cassava. I don't have a shower—no indoor plumbing—but a sponge bath might be the thing. I'm exhausted, restless, and jittery from discomfort. Fresh air makes everything better, right? I shuffle over, lift the handle, and muster the energy to trudge outside to the nearby water pump, wincing in the sunlight.

Meghan, my neighbor, fellow Peace Corps volunteer and HIV-prevention coordinator at the clinic, is there chatting with other women in fluent Chichewa. Her upper lip is too heavy for the lower, and dips into an almost-but-not-quite frown at my approach. Pretty sure she secretly believes I'm a total wimp ass.

I take my place at the end of the line and hope it doesn't look like my intestines are contorting themselves in figure-eight knots.

Meghan adjusts the intricately patterned *chitenje* that wraps her otherwise thick black hair. These large fabric squares are cheap everyday wear in the village, and I have one tied around my T-shirt and skirt as a sarong. Envy constricts my rib cage as she balances a full-to-the-brim bucket on the top of her head with casual ease. I've yet to manage such coordination, much to the merriment of the village women. It takes time to learn the little skills that make you invisible. Aside from the glaring difference of my pigment, I'm still too conspicuous, prone to making a dozen tiny errors in a single outing. The teasing is never mean, but sometimes yeah, I wish I fit in better.

"What's up, T?" Meghan's sharp gaze takes my measure. *Can the newbie hack it?*

Africa has the highest volunteer dropout rate of any continent. There is no way I'm going to early terminate. The very idea is taboo. I gave the Peace Corps a two-year commitment. Here's my big chance to show my spirit animal isn't a scaredy-cat. I'm a girl with fortitude, spunk, and great gobs of mettle—need to dig deep and see this decision through to the flip side.

Meghan tries to hold my gaze, but I don't let her. Instead, I study the ant marching across my bare foot. "Sorry if I seem pathetic—can't kick this stupid bug."

She's from North Carolina, and her twenty-four-month contract finishes next month. After Malawi, she hopes to score an aid position elsewhere in the sub-Sahara.

"Got to keep on keeping on." Meghan squints at the horizon with a thousand-mile stare.

"Doing my best." I take a deep breath through my nose. When people toss out those empty phrases, I kind of want to pat their heads, with a hammer.

"Sorry I haven't checked in on you since getting back."

She's going all hot and heavy with one of the two clinic doctors, a lanky Médecins Sans Frontières guy from Belgium. They recently returned from a week-long getaway climbing Mount Mulanje in the country's south. She's strong and independent, exactly who I aspire to be. In the meantime, I crave her approval. I want her to think the best of me, even if that means hiding my worst. The fear. The uncertainty. The moments of sheer I-don't-know-what-I'm-doing terror.

I'm unable to speak as my abdominal knot tightens.

"Stomach again?"

A wave of dizziness tumbles over me. I nod, not trusting my voice.

"That sucks. Hey, we all get sick. Adjustment takes time. I had giardia three times my first year. Lost almost twenty pounds."

My own clothes hang off my frame. I've never been big, but I sported more curves than not. These days my body's flat, battening down the hatches, reduced to two dimensions.

"Lay low and rest."

"I'll brew a pot of ginger tea," I mumble. "There's a bag left over from my last care package."

"Good idea, and, hey, if you need anything, you know where to find me."

Wow. Quick, someone nominate my fake smile for a Best Supporting Oscar, because Meghan's answering grin makes it seem like I'm not this big bummer.

Screams rise from the direction of the lake—the good kind—laughter harmonizing with joyful squeals. The women around me abandon the pump and race to the water. The weird cloud from earlier hits the shore, breaks apart in furious wings and discordant buzzing. Flies. Everywhere. I swat my face, strength depleting faster than bathwater spiraling into a drain. Women and children swing any available container through the air, collecting as many insects as possible. No one passes up free protein in this region.

Pain lances my side, an invisible knife ripping through my torso. What's happening to me? No way anyone hears my useless squeak. My heart flops in an erratic rhythm as blue stars cascade past in a psychedelic stream. Flies hum in my ear, crawl over the back of my neck.

Help. Please. I need help.

My knees hit the soil and I pitch forward, grappling the *Hey Darling* letter pressed to my heart. Bran is my sanctuary. If anything will keep me lucid, centered, it's him, but the blackness pulls too strong, rushes through my brain like a wild flood, dragging me into the shadows.

———

"Talia? Talia, can you hear me?" That deep rumble could be mistaken for calm and in control until the under-the-breath expletive. "Fucking hell."

My fingers slide to a narrow wrist, a leanly muscular forearm.

A flash of recognition. I read this body like braille. A name flits past, a firefly illuminating the darkness, but only for a split second.

Bran?

No way. That's impossible. He's on a boat in the Southern Ocean.

Can a hallucination brush warm lips across the side of my neck? I blindly clutch the strong fingers laced with mine, trace faint calluses. This contact is an anchor, holds me fast, safe from the hungry dark.

Bran.

A wordless prayer. For a moment, wild joy blooms. He's so close. I want to tell him I'm within reach, but speech is impossible, like trying to smile without a mouth.

"Don't bother bloody dying because I swear to God I'll hunt you down and drag you back."

Hot tears burn beneath my lids at the familiar accent. I clutch each word, his presence a safe harbor.

"Sir, I'm going to ask you again, step away from the patient."

"Not a chance," he snaps.

"I need to check her hematocrit and switch out the quinine." A woman speaks with unfamiliar cadence, hitting each consonant hard like she wields a hammer.

"Work around me." The pressure on my hand increases. "Don't worry, I've got you, sweetheart."

There's a sharp prick on my upper arm. Nothing compared to the pain dimly lingering in my memory's recesses—a skull-wrenching, chromosomal-deep agony.

Strange to feel so numb now.

There's an unpleasant tang to the air—disposable rubber gloves and disinfectant? A hospital smell. Claustrophobic panic wells in my throat.

"Damn it, Talia. Wake up." The fierce order is a tether out of this limbo.

My eyes open.

Bright. Ouch. Holy shit. Way too bright.

Everything is blurry without my contacts.

A hospital bed rail.

A shadowy outline of an IV pole.

A face.

The only face.

Bran moves with a suddenness that makes my heart skip. My limbs become aware of their existence, nerves revving to life. "You're back," he says quietly, firmly, as if there's to be no arguing the point.

He looks like someone pushed to the brink and kicked off the side. Thick, dark hair juts in odd angles. His eyes are chipped jade, but bloodshot and wild, ringed by sleepless bruises. A muscle bunches deep in his jaw, nearly undetectable beneath the days-old scruff.

He's beautiful.

But he's not supposed to be here.

2

BRAN

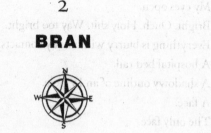

The hills outside the hospital window slump like the hinds of tired elephants. Maybe I shouldn't stare into the sun, but fuck it, Talia shouldn't be in that bed behind me either. People look with their eyes, but there's so much we can't see. Venus at noon. Dark matter. Malaria ravaging red blood cells inside the girl I love. She coughs, stirring. She's returned to herself in slow inches throughout the afternoon.

"Am I dying?"

"No!" I spin around and move to her bedside. She stares up with haunted, overlarge eyes. Jesus, when I pull her into my arms she's a fragile layer of skin pulled tight over sharp bones. "Don't you talk like that, hear me? Don't even think like that."

"Okay."

I hate her uncertainty. I hate even more that I'm not bloody Prince Charming, who can bestow a bullshit Disney kiss and transform this sterile room into happy-ever-after land. Nothing I do will make bugger all difference to the parasites swimming through her veins. Goddamn it though, I want—need—to punch something hard and furious until it breaks beneath my split and shattered knuckles.

Anything to avoid feeling this impotence.

Instead, I hold my breath a beat and exhale slow as if I'm a pillar of strength or whatever. "You're going to be fine. I'm here and won't let anything bad happen." I close my eyes so she won't see my brave words are nothing but a grand illusion. I have to front unshakable confidence that she's going to get better, that way she'll believe it too. I smooth back her hair and step away, fighting the urge to hold on tighter and face the wall to regroup.

"Where are we?" She asks, still groggy.

"Pretoria."

I can hear the wheels crank inside her head. "Wait, South Africa?"

"The Peace Corps medical officer based out of Malawi determined you were in critical condition and ordered you a medevac flight here. It's the region's most advanced intensive care unit." I turn back and lace my fingers with hers. "You've been in a coma for three days."

Three days? Her lips move but nothing comes out. "How…" She swallows and pushes herself to a half sit. "How are you even here?"

"Bad weather ended our Antarctic season early. We came to New Zealand to resupply before setting out for Japan and the dolphin hunts. The moment we hit dry land I took off in search of a calling card. When I got through on the number you'd sent, some Peace Corps volunteer, Meghan, answered your mobile phone from a truck carrying you to the hospital. She kept me in the loop after that. You…" I break off, my voice getting gruff. The past seventy-two hours have been the most goddamn awful in my life, and I've had some shithouse days. "You weren't able to speak."

Her bottom lip quivers—just once—and stills like nothing ever happened. When it comes to this girl, I don't miss a trick. "Don't worry, okay?" She laces her fingers with mine. "I—I can't have you scared."

"I know."

She's afraid she won't make it.

I'm freaked the fuck out that I'll lose her.

"You got this, Captain." All I've got are nothing words and optimistic posturing. I'd beg, plunder, and steal to swap places. Me for her. It should be me in that bed. I can bear anything except watching her scared and suffering.

"I'm thirsty," Talia whispers.

"Coming right up." I jump at the chance to do something, no matter how small. "Here we go." I snatch a cup off the otherwise empty food tray and lift it to her mouth.

"Sir." The grumpiest of the ICU nurses strides into the room without a preliminary knock. "You need to consult with a doctor before giving the patient anything."

"Why don't you find one for me? I want her checked over while she's awake."

Grumps flashes me her best stink eye.

She clearly doesn't know whom she's dealing with. I level her a look of my own. "Her name is Talia, and I'm giving her the water."

"We'll see about that." The nurse beats a retreat with a disapproving headshake.

"Don't worry about her." I bend and kiss Talia's clammy forehead. "Drink."

"Maybe I shouldn't."

"Yeah, you should." I press the cup's rim with insistence against her lips, and water splashes her chin.

"Jesus, Bran. Here, give that to me." She jerks the cup from my grasp and takes a sip. "There. Yum. Yum."

"Want something else? Orange juice? I'll shake down the nurses."

"No, please, don't bother anyone."

"I don't mind."

"You're driving everyone crazy here, huh?"

"Probably." I drag a plastic chair next to the bed. "But I don't care about them. I care about you."

"A three-day coma?" She rocks her head back against the pillow. "Where are my parents?"

"You didn't list your mom on the emergency contact record. As far as I've tracked down, she's on some silent meditation retreat. Your dad was taking his university class on a field trip in the mountains. No cell reception over the weekend, but I got through to him this morning."

"Thank you. God, I hate making him worry." She covers her face with hands the same stark white as her hospital gown. "It's crazy not to remember anything. It's like someone erased my hard drive."

I don't tell her that I have the opposite problem. I can recall every last detail in high-definition.

I remember the sucker punch in my solar plexus when I learned a mosquito infected Talia with malaria's worst strain, *plasmodium falciparum*.

I remember the total helplessness as within hours the illness tore through her, deteriorating into cerebral malaria.

I remember how she slipped into a coma while I waited at the airport to board my Emirates red-eye to Johannesburg.

By the time I found my seat I was praying. By praying I mean raging, begging, and pleading with the universe. When the wheels broke contact with the tarmac, I didn't even shudder. My entreaties coalesced into a single, ceaseless mantra: *not her, not her, not her.*

I offered to sacrifice myself or any of the random people surrounding me.

Take me, not her.

Take them, not her.

First, my father catches dengue fever and now Talia gets malaria. Can someone get on annihilating all bloody mosquitoes?

"None of this makes any sense." Talia drops her head against the pillow. "I took tetracycline every day and slept under a freaking mosquito net."

"The medical files from Malawi mentioned you'd had a stomach bug."

"Yes, but what's that got to do—"

"Didn't keep much down?"

"No, nothing."

"Including antimalarials."

Her face contorts into an expression of horror. "Oh my God. I'm such an idiot. It was like I hadn't even been taking them." She seems to almost say something else but changes her mind.

"What is it?"

"I don't know."

"You do."

"It's just…" she worries her bottom lip. "It's just that coming to Africa was supposed to be my big chance to prove my mettle, show what I was made of. It's early April, Bran. I lasted four months. Four pathetic months." Her heart rate monitor beeps, accelerating. "It's laughable really. Look at me, I'm a bona fide joke."

"More water."

She gives the proffered cup a halfhearted backhand. "No, please."

"I'm serious, you need to drink, rehydrate yourself." *Get better, stronger, less goddamn pale.*

The green digital numbers show her pulse rate passes into the high nineties.

"I know." Her tone is testy.

Pulse is in the low hundreds.

Hasn't she suffered enough? "Talia, calm down, sweetheart."

"Gah, I'm trying." She drills her fingers into the side of her temples and takes a ragged breath.

"Try harder!" I snarl, pissed at myself, the unfairness of the world.

For a moment, shocked silence reigns.

Her mouth quirks in amusement. "You don't scare me, buddy."

There's a staccato knock on the door frame, and a doctor enters, the same one who poked in earlier, low-key and to the point. Talia will be comfortable with him. I resume my position by the window, cross my arms, and watch the cars below. He conducts a quick examination, his hands light on her body.

As much as I'm grateful, I hate that there's another man who can actually do something useful for her.

The doctor straightens. "It's early days, but so far there doesn't appear to be neurological damage. We'll keep running tests, but for now, I'd say you're a lucky lady."

"Really?" The hope in her small voice flays my defenses.

"She's going to be okay?" I mutter, wanting to believe it so bad that my teeth hurt.

"Things are optimistic. Waking from the coma means the worst is over, but she's not out of the woods yet."

All the tension I'd held in my body rushes out in a tsunami-sized wave.

The second the doctor exits, I pounce forward and wrap my arms around her thighs.

"Tighter," she whispers, burying her fingers into my hair. "Please, hold me tighter."

"You're going to be okay. Thank Christ." I can't hold back the violent shudders.

"Do you . . . do you really think so?"

"I know so, Captain."

Her face softens when I use my favorite nickname for her. "Looks like you're stuck with me."

I force down the sob clawing from my throat. "I missed you so much."

"Really?"

"This is something you doubt?"

"No." The faintest smile. "But that doesn't mean I don't want to hear all about it."

"The crew got so sick of listening about you that I resorted to conversing with animals." I sit up and wipe my nose with the back of my hand. "Whales make pretty good confidants actually. The cetacean world must be buzzing with rumors of the hottest teacher in Africa."

"You told whales about me?"

"Yes. Is that a problem?"

The skin around her eyes crinkles. She gives her head a bashful shake.

"And don't forget about birds, love." I stand and lean forward, peppering kisses along her forehead. "The albatross were sympathetic. They mate for life. They understood where I was coming from."

"But wait." She stiffens. "You're supposed to stay on with the Sea Alliance for the northern hemisphere summer, go to Japan and all that?"

"I quit to come here."

"But…but…" She fumbles her words. "Bran, the dolphin drive hunts—"

"The crew leaders have time to sort staffing. This is where I need to be. I'm in exactly the right place."

"I'm sorry." She squeezes her eyes shut. "I made you quit."

"You didn't make me do anything. I wanted to be here, more than anything."

"I'm weak." Her hands form two fists. "You had to give up everything we fought for because I couldn't hack it."

"Come on, sweetheart." I don't like how she's breathing, too quick and ragged. "Hang in there."

"Don't feed me some motivational kitten poster line." She rolls away, giving me her back.

Oh, hell no. "We're not playing this game, Talia."

"What?"

"The one where you refuse to tell me what the hell you're thinking."

She grimaces. "Trust me, you don't want the all-access pass to my head."

"Let me be the judge of that."

Two lines appear between her brows. "I'm tired."

"Talia."

"Think what I've just been through. This is a lot to process. Besides, I feel like shit, smell like shit, and I haven't seen a mirror yet, but I'm a hundred percent certain I look even worse."

"You're you. Perfect."

"Enough. Stop talking."

"I'm dead serious." I bend to kiss her.

"No." She claps a hand over her mouth. "I haven't brushed my teeth."

"I crossed an ocean for you. Do you think I give two fucks?" I gently pry back her fingers.

"But I—"

My lips cover hers, and then she's returning my kiss with such fierceness my breath stops and I hear colors. Our bodies entwine and I inhale deep like she's a wildflower that blooms only for me as my fingers trace the delicate skin beneath her jaw. Each touch is an ode, a secret sonnet, composed just for her. I caress in lieu of words, want to give her myself, at my most basic—my body—blood and bones. Everything, every damn thing I am, or ever will be, is hers now and forever.

She breaks away, panting. "Holy hallelujah."

"Yeah."

"That was—"

"I know."

"Hang on, I need a minute." Her lids flutter closed. "Saying I missed you doesn't come close. I require you."

"I'm familiar with the feeling."

She sniffles.

"Here's what's going to happen." I smooth back a wisp of her hair. "You work on getting better and I'll figure out how to take you home. Back to your family."

Her irises darken to a bitter coffee brown. "What family?"

"Your dad. When we spoke this morning he made it clear he wants you to recover in California."

"God, I can't believe I'm doing this to him." She gives a low, keening moan. "I'm the only kid he's got left. My whole point should be not to cause unnecessary stress."

"He's fine. No worries."

Fine if you leave out the part where he broke down, got himself under control, and then sounded like he'd enjoy nothing more than strangling me. I get it, this situation is stressful and he's far away. Scott Stolfi didn't get into specifics, but apparently his girlfriend is also in the hospital over in California. The bloke is getting slammed on all sides. Did my reassurances that I'd move heaven and earth for his daughter endear me to him?

That would be a no.

I have no idea where in the hell Talia's mother is, and I can't leave. This is all on you and here's how it's gonna go, bud. You bring her back where she belongs, and then get the hell out of her life. You've hurt her enough. End of story.

"Fine, huh?" Talia's look is skeptical. "He tends toward overprotective."

"That's good. He should. You deserve that."

From both of us.

"Please don't make me out to be this delicate thing."

"Says the girl fresh from a coma and down ten kilos. Should I try to track down your mom?"

"No."

"Are you—"

"Maybe you should go and wrangle some orange juice."

"You're not getting off that easy."

"What about my blood sugar. I'm so weak and all."

Fucking hell.

She fiddles with her sheet. "Look, I really am so sorry about the Sea Alliance."

"There's nothing to apologize for. The mission was a success. We located the whalers and their factory ship, put a complete halt to the hunting season. The only thing left to do was ramp our media efforts. Dial up the PR machine."

Yeah, the mission was a success, except for me being a bloody idiot and damn near ruining everything.

I halt the bitter thought at the gate. *You shall not pass.*

The accident, the whole shit storm from that final day at sea is over and done with. This, right here, getting Talia better, that's what's important.

"You were supposed to stay on until October."

"Did you honestly think anything would keep me from you?" I straighten and push up my sleeves.

She won't stop moving her hands, fidgeting with the sheets, her hair. "What am I going to do? I mean, early terminating? Quitting the Peace Corps? Everyone expects me to be in Africa for two more years."

"Wait—what? You can't think to stay."

She nodded. "During volunteer training they said that if we get sick, like really sick, we can go home, recuperate, and return within forty-five days. It's called medical separation."

I want to respond with no way in hell, but that's the type of reaction that drove us apart in December. I scuff my Vans against the linoleum and clear my throat. "What are you thinking?"

"I'm not sure." She exhales hard. "It's a lot to consider."

"For now keep the focus on recovering. Rally."

"Rally?" She crinkles her nose like the word smells. "That's what I always do. Throw on a happy face and march into the world."

"I know, I know you do."

"But the world doesn't care." Her voice cuts like a knife-edge. "No matter what I seem to do, how much effort I make, the world face punches me and says 'Screw you, Talia.'"

This time when she rolls away, I let her go. Give her some breathing space. It can't be easy, getting so sick and then finding out you've been in a fucking coma. She's all over the place, moods crashing together like waves after a storm. She survived a nightmare. If she needs time and space to settle, that's a small thing for me to give. I'm taking her home. Afterward, I'm not sure what will happen. No matter what her dad says, I'm not leaving her side unless she tells me to.

It's not that I don't give Scott Stolfi respect for wanting me out of Talia's life. If I were her father, I'd want me gone too. I'm the wanker who hurt his little girl.

And somewhere inside me, the guy who did that is still there.

I love Talia more than my next breath, and I hurt her worse than any enemy.

I can't do that again.

Her place is in the sun. Am I enough to bring her there, or will I only cock this up and make everything worse? Drag her down a slippery slope the way I always manage to do despite my best intentions.

My whole life I've fought love.

Fuck it.

Some battles deserve to be lost.

3

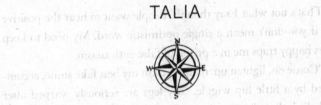

TALIA

Time blurs in a hospital until it becomes impossible to determine a break between days; each hour gloms to the next. I would never have described myself as a person who can't bear to sit still, but after two weeks cooped up in a bed, resting except for physical therapy appointments and the occasional bathroom visit, my muscles plead for movement.

That's why when Bran disappears after we land in San Francisco Airport, I shake my head when he returns pushing a wheelchair. "Nope. Nuh-uh. No way, home-skillet."

"Sit." He dials up his signature fierce look, the one that causes our fellow disembarking passengers to rubberneck. Fine, so his eyes are insanely mesmerizing. And when he channels his force of will through them? Yeah, a mite hard to resist, but if I yield to his overprotective act by an inch, he'll overwhelm me with attention. My weakness needs to end. We're here, segued in this unexpected California detour. It's important to face this moment on my own two feet—literally.

"I'm walking."

"Captain."

I stiffen even though he doesn't mean anything mocking by his old endearment for me. I'm not Captain America. My only super-power is a bottomless ability to fail.

That's not what I say though. People want to hear the positive even if you don't mean a single optimistic word. My need to keep others happy traps me in a prison of false enthusiasm.

"Come on, lighten up, mate." I flash my best fake smile, accompanied by a little hip wiggle. "My legs are seriously warped after that hellish flight."

"I'm not messing around." He slouches and balls his fists into the pockets of his red zip-up hoodie. With Bran there is a negative correlation between his lazy demeanor and his ratcheting temper.

"I can't ride in that thing." My legs wobble in a silent counterpoint.

His eyes hood and his cheeks twitch like he's biting the insides. He's been doing that a lot lately.

The atmosphere quivers. Tension drapes an invisible arm around my shoulders, the cool weight sending pinpricks down my spine. The silence spreads until it's huge, restless, an uncaged lion pacing in the corner.

What if—what if we can't work? What if he's going to find out that I'm nothing but a——

"Let me in, please, sweetheart. I'm trying…I've…I've got to do something to help." His soft accent falters, pushes over my rising panic like so many dominoes.

I hurl into the stupid chair with a heavy sigh like a total brat.

"Thank you." A stiff little word but I know what it costs him, trying to keep control. Maybe his exhausting confidence of late is an act too. What if he's faking as hard as I am? He might not know what to do either.

I'm not sure whether the idea is reassuring or terrifying.

I want to be the kick-ass girlfriend, spurring my guy on to chase impossible dreams. Instead, I'm sick, weak, and terrified that maybe malaria's not done with me.

Who was I when I first fell in love with Bran?

A person who had courage to stare down an unfeasible situation and say, *Sure, I'm up for the challenge*.

Who was I when Bran threw himself at me like a wounded animal, all claws, abandonment fear, spit, and fang?

A person who accepted that the moon has two sides, light and dark.

Who am I now?

I feel like a lost soul rocking in the corner, fresh out of ideas.

Bran pushes me through the long line until it's our turn at the passport desk.

"How long do you plan to stay in the United States?" The customs official glances from Bran's face to his passport photo and back again.

My stomach squirms like a writhing snake. We've avoided any discussion about future plans, focused instead on the short term. I had to accept the reality that I couldn't return to the Peace Corps, even with the medical separation. I was too sick, too shattered. Our discussions about the logistics of leaving Africa were easier to concentrate on than the looming issue of what *we* were going to do with each other. I treated the topic like an abandoned lot, filled with weeds and rusting cars, a subject to walk past and pretend to ignore.

Now a stranger is forcing the issue.

"Until this one gets better." Bran cocks his head in my direction.

The woman scoots forward, peers at me with a faint frown. "May I see proof of a return ticket, sir?"

Bran digs out the photocopy of his itinerary. When we bought the tickets, he had to borrow money from his dad. He hasn't said much, but I know the fact must eat at him. Add another bitter drop to my guilt bucket—soon it's going to overflow.

"You're on a temporary tourist visa." The customs agent flips the passport to a blank page and stamps with obvious relish. "You have three months, starting now."

Here we go again.

Visa issues.

Ticking clocks.

People imagine international romance is excitement, hot accents, and adventure. They don't want to hear about the bureaucratic drudgery that threatens to harden the arteries of even the most passionate hearts.

I thought I was going somewhere.

Nope.

I am an idiot Icarus who flew too close to the sun.

Bran leans forward, his lips hover an inch from my ear, his breath a hot caress on my cool skin. "You okay, Captain?"

"Fine."

"What are you thinking, thinker?"

"I'm just sitting here, a sitter."

We roll past an American flag overhanging a framed photo of the president. His smile seems smug, as if to say, *You really thought you'd get away?*

Yes, sir. I kind of did.

"We're up next." Bran hands a final customs form to yet another officer who waves us toward big silver doors that open and shut like gnashing teeth. On the other side is California. I can't shake the disorienting sense we're heading in the wrong direction.

"Ready?"

Nope.

Bran crossed an ocean for me. I have to find the way out of this black swamp, but I'm manacled to an island of self-doubt, and the tide is rising.

The airport terminal is vast and airy. Eager strangers lean over the metal partition rail, clutch flowers and balloons. One familiar gaze locks with mine. I know those eyes—the same ones that stare back from the mirror.

"Peanut." Dad slides under the rail, drops to one knee, and hugs me close. I wrap my arms around his broad shoulders and breathe in the spicy aftershave he's worn since my earliest childhood memory.

"Daddy." When I was little he was the one I went to when things broke. Toys. Shoelaces. He could always fix it. Growing up is a bitch at stripping away the illusions of safety. He couldn't fix my sister's broken body, his disintegrating marriage, or my defective brain.

He's a good guy, my dad, one of the best, but he can't fix everything.

"I'm so sorry," I whisper.

"For what?"

"This mess." I wanted to become something amazing and fell on my face.

"You're going to be fine, Peanut. Just fine. Let's get you home."

I start to push myself to standing, when Bran rests his hand on my shoulder.

Dad snaps to attention, his gaze narrowing over the top of my head. He'd focused on me so hard it was like he forgot Bran was there.

Dad rises to his full six foot five inches. Bran's got his own sexy, lean muscular thing going on, but he's also around seven inches shorter.

"Mr. Stolfi," he says, stiffly.

Mr.?

"Brandon."

I swivel my head between them. They wear identical tight expressions. I swear, the same muscle twitches in the same place in their upper jaws.

"Um, what is going on?"

They both blink.

Dad speaks first. "Right, let's get a move on. I'll push. You got the bags, bud?"

"Yes, sir." Bran's words are polite but the tone is curt.

Their dynamic is all kinds of odd. It's not that they were best friends last year when Bran came to visit, but they didn't circle each other like posturing alpha dogs.

We head from the airport to the parking complex. The last time I was here, I was flying to Africa, uncertain, nervous about the next steps and ruined about Bran, but still, I had hope. Now my heart is a cracked, barren landscape.

Bran throws our two bags into the rusty blue 4Runner Dad's driven since forever. He's from working-class Monterey roots. Mom's family comes from the opposite side of the peninsula in cashed-up Carmel. Dad earned decent money working for the U.S. Geological Survey and wanted to support us without all the old money bling. When Mom bailed, she ran straight back to the wealth. She currently freeloads full-time at my grandparents' second home, an estate on the Hawaiian island of Kauai.

Did she know I was in the hospital? There's no way I can ask Dad if they've spoken. I'm too afraid the answer might confirm my suspicions she's really disowned me.

Dad maneuvers us out of the sprawling parking complex and into traffic. I almost call out that we're going the wrong way. Santa Cruz is the other direction. Instead, he turns east, toward Sacramento where he lives with his new girlfriend—Jessie—a postdoc in wildlife biology at UC Davis. I've never met the woman, only seen an e-mailed picture. They met while working as guest lecturers on an expedition cruise ship in the North Atlantic last year. She's leggy and blond, like Mom, except trade yoga wear for quick-dry pants and a Patagonia fleece.

I fiddle with the door lock. "How are you liking Sacramento?"

"Good. Real good." Dad nods. "Great."

"Excellent."

He clears his throat. "I've got you booked in to see a top-notch doctor in Davis tomorrow."

"Dad, I was at a perfectly good hospital in South Africa." I swallow the edge from my tone, use the same neutral tone I've been giving Bran. All is great. No worries. Nothing to see here. "I received the best care possible."

"I'm your father and want you checked from head to toe."

I slide my hand to unlock and click the seat belt again for the fourth time, and it still doesn't feel right. After a second, Bran takes my hand. The muscles in my stomach quiver; no butterflies today, only hornets. The urge to shake free from his grip and redo the buckle sets my teeth on edge.

After Pippa died, my health anxieties spiraled out of control, and seeking reassurance from doctors became a crutch. I'd go in with some phantom ailment, a lingering headache or mysterious twinge. They'd check me out and say I was fine. To get more sleep. Drink less coffee. I'd feel better for an hour, a day, a week, and then some other sensation would flare and start the whole gong show off again.

Things are different now. There's no brief reassurance to be had in getting a checkup. Before departing Pretoria, the South African doctor informed me the strain of malaria I contracted could lead to all sorts of unanticipated repercussions like cerebral venous sinus thrombosis or cortical infarcts. Fancy-sounding names for terrifying outcomes like strokes or blood clots.

My prognosis is that I could be totally healthy...or a ticking time bomb.

The uncertainty is throttling any hope for inner calm, eats at me with a termite-like tenacity, leaves behind nothing but rot and carnage. None of my usual coping strategies are working. It's like I'm sliding down a steep embankment, digging nails in the soil but the earth keeps crumbling.

Is my heart beating harder? Yeah, crap, my pulse is racing, but I'm just sitting here, not exerting myself. Is this panic or a sign malaria has destroyed my internal organs? Bran gives my hand another squeeze and his tenderness makes me want to cry.

We zoom past a billboard for medical marijuana. Hey, I wonder...not a bad idea, might help take the edge off—

"Earth to Talia, have you heard a word I said?" Dad says.

"Sorry, I didn't sleep much on the plane." I snap to, realizing I'm unconsciously running my tongue along my teeth, counting each incisor, bicuspid, and molar. *Losing it, you are losing it.*

He meets my gaze in the rearview mirror. "You're going to the doctor tomorrow. Not up for debate."

"Fine." I cross my arms and glare out the window. Soulless strip malls fly past the window. Up on the hill, white concrete words spell out: SOUTH SAN FRANCISCO THE INDUSTRIAL CITY.

"You miss the ocean?" I ask after a few minutes of awkward silence. My dad has always lived and breathed surfing. His new home is in a Sacramento suburb smack-dab in central California.

He shrugs. "There's a river."

"O-kay. Not exactly the same though, is it?"

"I paddleboard most days."

Looks like I'm not the only one making the best of a subpar situation.

"And the new job, you liking that too?" He's adjunct faculty in the geology department at Sacramento State.

"The job? Good, good. Yeah, it's all good."

I fumble for my water bottle and flip off the cap, take a long sip. "How does Jessie feel, you know, about us staying?"

"She's excited to meet you."

The fact he doesn't include Bran in that statement doesn't escape my Spidey sense. They haven't spoken a word to each other since we left the airport. We turn onto the Bay Bridge. Dad taps a beat on the steering wheel the whole way across.

He only does that when he's stressed.

Crap.

Despite his words to the contrary, I am a hassle. He's set up a new life, a sweet little love nest, and got stuck with a twentysome-thing failure-to-launch daughter barging in with her boyfriend.

"Hey, so I've got news." He rumples his thick hair, the first traces of gray at the temples. He didn't have those the last time I saw him. "Jessie and I . . ."

I'm hit with an unexpected adrenaline rush. Oh God, he's

getting married. Got to suck it up, be happy or at least fake it convincingly.

I lean into Bran and he wraps his hand around the back of my neck, responds with a hard squeeze that delivers a dose of courage straight to my heart.

"We... well, we're..."

"Hey, it's cool. You can share the good news. I really am happy you met someone." That sounded believable, I think.

He cracks his neck. "It's hard to actually say the words out loud."

"Let me make this easier, are congratulations in order?"

"Yeah. I guess so. Wait, I mean, yes! They are. Of course, they are. Jessie's expecting."

My mind blanks and the muscles in my back go rigid. I should grasp something important, but I'm all thumbs and fumbles. "She's expecting what?"

"A baby, Peanut." His smile is all goofy and sheepish.

"Wait, what?" Does not compute. "A baby baby? Like a baby human?"

"I sure hope so." Dad does his forced nervous laugh. The one that goes *heh-heh-heh* like a misfiring machine gun.

My thoughts slam together like a bunch of cars hitting an unexpected red light. A baby, a new child? "But you're like what..." I do the calculation. "Forty-eight?"

"Yep."

"And Jessie? Oh, God, she's not my age is she?" She was kind of blurry in the photo. My dad is my dad, but I'm uncomfortably well aware that my friends harbored little crushes on him over the years. He's a big, strapping man who tells dumb jokes and surfs like a beast.

"No! What do you think of me? She's thirty-five."

"Oh." My throat reopens. "So kinda old."

"Not really." He laughs for real this time.

"Does she have other kids?"

"No."

"Psycho ex?"

"She's never been married."

"Former lesbian?"

"None of the above. She's been focused on her career. This...
uh...development is a surprise for both of us."

All of us.

"Are you okay, Peanut?"

"When's the big unveil?" I ask faintly.

"August." He shifts in his seat. "She's seven months along."

I do the math. *What the actual fuck?* "Wait, did you know
before I left for Africa?"

"Uh, yes, but only for a few weeks. I—we—didn't want to say
anything while it was still so early."

"Are you kidding—"

"It was touch and go the first trimester and a half...lots of
intermittent bleeding." He coughs into his fist. "After that, you and
I played phone tag—"

"You left messages that said, 'Call me sometime,' not 'I'm having a kid.' Jesus, Dad." Bran's bones must be made from rubber
because I'm crushing his hand and he's not even flinching.

"You were busy getting set up—"

"I had time for this—"

"Jessie's been unwell. She was hospitalized for a blood pressure
issue right before you contracted malaria. She's better, but gets easily tired."

"I can't believe I didn't know. Not cool. Not cool at all."

"Listen, if you want to be upset, take it out on me. Jessie's still got the whatchamacallit, morning sickness."

Dad gets supremely uncomfortable with woman issues. He lived in a house with three of us. We'd synchronize periods and he'd double down on the surf sessions. I'm pretty sure he suffered a minor heart attack the one time Pippa requested that he pick up tampons.

Bran keeps squeezing my fingers in a steady rhythm.

I'm here. I'm here. I'm here.

Gratitude. Love. Weak, white words we assign to feelings so vast and profound that it's absurd we even bother to try.

I grip Bran's hand harder, hanging on like I'm in a movie, playing the person dangling off a bridge.

Please, please, please don't let me go, even if it would be the easier option.

4

BRAN

Talia and I stand before the kitchen sink in strained silence. I give her a sideways glance. Her cheekbones are sharply defined and her under-eye circles are the only color on her face. The doctors say she's fine physically. Mentally? Not good.

Jessie and Scott are walking the dogs. My offer to wash the dinner dishes wasn't a brownnose move for her dad's benefit; nothing will alter his opinion of me. Scott set his mind before I arrived—probably since Talia fled Tasmania—that my future isn't with his daughter.

"Sorry, bud," Scott had said the day we arrived, two weeks ago. He appeared in the doorway as I dropped our bags in the guest bedroom that was halfway to becoming a nursery. "You're downstairs. House rules. Jessie set you up with clean sheets on the veranda." In other words, the heatless porch on the front of the house with a lumpy futon and litter box.

After he left, I stared at Talia. "What the hell? We're sleeping apart?"

She'd shrugged, avoiding my eyes. "He's a lapsed Catholic."

"I'm not religious, no idea what that means."

"He turns his morality on and off like a tap." She gave a heavy sigh and sat on the edge of the bed. "Roll with it for now, okay? He'll come around soon."

I've been in Sacra-fucking-mento for fourteen days, and Scott hasn't come anywhere. The bloke bides his time, thinks our relationship is a lost cause.

He underestimates me. When it comes to Talia, I'm not mucking around anymore. The real reason I roped her into dish duty tonight was to force her into the same room with me, alone, for more than five seconds.

She's hiding in her room up to twenty hours a day. "Catching up on sleep" is her official line but she's not a goddamn koala. The current situation needs to change, starting with her telling Daddy to piss off. I've given parental respect a fair go, but enough is enough. Scott is sailing the river of denial, pretending Talia's fine, just needs space and alone time.

He doesn't grasp it's a bad idea for Talia to be by herself, hour after hour, avoiding the world. Last night I woke to the sound of her locking and relocking the front door. By the time I came out of the veranda, she'd dashed up the stairs. I'm not sure what to say because I don't want to cause her more anxiety or continue to feed the OCD cycle. This morning, all the electronics in the kitchen were unplugged. If only I could hold her, talk, maybe it would make a difference, help her feel like she's not facing this alone, but I can't even get close.

A cat brushes my leg and I almost leap from my skin. This is the fat orange one. Pumpkin? Persimmon? The house is a bloody menagerie. Jessie has three cats, two dogs, four fish tanks, back-yard chickens, a blind rabbit, and a chinchilla. Step in any direction and you're bound to collide with a wagging tail or ball of fur. I never grew up with animals, and I'm not used to them. The cat purrs against my ankle; this one's staked me out as some sort of favorite.

"Hey, guess what? I got an e-mail from Karma." I select a neutral lead-in, an update on my old office mate at the University of Tasmania. We became the black sheep of our environmental studies program, dropping out of honors before completion. "He's traveling around Australia."

She gives an absent nod in lieu of a response, wiping the same plate over and over.

"The dirtbag sent me a picture of a pig's ass from out Innamincka way, on the Strzelecki Track."

No response.

"Talia?"

All through dinner she chased salad leaves around her plate. If she took three bites it was a miracle.

"Sorry." She glances in my general direction, stops, averts her gaze. Her fringe falls forward, shielding one eye. "You were saying something?"

"Nothing, no worries."

Her shirt hangs loose around her collarbone, skims one shoulder enough that her black bra strap peeks into view. I know this one. It used to be my favorite. A frustrated anaconda coils my spine—any second it will crush the bones. Forced abstinence sucks ass through a straw, but there's a deeper aggravation. I am bloody useless, doing nothing but watching her unravel. She hasn't shut me out. She's taken away the door. Three's a crowd in any relationship, and right now it's me, Talia, and her OCD.

"You ever notice how Jessie watches him?" Talia mutters—whether to herself or me is impossible to say. "She's got a raging lady boner for my dad. All those flirty touches and cheese dick smiles?" She makes a huffy noise. "God, it's so nasty."

"Jessie?" Scott's girlfriend is actually pretty cool. Still, Talia's talking at least, so that counts for something. And we're alone; all that separates our bodies is air.

"Look at me," I murmur.

Her breath picks up speed. "Can't."

"Why?"

"You have those eyes." She continues to dry the plate. Something about the way she grips the holey, faded tea towel gets me hard.

This situation is in a giant hurry to go from weird to fucked.

Talia turns toward the sink, starts to rant. "And please, Jessie's plaid shirts? Those hiking boots? Whatever. It's not like she's hitting the Pacific Crest Trail anytime soon. And Dad? When he runs to Safeway to buy her that full-cream maple yogurt. Jesus. You'd think he hunted her a gazelle at the local watering hole."

Where is she going with all this? "Yeah, it would be way cooler if he sat on the couch with a beer and watched her vacuum."

She flings her hair back, gazing at me over one shoulder. For a moment her eyes are shiny, focused. I'm here. She sees me—even if it's for the wrong reasons, like the time I called my mum a stupid cow when she arrived at a swim meet after I'd already won. I got her attention all right, and was shipped off to boarding school the following year.

The front door slams, and there's a mad scramble of dog paws raking the hardwood. Milo and Otis, the golden retrievers, fly into the cramped galley kitchen and head straight to Talia. They love her and the feeling is mutual. She sinks to her haunches and hugs them with all her might.

My stomach flip-flops. Great. I'm jealous of a pair of drooling dogs.

I want to push but how hard? She's so thin, fragile, and half the time hovers on the verge of tears. Bloody Scott, with his sleep-in-the-veranda power play.

"Captain."

"Yeah?" Her face is buried in thick fur.

"The separate bedrooms——"

"Look, Bran, after all our drama from before, Dad needs time to trust you. As it is, he's acting like it's a big favor to let you stay at all."

"Do you want me here?"

"Yes." Although she doesn't look at me when she says it.

"Fight him on it."

Fight for us again, for fuck's sake.

"Maybe I need space, okay?"

I force myself not to shoot back, *No! Not okay.* Instead I ask, "Want to go for a walk? Or slaughter me in Monopoly?"

This is what I'm reduced to, boring piece-of-shit board games.

She stands, gives the dogs a final pat and wipes her hands on her jeans. "I'm tired."

"We need to talk about——"

"There a problem in here?" Scott fills the door. The dude is built like a mastodon, and he's not afraid of throwing his size around, especially in my direction. He gives me a look like, *Just give me a reason, bud*.

"No." Talia's widemouthed yawn isn't fooling anyone. "I'm going to bed."

I glance at the clock. It's 7:45 p.m.

She catches my look. "I told you, I'm exhausted."

"'Course you are, Peanut. It's normal after what you've been through," Scott says.

She steps toward him and he wraps her in a hug, holds fast, and slides his gaze to the ceiling fan. His jaw clenches and for such a big guy, it's obvious he feels weak as fuck. "Love you," he growls.

Jessie strolls into the tight space and joins the cluster that's me, Scott, the cat, and two dogs, all crowding Talia. All eager, too eager, to help.

"Okay, I'm out." Talia jumps back, wipes her eyes, and makes a quick exit. I'm blocked by everyone else.

Cocksucking bloody hell.

I grab the teapot and throw on the sink tap as Scott bails to watch television with the animals. Only Jessie lingers, poking around the fridge, one hand splayed over her swelling belly.

"Want a cuppa?" I ask, striving for politeness. This is her place after all.

"Mmmmmm, that would be great, thanks." She shuts the door and pulls her hair in a loose ponytail. "How's T doing, really?"

I shrug my answer.

"Still not talking much?"

"No."

"Has she committed to going to her graduation this weekend?"

"That whole not-talking part makes it difficult to tell."

Talia graduated in December. She's eligible to walk in the commencement ceremony at UCSC, but refuses to say if she wants to attend.

Jessie gives a sympathetic smile. "I know this is hard. Keep trying. Whenever someone's pushing the world away is right when they need love the most." She grabs an apple off the counter and takes a big bite.

"I'll take that under advisement, Yoda." Jessie's solid. If she asks a question, she cares about your answer. I like that.

"Hey now." She waves the fruit in my direction. "I handle the dad, remember? Those two push their stuff down deep. You need patience."

"Not one of my particular strengths."

"She's been granted a clean bill of health?"

"More or less. Doctors are saying she'll probably be fine, but there could be unforeseen complications. They were surprised she ended up as sick as she did."

"She must have run herself down over there."

"Yeah," I sigh bitterly. Or before, during our fallout in Tasmania.

"I've been meaning to ask, Scott calls you Brandon. Do you prefer it?"

"No."

"He's a Daddy Bear." Her eyes crinkle in restrained affection. "Has a hard time adjusting to his little girl in love."

"I can see that." Scott's not my favorite at the moment, but he's the father of Jessie's kid. Not going to travel down that shit-talking road. "Hey, speaking of adjustments, you excited for the baby?"

"There's still lots of time—two more months. I'd be happier if the due date was tomorrow." She leans back with a deep sigh.

"Two more months?" Her bump is at watermelon proportions. How much bigger is she going to get? Another thought slams me with equal parts relief and foreboding. Talia's stalemate can't last forever. That baby's coming out. At some point, the dynamic will change. "You're going to need the nursery soon."

"Soon and not soon. I've got around sixty more nights of peeing twenty times an hour. But, Bran, I got to say, I'm ready to be done. Even the smell of lettuce makes me queasy."

"I wasn't aware lettuce is odorous."

"I know! It's like I've been granted superpowers and became a bloodhound."

"Or a vampire."

She laughs.

The kettle boils. I pour water into the mugs.

"You know something, I never planned to have kids." She smiles. It's her mouth's default setting. Jessie is the most smiley person I've ever met.

"For real?"

"No strong maternal urge, you know?"

"Um, not exactly."

"Ha! What I mean is that this pregnancy came out of left field. I was on birth control. The statistical chances of conception were nil."

Jesus, I like Jessie, but do I want to hear about Scott Stolfi's super-sperm? No. No I do not.

"All I'm saying is, things don't always go as planned and that doesn't have to be a bad thing." Her features soften into a private expression of contentment as she idly rubs her belly. "Sometimes it's in the unexpected where the magic happens."

I set her tea on the counter to cool. "You sure you're not Yoda?"

"Hey, maybe you're onto something. I'm as green as he is most mornings." She grins and glances up. Talia's room is directly above us. "Go talk to her."

"She doesn't want to."

Jessie picks up her tea and blows against the rim. "She does, she just doesn't know how to start. Trust me, I'm getting to be an expert on Stolfisms."

That's how I end up giving the guest room door a cursory knock two minutes later. Jessie's right, Talia and I need to start somewhere. I need her to know I'm sticking around, no matter how hard things get. I walk in before she has a chance to turn me away. "Hi. Want to hang out for a bit?"

Talia sits on the bed, cross-legged, staring at her phone. "Um..." She glances up with a guarded expression, watching me lean back and close the door. "I guess so."

"Don't sound too excited."

She sucks in her top lip and worries it a little between her teeth.

"Checking out that job?" At dinner Jessie mentioned a position advertised at the local history museum for a program coordinator. Do I want to live in Sacramento? No, but I'll work under the table, scrubbing petrol station toilets, if it meant snapping her out of this funk.

"Nope."

"What are you doing?" I pluck her phone from her grip, half in jest and half to get her attention. "Playing online Scrabble or something?"

She tries to grab it and misses. "Hey, give it ba—"

"Wait." My chest tightens when I look down at the screen. "Talia, is this an app for—"

"Medical marijuana." Her cheeks flush even as her jaw sets in defiance. "The site is remarkably organized." She adjusts her glasses like the action gives her scholarly authority. "The reviews rank different varieties on criteria such as the potential to cause paranoia or decrease anxiety."

"You're shitting me?" My arms drop to my sides. "Please don't tell me you'd rather research weed than hang out together?" My company isn't legendary, but this is a fucking ego blow of the first order.

"Pot helps lots of people. I'm taking anxiety medication again but it's not working fast enough. I thought an indica strain might take the edge off—"

"Sweetheart." I sit down, toss the phone to the end of the bed, and rub the small of her back. This isn't about me. I need to remember that. Talia's carried a whole suitcase of stress back from Africa. "Everything is going to be okay." Her eyes fix on the window, and who the hell bloody knows if she even hears me. Her vertebrae jut beneath my fingers. She's too skinny. "I'm here for you, always."

"Are you, or are you just sorry for me?"

I throw up my hands. "What do you want me to say?"

"I . . . I . . . look, I can't face it if you stop, okay?"

"Stop what?" I try to catch her gaze but she ducks. Her blond hair veils her features behind a golden curtain.

"Us. I'm not exactly a barrel of fun, am I?"

My nails bite into my palms. OCD isn't about logic, it's about anxiety. I need patience, fucking buckets of patience. "Talia, I love you. No matter how hard you fall, I'll be there to catch you in the end. You've put up with my bullshit time and time again. No way am I leaving because you're down. I meant every word, we are in this together. You've fought for me and deserve no less in return."

She digs her fingers into her temples. "I can't hold everything at bay—the bad thoughts, the fears. My brain keeps taking me to the worst possible places." Her face crumples. "Like what if someday you think of me the same way as the Lockhart Foundation?"

"My father's charitable organization?" I wrinkle my brow. "Not following, Captain."

"He wants you to be involved still?"

Her tone is dead calm, but that's in no way reassuring. Red blinking alarms flash, *Warning! Warning!* in my mind. "Sure, yeah, I guess so."

"And have you committed to them?"

"No."

"Because you're waiting for the other shoe to drop." Her voice fades to a whisper.

"Talia..." I draw a deep breath, and another for good measure. There are already enough fires to put out without throwing my dad and his new foundation into the mix.

"What I'm trying to say is you expect the worst from your dad. You are so sure, despite every shred of evidence to the contrary, that somehow your family foundation's environmental work is going to be nothing but greenwashing, a bogus front to make his company's shady exploits more public friendly."

I got nothing to offer in response because she's right. This is something I worry about. I evade my dad and sister's efforts to bring me on as staff with the foundation because I'm afraid they'll only disappoint me again, or I'll disappoint them. But why is she grabbing this issue like a dog with a bone?

"You expect people to let you down."

"Not you," I growl back.

"Not yet." She flops to the mattress, deflated, and throws an arm over her eyes.

"I love you. No way am I going anywhere."

"Please go, get out. I can't stand you in here, seeing me like this, popping pills, researching medical fucking marijuana because I can't deal." She draws her knees up, curls into a fetal position. "It's shaming. I can't stand myself."

I lean toward her, stroke her hair. "Let me try to——"

"I didn't live up to what I wanted to be in Africa and hate myself for it, okay?" She wriggles away. "I can't give you my best. This shitty, weak self is all I've got to offer. You don't understand. Things work out for you. When you try, you succeed."

She is wandering so far from right. I've crashed and burned a good many times. "Listen, Talia, about when I was Down South——"

"I don't want a pep talk."

"You need me."

"What I need is a brain transplant."

"Sweetheart." I jump off her bed, circle the room, lost. "I understand you're wired differently, but to me that's not a bad thing."

"Why?"

"You are the only person who's ever accepted me, even at my worst." Jesus, I'm exposing my every weakness here and she can't even meet my eyes. A vein pulses in my neck. For so long, I shut myself down, believing it was the safer option. Talia opened me up, to life, to hope. She gave me courage to believe. Why can't I do the same for her? My mouth dries. I need to do better, try harder. "Your heart is big because you understand hurt. Who else would have ever believed in me? Trusted that I could get out of my own way and be the guy you deserve?"

"I don't want to understand hurt, Bran." She rolls away. "I'd give a limb to stop thinking. But there's no way to escape my mind. Or undo how I fucked up by joining the Peace Corps. I wasn't cut out for it and now everyone knows. I keep getting these sympathetic 'it was for the best' messages." She grabs a pillow and shoves it over her head. "All I want to do is never feel anxious ever again and no one can give me that, least of all myself."

"What about going to Santa Cruz for your graduation ceremony? You worked hard to get there. Why not take some time to focus on what you've achieved. Celebrate? Remember, great things are done through lots of small steps."

She stills. Maybe I'm getting through.

"Stop trying to untie my knots." She begins to cry, great sobbing wracks. "I just want to be left alone. Do I have to fall on my knees and beg?"

I'm at her side in two quick steps, all frustration evaporating at the sound of her weeping. "Hey! Calm down, please, you're going to make yourself sick."

"I want you to go downstairs." Her voice is muffled under the pillow. "Leave me alone."

That sentence, it's a knife to my gut. "Let me fix this."

"You can't whip out a tool belt and go to work on me! It doesn't work that way."

"That's not what I'm saying." I touch her leg. "Talia—"

"Go, go, go, go—" She grips the pillow, chanting the word.

I came up here to try to make a connection. Instead I've pushed her even further into her OCD spiral. Fan-fucking-tastic job. When

I pull her bedroom door closed it takes every ounce of willpower not to slam it off the hinges.

I'm out. Alone. Not enough to help her. Scott glances from the television as I barge through the living room. He's only made the problem worse with his enabling excuses, not challenging the status quo. If I wasn't here, how long would Talia be allowed to haunt the bloody shadows in some sort of half-life?

It's doing my head in, but I've got to stay. She needs me and I won't let go.

I throw on my runners, hit the empty street, and push hard. I lose track of the distance after ten kilometers. I run and run but can't escape Talia telling me to leave. The sidewalk peters near the freeway. I prop myself against a lone tree and stare out, concrete in every direction. Cars speed past—all these people with someplace to go. What am I doing? For such a smartass, I've got no answer.

I throw back my head and scream at the overcast sky. My girl-friend won't speak to me. I have no money. I owe ten grand to my dad because I spent everything I had on getting to South Africa. Family money was strictly a no-go for me, until Talia got sick and I needed to be with her here, in America, where I can't work. Or do school. Or do anything but climb the walls and avoid e-mails from my dad about the Lockhart Foundation. He's all business, all the time. I get that's how he functions but an occasional *How the hell are you doing, mate* call would go a long fucking way.

I'm stuck at this invisible crossroads, unsure which direction to take. So in the end, I do the only thing there is to do: I run back to the house.

Upon my return I fill three pints of water and drink them in quick succession. The liquid hits my gut, leaving me nauseated, and I wander to the veranda. There's a scuffle from the cage in the corner. Chester the chinchilla. My furry mate. My comrade-in-arms. What the? Is he doing what I think he's—

The fucking chinchilla is self-fellating. I don't know where to look.

"Bloody hell, don't mind me, mate."

Chester carries on like I'm not even there.

I fall on the futon and slam my foot against the lumpy mattress. I don't know what to do, but I'll be damned if things can't get much worse.

5

TALIA

Crib sectionals are stacked against my bedroom's far wall.
Correction—not mine—this ten-by-ten patch of real estate
belongs to the Sea-Monkey. Dad's replacement child. He's rebooted
his family and is up and running with a new system. I'm like a virus.

Jessie finished painting the future nursery a shade called
"Lemon Twist." "Morning-After Curry" is more apt. Poor kid, it's
got plenty of nauseous hours to look forward to in here.

Jesus, listen to me. I sit on a throne of assholery.

There's a creak outside my door. Bran? My thighs clench. My
emotions for him are all over the map. It's amazing that he's still
here. I can see him trying, putting himself out there, being vulnerable in the hopes I'll do the same. But all my good is being eclipsed
by ugly, black fear and malignant shame, and I hate he sees that; I
hate it so hard.

There's a feminine giggle out in the hall, followed by a muffled
groan. Oh, hell no. Jessie and Dad are making out? Clearly they
touch each other, Jessie's gigantic womb is proof enough, but I don't
want to hear actual evidence. A wall bumps. I eye the window, seri-

ously considering leaping out Superman-style. I'd rather plummet to the earth than listen to my dad get jiggy.

There's more furtive laughter, followed by audible shushing. A door slams with a little too much force.

It's not that I want my dad to be miserable and alone, but the fact his relationship is so relaxed and happy? Their brightness only makes the rain cloud I'm trapped under all the darker and more dismal. A faint noise of running water starts down the hall. Bran must have gotten in the shower, because Dad and Jessie have their own bathroom in the master suite. A sob breaks from me, a single, sharp wrenching note. Oh God, please don't let me crush him under my mountain of crap until his love is squeezed away.

After he stormed out earlier, I bit off all the new growth on my fingernails. Then I gnawed an angry sore on the inside of my bottom lip. Then I cried in the closet, next to a stack of tiny cloth diapers. Finally, I canceled my appointment with a local doctor to get the written documentation necessary for obtaining medical marijuana.

My outburst at Bran was crazy town, and I don't want to live there anymore. I tip my head back and offer my next breath to the universe, imagine it spiraling to the sky, leaving the atmosphere, carrying my confused longing to the invisible stars. I can't see starlight right now, but that doesn't mean it isn't there. That's how my feelings are for Bran. I can't feel…anything…in this awful place, but I know love is inside me, locked away.

When we were together in Australia, I felt attuned to him. Sure, we had our share of discord, but I became pretty dang skilled at sensing his rhythms. Lately, it's like I'm forgetting the words to a familiar song. What-ifs, my old enemy, keep paying insidious visits. What if he doesn't even want to be here? I mean, why should he? He lives for activism, the thrill of grabbing a cause, righting wrongs. I've forced him into this quiet, midcentury house, where he paces the halls like a captive panther. He's not the type to chill in the suburbs indefinitely, go to the mall for fun.

Imagine him in line at Mrs. Fields Cookies.

For me, this Sacramento suburb, Bankside, is the perfect place to hide. No one questions me about taking the cop-out route from the Peace Corps, choosing early termination. Sure, malaria is a good reason on paper, yet I can't shake the fact it's an excuse. I secretly didn't want to be teaching English as a Second Language for the next two years, and it's like my body decided to up and do what my brain would not. It got us out of there.

But where am I? Not home. Not even close. The idea of going to Santa Cruz for graduation, getting asked by everyone what I'm up to. What's my next plan? Holy Christ on a cracker, that's a torture I'm not ready for.

My phone buzzes. S'up, homeslice? It's a text from my friend Sunny. There's a person who doesn't stress. She spends her days chilling at the beach, works a hassle-free job at an organic grocery store, and bed-hops around town. Sure, she got a degree in art, but she's not having any sort of existential, what-am-I-doing-with-my-life dramas. She lives in the moment, damn the torpedoes, full speed ahead.

How's the thunder from down under? ;)

She checks in every day, and so does Beth. But I've asked them not to visit, not yet. Made excuses that I was too tired, too sick, when really I'm just overwhelmed and embarrassed. They are both going places, and here I squat at Jessie's house like a big ol' failure to launch.

All good, I respond. Because what do I say? My sex drive has taken a one-way vacation to Pluto? I can't bring myself to talk to my boyfriend, let alone engage in a whole body dialogue. I roll over and muffle my groan. At this point, I'm not even sure what would make things better. I want to reach out to Bran, but I am trapped in this revolving door. Every time I push, I end up exactly where I started, a place of self-loathing and life doubt.

Haven't heard from you in a while.

I fire back an airy response. I know, sorry! Been busy. Watching puke-colored paint dry and shutting out my boyfriend.

Busy? Yeah, right. Busy with bow chicka wow wow. I want to see you soon, okay? I miss you xxx

LOL. Miss you too! I hit send and throw my phone onto the rug.

Shit, I have to chill out. Otherwise I'll do something stupid, like count heartbeats. That's one of the worst rituals because it means I can't stop looking inward. Can't escape my own body even when I wish to flee my flesh like Peter Pan's wayward shadow.

Double shit. I forgot to take my medication tonight. Nice one. Because nothing says "I want to cease being a pathetic loser" more than spacing the thing that has a chance in hell of curing me.

The problem is that my pills are in the bathroom, where Bran's currently showering.

Stop being a whiner, sneak in and sneak out. He'll never know you're there.

I tiptoe down the hall. There's no light under Dad and Jessie's closed door.

The shower is still going full throttle. I turn the knob slow to minimize the noise. The orange pill bottle is on the counter. I'm going to get away with it.

"Talia."

Bran's voice rumbles from behind the shower curtain.

Damn. I close my eyes. "Uh, yes?"

"You need me?" His words come out gruff like he's expecting to be rebuffed.

Yes.

No.

I don't know.

Here's a guy who still needs convincing of his own lovability, and I've put a prison glass partition between us.

"I'm all good." My accompanying laugh is hollow. "Forgot to take my pills."

He doesn't respond.

Maybe I should give him a kiss, couldn't hurt. I mean, it's a normal part of the girlfriend job description. I can't remember the last time I did it—which is so fucked up and a testament to how far underground I've gone. I've been a terrible girlfriend. I've got to get things under control—a large task, but a kiss is a start. I pinch the shower curtain and pull it aside.

Bran stands, back to the spray, regarding me with glittering, hooded eyes. My gaze drops over the bare chest that my mouth and hands are so intimately familiar with, and lower still, past his flat stomach. He's got a hand working his dick in a rhythm so private, so personal, I feel like I should cover my eyes. Apologize. Get the hell out.

He doesn't stop. Or look away.

His irises are an impossible green, like a thermal pool, hot, dangerous. You know you shouldn't touch, what will happen if you do. It will scald. You won't even be left with skin. But this is the kind of look that overrides good judgment, despite, or maybe even due to, the danger. Even though I was the original architect of this safety fence, I'm tempted to jump the rail and burn.

His top teeth jut out, far enough to catch his lower lip and bite down. Yearning compresses my capillaries. Slit my wrists and rubies will spill forth.

He increases the pace, his heavy-lidded gaze one part desire and one part amused. His mouth crooks in a slow, wicked smile.

Cheeky.

He knows exactly what he's doing.

He doesn't ask me to join. He doesn't ask me to leave. His eyes don't swerve from mine. "I love you." A low huskiness threads his words.

A hot surge fires through my hips. "I'm not sure I deserve it."

"You do, but I'm not loving you for you alone. I love you for me too." His groan carries a hoarse note as his dick slides through his grip, root to tip. I know how it feels, having him inside me—like I went to the lost and found and discovered the exact thing I was missing.

My fingers twitch. It would be such an easy thing to reach out and touch. I'm Sleeping Beauty, my desire an evil Maleficent. His next noise is raggedly intense, dragged from a secret location that's strictly ours. I'm the only person who takes him to this place. He's the only one who takes me to mine.

Typical Bran. Right when I think I've hit the depth of my longing, he does something like this, the ground splits, and I uncover whole new caverns of wanting.

He thrusts harder and my knees turn traitor. I sink to the tub's edge and sit on my hands, not trusting myself to touch, 100 percent unable to avert my eyes. Nerves knot in a bundle between my legs.

His free hand reaches to clench his hair. His throat is red from the water's temperature and his own mad want. He's still not looking away and I'm not looking away and somehow without him laying a single finger on me, this is the most erotic moment of my entire life. His teeth tighten their hold on his lips as his ribs start to rise and fall. His abdomen pulls in, every muscle in his beautiful body tightens.

"You're gorgeous." I mean the word to the moon and back. He's nothing like Michelangelo's *David*—too short for starters, and his dick's too big. With that near-black hair and perfect skin, he's a fallen angel, one who raged out of heaven, but isn't quite at home in the darkness. He spreads his feet farther, bracing himself. His second toes are the longest. The top of his nose is a little too broad. It hasn't been broken, a surprise given his propensity to deal with big feelings through his fists rather than words. His lips are a shade wider than they should be, but the exact perfect shape to fasten on my body.

"Fucking hell." The urgency of his feral growl constricts my stomach.

Steam cloaks us. He locks his hand around the back of his neck. There's no possible way his abs can tighten more. I fixate on his navel and it relaxes me a fraction. Proof he's human. Not a strange creature conjured from my own personal Garden of Temptation.

"See how I want you." His agonized whisper is barely audible over the water lashing the tiles. His hips lose their slow, lazy tempo. He pounds himself deeper, harder.

An intense ache spreads from my belly through my breasts. I've forgotten what it feels like to be turned on. Muscles tighten within my sex. I'm fast remembering.

"Want. You. So. Bloody. Much." He always sounds like this right before he comes, as if it hurts, like I'm pressing on a wound that's too much to bear. "Damn it, Talia."

I can't look away as he loses himself in a blaze. I'm a prism, refracting his light. His features spin through a kaleidoscope of emotions starting at brutal need and ending with an unexpected vulnerability. My fear about the future disperses so quickly it's hard to believe only minutes ago it felt inescapable. Bran isn't some scary what-if. He's a fact, a truth to hold on to against all life's uncertainty. Why have I been so afraid he'll see me as a walking disaster? He knows what it's like to mess up, to feel like a failure. I need to reframe my question. Rather than asking what if Bran gets sick of me, maybe I should ask, what if we've worked our asses off, and finally have a shot at a real forever?

He falls to his knees and grabs me before I can take a breath or do anything but throw my arms around his lean shoulders. Water soaks through the white cotton of my pajama pants until I might as well be naked too.

"Show me the way back to you." He buries his face in my neck, drags his lips to the place behind my ear, the headwaters for all delicious shivers.

"I want that so much."

"I'll do whatever it takes, go off the map."

"You will?"

"We're already there."

He's right. We've been explorers for some time. During the last little while it's as if a blizzard descended, we were stuck in a white-out, so close, but the snow made everything indistinguishable. At last, the storm's abating and he's right there, and I'm over here. Suddenly, we can see each other.

Within us is the way forward. We each possess half of the compass and must join together to find the right direction.

"You've got to know how much I need you." A lock of his wet hair twists in a boyish curl.

I go to smooth it down, but my fingers tangle in the thick waves, and instead draw him closer.

He bows his head, still panting a little. "You can't check out on me like that again. I can't live this bloody life devoid of you—"

I brush my mouth over his lower lip, that reddening mark where his teeth left imprints. "I won't. I'm so sorry. I-I'm ready to try. Thank you for believing in me."

"I'll never stop."

We rest our foreheads together, holding one another upright. Droplets fall from his hairline onto my cheeks, joining fresh tears. He's water, I'm water, and our flotsam and jetsam fit in a way that's strange, yet familiar. I have no idea where we're going, only that the way out is lined with broken feathers, bloodstains, marrow ash, and the serrated teeth of sharks.

This journey will take all I've got, a small price to have everything.

And that's exactly what this guy in my arms is.

6

BRAN

$\mathcal{I}$ settle my feet on the veranda's rough floorboards and bury my face in my hands. There's a vague hint of coffee in the air. Scott or Jessie must be awake. Might as well get up and fortify myself. Despite what Talia said last night, how she behaves in the grisly light of day is going to be the real test.

I have just enough hope to hang myself.

Furtive rustles emit from the wire cage in the corner. Chester the Sexually Deviant Chinchilla stirs. The little bloke's crepuscular, dawn and dusk are when he's most active, and that means... wait for it, wait for it... yep, little pervert's working himself over again.

"Mate, give it a rest," I mutter. "You're going to gnaw your bits off."

Chester's determination to eunuch himself finally forces me into action. If given the choice between watching a rodent self-fellate versus enduring a piece of toast alongside Scott Stolfi—the dad wins.

Just.

I open the door into the living room and collide with Talia, who's holding a loaded breakfast tray.

"Oh, hell, sorry, Captain." I reach to steady her. "Didn't know you were there."

You are awake before 2 p.m.

She's here. She's come to find me, and her shy smile makes my teeth hurt from the sweetness. "I wanted to fix you breakfast in bed."

"You did, did you?"

She looks me up and down. "Guess I'm too late."

"Hold that thought." I slip back onto the veranda and hurl myself onto the futon with such force that Chester emits a squeal and scurries into his den.

"What're you doing?" Talia stands over me, hesitant, but at least halfway amused.

"Morning, sweetheart." I make a production out of exaggerated yawns and eye rubs. "Oh, hello, what do we have here?"

She giggles and sits, settling the tray between us. "I thought you might accept frozen waffles and out-of-season blueberries as a suitable peace offering."

"When you're right, you're right."

She fiddles with the lid of the maple syrup bottle. An amber drop collects on her fingertip. "I just don't get it." She licks the sweet stickiness from her skin in an unselfconsciously sexy gesture.

"What's that?" My question comes out a hoarse croak. It's been five months since I've had this girl. My dick perks, sensing opportunity.

Down boy, don't scare her off.

She takes a sip of coffee. "I don't see what the big attraction is."

"Attraction?"

Bloody hell, the way she palms the mug——

"Are you getting a cold?" She peers at me. "Your voice is all crackly."

I clear my throat and direct my thoughts to things vaguely unpleasant: the prime minister's smarmy features, paper cuts, or cricket. Desire remains, trapped in a warped eddy, a frothing confusion of conservative politics, pain, and wickets. Quick, divert—what's 6,426 divided by 6? 1,071.

"Your attraction to me." She leans forward, provides an unobstructed view down her tank top. She's not wearing a bra, and her pink nipples are right there, looking a trifle lonely. "You're some kind of masochist."

"Let's clear this up once and for all. Every atom, every last one in my heart is yours. When I'm with you…" I wrap my hand around her fingers, still syrup sticky. "Bloody hell, Talia. It's the only time I'm not practicing at being alive."

Talia's eyes round, match her mouth's perfect O. "Who are you? It's like I've made you up in my head."

"No more make-believe. I'm done being Pinocchio."

"And you honestly believe I'm the Blue Fairy?"

"Whatever you are, you're some kind of magic."

Her sudden tears fall fast and silent.

I shove away the breakfast tray and pull her close. She buries her wet face in my neck, her fingers lightning quick on my skin. Her little touches aren't sexual, more like remembering.

"Tell me what's up."

She shakes her head.

I rock her gently. "What's the worst you can say?"

She doesn't move, if anything she grips tighter.

"Look at me, Captain. I need you looking at me."

She pulls back with a shuddering sigh. She's silent. I'm silent. There's a question she asks with that gaze.

"Yes." I answer. "You are worth it." I walk my fingers to the nape of her neck. Brush my thumb across the base of her skull. "I know next to nothing about love. But I know you."

"So you'll come to Santa Cruz? Suffer through all the pomp and circumstance? Clap wildly while I get a piece of paper that cost nearly six figures and will probably never lead to gainful employment?"

"It would be a pleasure."

She rests her hand on my heart. Her cheeks are red from wiping away tears. "Where do you think we're going?"

I muss her hair. "Everywhere good, Captain."

"It's time to get out of Sacramento, huh?"

"Leave Jessie's house? In a word, yes. In two, fuck yeah."

"Can we have a garden at our hypothetical new residence?"

I tug her close and flip her to one side so we're spooning. "Sure."

"A four-poster bed?" She nestles into me.

My knuckles skim the undersides of her soft breasts. "Um, I've no opposition on that front." Indeed, a whole dirty scenario plays in my imagination. Talia tied to a bed letting me have my way with her. Fucking hell, I have so many ways to try out.

A hint of an eyebrow arch, a cute-as-hell smile.

"Why, are you flirtin' with me, Miss Stolfi?" I do my best Texas cowboy impersonation.

"I do declare." Abject horror replaces her cheeky smile. She stares over my shoulder in the direction of the chinchilla's lair. "The hell?"

"Fucking Chester."

"Is he—"

"Yep."

"Whoa. Does he do...that...a lot?"

"Whenever he finds a spare moment, and seeing as he lives his whole life in a bloody cage..."

"You've been sleeping out here, with him, for two whole weeks?"

"Bypassed purgatory and went straight to hell."

"I am so, so sorry."

"I'd suffer through a lot more than a furry horn ball to have a chance with you."

"Would you print that on a bumper sticker?"

"Get over here."

She's Talia, so she laces her fingers in my hair and kisses with the same eagerness that used to equal parts frighten and fascinate me. Though so much is different, this rush of sheer disbelief at my own dumb luck remains the same. Our tongues sweep against each other, and everything is maple syrup, spearmint toothpaste, and possibility.

"Talia!"

Scott stands in the doorway, frowning.

Yeah, we have to get the hell out from under this roof.

"Dad?" Talia doesn't pull from my arms. She leans against me like she belongs there, and she does.

Scott gives us a deadpan once-over. "Brandon, come in here a minute."

"Are you for real?" Talia's arced up like an irritated dingo defending its territory. The sight is so bloody adorable I almost kiss her again, dad or no dad.

"I'm serious. You'll both want to see this."

The way he speaks dashes my good humor on submerged rocks. He looks perplexed, stares as if I'm this new stranger, worth consideration.

"Have you heard of a cable show called *Eco Warriors*?"

Shit.

"What's that?" Talia asks, giving me a puzzled look.

I can't search for words of explanation. I'm afraid for what I'll find. Goddamn it, just when everything is turning around—

"Bran?" Talia gives up on my stricken ass in favor of searching her father's face.

"It's going to be a new program on the Discovery Channel," he says. "They just ran a promo ad and Bran was in it, on that ship of his, down in the Antarctic."

"I don't understand." Her brows knit.

I shrug. Maybe it won't be so bad. Maybe—

"You're a wild man, bud." Scott's tone is awed. Impressed.

"Look, it's nothing." I shift on the bed, knocking into Talia's breakfast. Blueberries roll over the mattress. Only a minute ago, everything was easy, uncomplicated. Now it's—

"Come on, Talia, you have to see this. Bran is some kind of hero."

"I already knew that." Talia disentangles from me. "But I still have no idea what's going on."

I want to order her not to go. This so-called reality television is anything but.

I know the truth.

I'm no hero.

7

“There I was, with my morning coffee, watching Shark Week on the DVR, when this happens.” Dad grabs the remote, fast-forwards past an SUV advertisement, and hits play. Bran’s image fills the flat screen. He’s dressed in a black Gore-Tex jacket, a gray wool beanie tugged low on his forehead. Fog eddies around his meditative profile as he leans against the ship’s rail—an anarchist sailor, or a mind-bogglingly hot pirate. He turns slowly, as dramatic music commences.

Holy sweet Jesus.

His eyes catch the half-light and shine this unfeasible green. Cameras were invented to make love to his face. He’s not guy-next-door handsome. His features aren’t model perfect. But his aura is hypnotic. You’re simply compelled to keep watching.

The next forty-five seconds vanish into disorienting cutaways: a dead whale, the sea inky with dark blood, helicopters banking mid-air, surging waves, crew hastening around the deck, and shots of Bran, time and time again. The clips increase with frenetic energy until the final culminating moment, the one where my boyfriend leaps off the side of a ship that's rocking wildly on stormy seas, and lands in a Zodiac far below. A woman appears to be sprawled unconscious in the bottom of the small boat.

"All new episodes of *Eco Warriors*, coming soon." An intense, raspy voiceover breaks through the background music.

We sit in dumbfounded silence.

"Eco my fucking left nut." Bran jumps to his feet. "What a bloody joke."

"What is this about?" Dad leans forward, ignoring Bran's curse-laden outburst.

"A hell of a lot more than me standing around looking like a wanker." Bran paces in front of the TV while a hunting tiger shark swims on the screen behind. They share identical expressions.

"You jumped off a ship? In a storm?" The reality of his actions makes me restless. I take a deep breath and hold it, my knee knocks the coffee table, and a stack of surf magazines cascade to the floor. Losing Bran, the idea burns through my brain like my own personal hellfire. "You're not Batman. What if you missed the little boat?"

"The Zodiac?"

I nod, dazed.

"I'd be dead."

"Bran!" My powers of speech freeze, I'm bordering on incoherent. Where was I the day this happened? Probably in my village, teaching English. What if he—

"Captain." His face softens. "If I hadn't jumped over, Juz would have drowned."

"Juz?"

"Justine, the woman I almost killed." Bran's voice rises. He passes a hand over his face, and when his features reemerge they are stone. His eyes hood. "Did that clip show me cocking up? No. What you saw right there..." His voice is dead calm. Chills zing up my thighs as he points a shaking finger. "Everything they showed about me is bullshit. Fake Hollywood-style spin doctoring."

"I had no idea any of this happened."

"Well, you do now. Everyone does. A total cock up." He continues his pacing. Dad looks at me and raises an eyebrow. I shrug in response.

"Hey." I start to rise but he halts me with an upturned hand.

"Not right now."

"Bran—"

"Soon, okay?" He closes his eyes for a couple of seconds. "We need to talk, I need to talk, but give me some time. Better I go for a run first."

———

Bran's been gone for over an hour. From the way he looked before leaving, he's plotting a long-distance event. I halfheartedly distract myself by trolling through random jobs and internships on my laptop, postings in the U.S. and Australia. My focus is shot to hell. I don't know what he and I are doing.

Apparently I don't know anything.

After Bran took off, Dad and I watched the *Eco Warriors* promotion three more times before he left for work. Each viewing was more unbelievable than the last.

Why didn't he tell me?

Oh, yeah, because I was stranded on Self-Pity Island. How much has Bran carried while I've been loaded down with the weight of my own issues? I'd give anything to be a mad scientist and whip up new biochemical reactions for my brain.

Hello, what's this?

I hover my finger over the track pad for a second, two seconds, three seconds—I force myself to click the link: Production Assistant/*Put it Past* (San Francisco). *Put it Past* has an entry-level position on public radio with a new oral history program. All my qualifications fit the profile. It reads like my dream job, if I blotted out my worries and allowed myself to dream.

Yes, I want it, and feel shamefaced for this want.

Look what happened with the Peace Corps. Maybe I left with a justifiable reason, but there's no denying the smirking truth. I was relieved not to continue. It wasn't a good fit for me.

I'm nervous about chasing hope. Maybe I won't get the job and I'll fail again. Maybe I will get the job, I won't enjoy it, and I'll confirm to myself that I am this lame and shallow person.

But inaction isn't working either.

"I don't know what to do," I whisper to no one.

A ping from my laptop indicates a new e-mail and saves me from further navel gazing. I click open my inbox and see a message from my friend Beth. Odd. Why wouldn't she just text?

The heading says: *Bran?*

Figures we weren't the only ones who spotted the *Eco Warriors* spot. Beth scored a dream PR internship at an up-and-coming social media start-up, so she's hip to pop culture.

T—WTH? This is blowing up!

—Beth

Pasted below her cryptic message are a bunch of links.

Okay, random.

I open the first one.

Is this for real?

I open the second, third, fourth, and fifth before jerking back. My jaw is sore like I chewed too much gum.

Bran's all over the Internet. Clips from the *Eco Warriors* promo, and stills of his face, have been tweeted, pinned, reblogged, and posted. The online chatter hums the same tune:

OMG—heart palpitations!!!!!!

WHO THE HELL IS THIS HOTTIE?

Come and give me some of that yum yum . . .

Squeeeeeee—my new BF!

When is this show airing—must see (ALL THE GRABBY HANDS)

#EcoWarGuy is trending on Twitter.

This is twilight zone territory. If Bran sees this stuff he's going to lose his shit. Hell, I'm losing mine. My boyfriend's become international drool fodder. He's some fine eye candy, but to have the entire Internet lusting after him? Not sure how I feel about that.

I wander onto the veranda. A steady rain falls outside, rattling the eaves. The tree-lined street is empty, no sign of Bran. I curl up on the futon and bury my face in his pillow. The scent of leaves, soap, and him clings to the cotton.

I don't remember falling asleep. I blink my eyes, disoriented from a Southern Ocean dream, being tossed about in a little Zodiac. Bran stands near the edge of the bed, hair sodden, in a pair of knee-length jogging shorts. His white T-shirt is rain soaked and leaves nothing to the imagination.

Whoa.

"You were thrashing around."

"Bad dreams." I shift over, making space on the mattress. "You must be cold. Come warm up."

His eyes plunder me a long moment before he fists off his shirt.

There is nothing sudden about the gesture. The motion is slow. Deliberate. The beauty of his body is fearsome. A poem of flesh and bone.

My brain collapses and my heart explodes in fireworks that fall and fall but never hit the earth. He crawls beside me and the air is hushed, like the morning wind that blows off the sea.

"I miss you," he murmurs.

"I'm right here."

"There's been so much distance."

"That clip—"

"Was nothing." His phone rings.

"You going to answer that?"

"No." He throws it to the end of the bed.

"What happened down there, on the boat?"

"I messed up."

"What are you talking about? Don't tell me you regret joining the Sea Alliance."

"Not until today. The work we were doing was important. Crazy shit is happening in places that the world can't see. When they said a reality television show had contracted to film their new series about the illegal whaling, I thought it was a good idea. The crew seemed cool, like they were interested in the real issues, not spying in the bunks to see who rooted who."

"Like a *Big Brother*, Antarctic Version."

"Right."

"I want to know what happened, why you risked your life?"

Risked MY life. I couldn't survive losing you.

He closes his eyes as if the scene unfolds movie-style behind his lids. When he starts to speak his words come out in a quiet, monotone narrative. "It happened one of the last days. The weather turned foul, a big dirty low moved in, a storm system from nowhere, and with it came waves bigger than this house. At the same time, our last action was going down and a few folks decided to try to illegally board the whaling factory vessel."

"Why?"

"To get arrested, be taken to Japan. Draw international media focus on the country's illegal whaling activities in protected marine areas. The film crew was focused, all the cameras were out. Two of our people made it onto the factory ship safely. Everyone was coming back. I wasn't on a boat. I was a deckhand, helping secure the Zodiacs as they arrived back at our ship. The guy working the back crane told me to jump in and work the controls. Get the last Zodiac up. It should have been a straightforward action—I lower the hook, the woman, Justine, grabs it and attaches to her boat. Then I lift them out of the water, onto the ship. I'd worked the crane enough, but never in those conditions. The hook was big. Heavy steel. A rogue wave came in, far bigger than the rest. Our vessel pitched the exact moment hers lifted and the hook nailed her right in the face."

"Oh my God."

"The way she fell. I knew she was unconscious. But she was the only one in the Zodiac. Her passengers were over on the factory ship." He bunches his hands into fists, knuckles white. "If she had remained alone she would have been swept overboard. Even though she was wearing a full immersion suit, in those conditions, it would be game over."

My chin trembles. "So you jumped?"

"I didn't even think. It was pure reaction. I saw where I was positioned, where the Zodiac was, it was a perfect drop. If I hesitated even for a second, the moment would be gone."

I'm dizzy, black spots fire off on the edge of my peripheral vision. "You could have died."

"If I hadn't tried, she would have." His breath comes in shallow rasps.

"You really are a hero."

He blinks rapidly. "I caused the accident, Talia. It wouldn't have happened if it hadn't been for me cocking it up in the first place."

"Stop." I place my hand on his jaw, force him to look at me.

"What?" Muscles clench beneath my hand.

"Being so hard on yourself. The situation sounds like madness. I know it's different seeing it from television, but the conditions sounded totally rotten. You were a hero."

A shudder runs through him. "Can we stop talking about it?"

I scoot closer. "Fine, but none of that changes how I think about you."

"I miss..." He brackets my hip with his hand. "I miss talking with you."

"Me too."

Having him cuddled in close with no tension—the moment's almost too much. Sometimes good hurts, like if you've been out in the cold for too long and come inside. That first hit of warmth is enough to make you scream.

"Oh, Talia." He buries his face in my hair. "Talia, Talia, Talia."

"Every night I went to bed in my hut and I would imagine us, like this."

"Was it a nice place, this bed of yours?"

"The only furniture I had, besides a table and a stool. I did pretty much everything there."

"Did you now?"

"You turn the most innocent comments dirty."

"It's a gift."

"A sexual superpower."

He shrugs. "My thoughts have been gutter-bound since last night."

The image of him jacking off in the shower powers up my desire machine. Deep in my lower belly, a complex conveyor system of belts and pulleys delivers molten tingles between my legs. Holy crap, all systems are go. I need an effing hard hat.

"Yeah, um . . . so, it's been a while."

"Understatement."

I fiddle the sheet, play peekaboo with the hollow of his throat. "I'm not on the pill."

He frowns. "And I don't have any condoms."

A major logistical problem. I groan my frustration, torn between an urge to be responsible, and a wild urge to keep going, damn the torpedoes.

He rests his forehead against mine. "We can still be with each other, talk and stuff."

"After you left I told Dad I'd go to graduation."

"That's good, Captain. Really good." He traces the corner of my mouth.

I hope my smile covers my wince. I'm still nervous about returning to Santa Cruz, but I did work hard to get off academic probation. A bachelor's in history might not be much in the grand scheme of things. Still, it's a straw to grasp at. A sign that I've accomplished something. "He booked two rooms at a hotel on the bay. We'll all drive over tonight after they finish with work. Oh, and he doesn't want us sharing a bed."

"Talia—"

"I'll talk to him. Really, I will."

"We lived together in Tasmania. I want you close. Sneaking around isn't going to work for me."

"I know, I know." I scrub my face. "It's just my *dad*, you know? He doesn't make it easy and it's like I have to go, 'Yo, Dad, me and Bran, we want to bone down.'"

"Want me to do it?"

"I'll spare you the torture. You and me—this is an idea he's going to have to get used to. Where you go, I go. Where you sleep, I sleep."

"Thank you."

"Besides, even though you don't want to hear it, I think the sight of you going all wild man blew his mind."

"Bloody hell."

"I swear his Grinchy heart grew every time we hit rewind and watched again."

He bites my earlobe, lightly, right on the tip and removes the slight sting with the flat of his tongue.

"But remember we can't—"

"There are loads of ways to make you feel good, Captain."

"Oh?"

"And because it must be said, these are fucking sexy jams." He skims the fleece waistband of my lounge pants—the ones imprinted with hearts and grinning cartoon squirrels.

"They're ancient, from high school."

He emits a ragged sound. "Oh, that's a turn-on, not gonna lie."

I tsk-tsk. "Naughty boy." My giggles are eclipsed when he skims the top of my bare ass.

"No underwear?"

All I can do is shake my head.

His answering groan pulls from me this sound that hovers midrange between a giggle and a whimper.

"This makes things more interesting." He continues his exploration.

I lost so much weight in Africa. "The landscape is different. My butt's gone."

He hauls me closer, nuzzles my temple. "That ass was a friend of mine, but it's still there, just a little different."

"Like me."

"And me."

8

BRAN

I nibble across Talia's lower lip on a reconnaissance mission. We are alone finally, Scott and Jessie gone to work. The house is all ours. Curiosity tugs my gut. How much has she changed? I want to take us fast, but need to stay slow. Let us get reacquainted. Make her comfortable. Her mouth holds a wild herbal quality—chamomile tea and honey. I move in for another teasing taste and oh, hell yeah, there we go, that indefinably Talia essence.

She squirms, rubs her knees together in a herky-jerky way.

I slide my palms up until one hand cups her jaw while the other snarls her hair. Our tongue tips meet in hesitant greeting before an invisible thunderclap breaks. We storm each other in a desperate reunion. Our moans tangle. The kiss deepens until we tremble with the need for air. Her fingers are strong, locked between my shoulders like if she presses hard enough our atoms will form new molecules.

I rub my cheek across hers and move lower, over her tensed

neck, the rise of her breasts. "Remember the first time I ever touched you?"

"Like it was five minutes ago."

"I'd never seen anyone so sexy." I skim my fingers over her hitching lower belly, down to where soft hairs graze the back of my knuckles.

Her lids flutter. "That's a tricky thing to say."

"Why's that?" I slide my hand between her legs, circle, soft and light, the way she loves. Her hips mimic my rhythm.

"Of course you've seen hotter girls, that's an...oh, Jesus God... an empirical fact."

"But I—"

"I'm not trying to feed you an I-don't-think-I'm-pretty-so-that's-what-makes-me-pretty line. Yes! There. Keep touching exactly right there. You know, like in a movie where the girl is supercute, but wears thick glasses and—"

"Talia, are you ready to shut up and come?"

Her eyes widen.

"I want to love on you. Scratch that. I'm ready to worship." I cover her mouth with mine, fuck her with my tongue until her back arches, her core clenching tight. "I'll ask again. Are. You. Ready. To. Come?"

Her fingers roam my shoulder blades. "Holy Christmas, what's next? You'll tell me to sing for you, your 'Angel of Music'?"

"Hey." I pause. "I know that reference."

"Stop the presses." She rocks against me, urges my movement.

"My sister loves *Phantom of the Opera*." My index and middle fingers find the sides of her clit and glide down and inside. The move drives her crazy and only works when she's this wet.

Her reply is a ragged gasp, a writhe.

"You can sing for me. I don't mind."

Her panting breaths drive me crazy. She tosses her head from side to side. "Please…"

"Please what?"

She's slick and delicate; makes me protective, careful, like I've been given something precious. I slow down.

She bucks her hips in protest. "No, no, faster."

"Talia?"

"Mmmm?" She licks her lips.

"Eyes on me," I coax.

Her unfocused gaze catches mine. "Love you."

"Always and forever."

Her skin is scorching. Clit slick. Her legs jerk involuntarily as she comes hard, her orgasm milking my fingers.

"Holy God." Bliss coats her words as she collapses against me.

"Yes?"

"That wasn't a direct salutation." She's all dazed smiles and giggles.

"Can I at least get an amen?"

"Preach."

"I haven't even started." All it takes is a tug and her pajama pants tumble down. Bloody hell, I really do love these things. I free her ankles and toss the wadded fleece to the floorboards.

She props on her elbows. "You're joking, right? Because I can't possibly—"

"What are the last four letters of American, Captain?" I spread her thighs before she finishes her eye roll. The sight of her—damn, I need a minute. "When's the last time you came?"

"I…" Her brow knits.

"You've been touching yourself?"

Color fires her cheeks. "A few times, in Africa, but not since before I got sick."

"So it's been what? A little more than a month?"

"Longer. What about you?"

"Pretty much daily."

Her tongue dots the center of her upper lip. "You've made it a regular habit to masturbate in the guest bathroom shower?"

"Yep."

"I'd no idea."

"It's not a topic to raise with your dad and Jessie over dinner."

"I haven't made the last month easy."

"I prefer endurance to sprints."

Her lips crook. "You want to go the distance?"

"I've got a game plan." I slide a hand from her splayed knee to her center, enter a finger, draw out and return, this time with two.

"I seem to be winning."

"Ah, sweetheart, don't you see?" There it is, the secret spot, deep inside. I crook my fingers in a beckoning, come-hither motion and she bows. I do it again and she grabs her hair in two violent handfuls. The third time she screams. "I'm playing for keeps."

"Holy fuck, Bran." She looks bewildered and sounds drunk.

I drop forward, my face between her thighs. "There's a prayer I can get behind."

We drive from Sacramento to Santa Cruz with her dad and Jessie in the front seat. I can't bear to look at Talia in her tiny skirt beside me. I'm reduced to a horny seventeen-year-old trying to lose his virginity. We stopped at a petrol station twenty minutes ago, and

Scott cock blocked me from buying condoms by coming in to take a leak.

I've got balls, but not enough to buy rubbers under a father's nose.

"Dad," Talia pipes up.

He turns down public radio. "Hmmm?"

"I want to touch on the room situation for when we get to the hotel."

"You and Jessie will pair up, so will Bran and I." His tone is curt.

"Yeah, about that. Um, no."

"Come again?" Scott's hands clench and unclench on the steering wheel.

"Bran and I lived together in Australia. We are going to be moving into a place once we leave Bankside."

"Listen, Peanut—"

Jessie reaches a hand over the console. "I'm thirty-two weeks along, honey. I need my baby daddy close at hand."

Scott's shoulders drop. Jessie in for the win. Can't argue with a pregnant lady.

Talia glances over at me and does a furtive hip shimmy that doesn't do anything to improve the situation in my pants.

Scott's an overprotective father and that's fine and good, but Talia's capable of so much. She's right there, hovering on the edge and only needs to give herself permission to fly. When she does, everyone will gawk and say, *I never saw that coming!*

Except for me. I always knew.

Talia and I get a room overlooking Monterey Bay all to ourselves. We toss our bags on the king-sized bed and explore. The bathroom is massive. A sunken tub? Two nights? I can work with this. Inspiration strikes and I turn on the tap.

"You want a bath?" she asks.

I turn and lift her shirt, circling my thumb around her navel. "I want you to have a bath. Let me spoil you."

Her eyes hood as my hand rises higher, cupping her breast. "No complaints from this quarter."

I'd take her here, on the tiles, but she deserves care. Instead, I help her into the steamy water, kneel beside the tub, and massage shampoo through her long hair as she sighs. She looks like she does right after she comes, blissed out. The tub is filled with the hotel's complimentary jasmine bubble bath. The water temperature is hot, enough so that she sucked in her breath upon entry, her tight muscles relaxing despite herself.

"Mmmmmm...that's nice."

Bloody hell, she purrs like a cat.

"I want to take care of you."

"Aren't I supposed to take care of myself?"

"Fine, I'll settle for bath boy."

I've never washed another person's hair before, but with her, all the stuff, the little gestures that always seemed too intimate, too much, are just right. Every touch I put on her body is tender. Hell yes I want to take things further. The way she looks? All soaped-up nakedness? Hotter than blazes. During the drive to Santa Cruz, I mulled 3,406 dirty ways to have this girl. But she unwinds under my hands, distracted from her worries, and that's what slows me, keeps me gentle, careful.

After all she's been through, I want her feeling safe, adored, to understand no matter how bad her darkness gets, I will always believe in her light. I don't speak these words though. Sometimes touch makes for better communication. Words only go so far.

Talia is the only person I've encountered at the perfect inter-section between mind and body—the sweet spot on a Venn dia-gram. I rinse her pretty hair clean, careful not to get any water or soap in her eyes. She doesn't squint or squirm. She trusts me. God knows why, but to her I am a hero.

She makes me want to be the best version of myself.

I'm trying, and it's bloody hard work. She deserves a man not a sulky boy who pitches a fit when things don't go his way.

Of all the things she teaches me, the most important is drop-ping defenses without fear of where the next punch will land. I have loads to learn, but I'm getting there.

When she starts to cry I don't make a single *shhhhhh*-ing sound. Not all tears are bad. Better to have her cleansed inside and out.

"Get in here with me," she whispers.

"You know we can't do anything without—"

"Yeah, I know."

I've gotten a girl accidently pregnant before. I'll never be so careless as to put another person, or myself, through that again.

"Hey, I love that you're careful with me. I just want you closer, skin to skin."

I stand, strip, and drop into the opposite end of the bath.

Bubbles part around her body as she moves forward, crawls on top of me.

The feel of her is so good I almost cry out. She's it for me, for-ever, the last girl I'll ever love.

She drapes her arms around my neck and we kiss and kiss. Even though I'm rock hard, I don't let my hands slide below her shoulders.

"Brandon."

I freeze. Talia never calls me by my full name.

"You know how I say I love you?"

"Yeah?"

Her lids close for a millisecond and then that warm brown gaze is back on me. There's this weird sensation in my chest like she's got magnets in her eyes and they tug at my heart.

"It's not enough."

Fear rushes through me. I'm trapped inside myself, clawing walls of flesh and bone.

"The word..." she says with a gentle wonder, like she hasn't annihilated me. "It's not big enough to explain what I've got going on in here for you."

My limbs go shaky, uncertain, like I'm a newborn foal. I don't know where the next seconds go. Her pupils are so dilated that my face reflects back. If I stare harder, maybe her eyes will be reflected in mine and vice versa, and I can follow the chain back to the origin of our universe.

She traces my mouth. "I supernova you." Her fingers slide over my jaw, down my neck, my chest, lower. I don't move. Or breathe. Lower. Lower. Is she? Is she?

Fuck.

Her gaze remains locked on mine as she encloses my shaft. Deliberately, rhythmically, she twists both hands in opposite directions while sliding up and down.

"Nice?"

I can't speak. A single nod must suffice.

She works me like that in the warm, silky water until I'm half-mad. The moment she cups one hand around my balls, glides the heel of her palm along my base, I launch backward, half out of the water.

She crawls after and nudges me to the side. I haul onto the edge of the tub and she kneels between my legs. The sight of her staring at my dick with those heavy-lidded sexy eyes nearly brings me off. She takes me all the way down. Bloody hell. I jerk, impossible to hold still. Her tight mouth is even hotter than the bathwater. She takes me slow and steady, pausing occasionally to swirl her tongue just below my head. Fuck. I'm so close. She offers up a little moan, the urgent vibrations push me closer to the brink.

She pulls back and whispers against my skin, "Come in my mouth."

"Yeah?" I've done it before, in the past, with other girls, but I'm never sure if it's right.

"I want this." She takes my hand and rests it on the back of her head. "I want you."

I knot her hair in a loose fist and she's everywhere, lips, mouth, eager tongue. The fact she's so into this, into me, here we go, I can't keep control. Talia is right, love doesn't cut it. Together we're a goddamn supernova.

Talia drags me across the street to the boardwalk. The sun has properly set, so the place is a surreal mosaic of neon lights. A forty-meter tower rises to our right. People queue to be strapped into the seats, heaved to the top, and dropped.

"Oh, look! The Double Shot. I threw up my cotton candy riding it once."

"Hot."

She slaps my chest with a laugh. "Man, I love this place." She points to the merry-go-round. "My first memory is that carousel."

"Really? How didn't I know?"

"My first memory?" She gives me a funny face.

"I want to know everything about you."

"Women should have their secrets." Her flirty side eye sends blood rushing below my belt. "I have one now. A place we could go."

"Do you?"

"Indeed. You have the goods?"

"7-Eleven mission completed. Thanks for being my wing-woman." The condoms are in my back pocket. Condoms I scored while pretending to buy a drink at the convenience shop after dinner while Talia distracted her dad and Jessie with a desire to watch the sunset.

"I have a vested interest, and the perfect plan."

"Which is?"

"A secret isn't a secret if I tell."

"I have ways of getting you to talk." I pull her close and our kiss is long and deep. The air is thick with sugary smells, candied nuts, and fried donuts—sweet but fake. Talia tastes like the real deal. She deepens the kiss and for a second I almost forget we're in a family setting.

"Interrogation by tongue?"

"You disapprove of my methods?"

"Au contraire."

I tickle her sides. "How about a turn on the Ferris wheel?"

She pokes out her tongue. "I'm afraid of heights, remember?"

"You can sit on my lap. Close your eyes."

"A regular romantic."

We wander past the haunted house with its eerie organ music and evil-looking gargoyles.

"They filmed *The Lost Boys* here." She's doing her nervous talk thing.

"Okay."

"You know that flick, right?"

"Should I?"

"Hang on a sec. I need to process... you're down with Andrew Lloyd Webber but—"

"Jesus! Quiet, Captain." I cover her mouth. "Never speak of that."

"For being an Internet sensation you know nothing."

"I. Am. Not. A. Sensation."

"I'm surprised no one has asked you for your autograph yet."

I don't smile.

"I'm sorry, okay. No jokes."

"Not about that." I'm trying, but that *Eco Warriors* shit cuts close to the bone.

She runs her hand up my arm. "Hey," she says quietly. "I get it. Not everything is fair game for comic relief."

"Thank you."

"Notice how I refrain from teasing you for not knowing *The Lost Boys*. It's an old-school vampire movie, by the way. It starred those two Coreys who were big in the eighties and Kiefer Sutherland. He plays a—"

"I know who Kiefer Sutherland is."

"You do?"

"Gaby had a poster of him on her wall. I caught her making out with it once."

"Oh my God, I used to do the same with my NSYNC door poster. I wore off Justin Timberlake's mouth."

I grimace.

"TMI?"

"The mental image of you tonsil-licking a photo of a boy band?"

"Suppose you don't want to hear about my torrid affair with a Harry Potter pillowcase."

"Abso-fucking-lutely not."

"You're no fun."

"I think our definitions differ."

"Do you want to take a ride?"

I give her a look.

She blushes. "I meant like maybe the swings."

"I'm good."

She waggles her brows. "Straight to dirty deeds?"

I extend my hand.

She leads me through the press of bodies. We don't talk. We don't even look at each other. My mouth goes dry as I imagine her soft, hot wetness. She twitches because I made a noise, something animalistic, deep in the back of my throat. It's been five months since I've been inside this girl. For the last month I've waited.

Waited.

And waited.

I cock my chin toward the beach. The wide strip of sand disappears into the dark. "How about out there?"

"Beach hookups are romantic in theory. The reality is sand in uncomfortable places."

"What about under the wharf? I could—"

"No!" Her voice raises an octave. "Not there."

I frown. Wait, this must be *the* wharf. The one where she lost her virginity with her sister's ex, a guilt she carried even when she'd done nothing wrong. She stares up at the night sky, her features tight, and I make a decision to let it go. Not push. I don't want to know everything about her, despite what I said. Just like she doesn't need to know every last detail of my own past. The important thing is that we know each other's future.

I lean in and kiss the side of her neck, breathe in the sweet jasmine smell of her shampoo. "How about we go back to the room and—"

"I've always had this one little fantasy."

"Go on…"

She bites the corner of her lip, considering. "It's better if I show you. We have to cut through the rest of the boardwalk."

"Lead the way."

We reach the end of the boardwalk. Water splashes from the log ride overhead as she steers me through an old-fashioned turnstile. I follow her into the tight space. Her ass collides with my pelvis. I do a quick check and don't see anyone close, so I wrap my fingers around her breasts and grind a little. Let her feel my want. Her head falls back against my shoulder. I nip the top of her ear, soft, even though I'm so hard.

"Not far." She leads me down the hill. The boardwalk is built right on the beach and alongside a river. There's enough light to reveal the shallow water and wide sandbars. Is that where she's taking me?

She stops and starts to kick off her shoes.

"Let me do it, Captain." I drop to one knee and ease them off.

"It's low tide. We have to wade across. A bit of a mission but it'll be worth it."

She gives me a smile as I run my thumb down the arch of her foot—one that's all naughty promise.

Bloody oath it will.

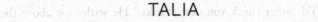

9

TALIA

I lead Bran to where the San Lorenzo River loses itself at the Pacific. It's low tide, so the depth is only ankle-deep. He snatches me around the waist and flings me over his shoulder.

"Whoa there, cowboy, my feet are in fine working order, thanks very much."

"If you walk, I can't do this." He gives me a light slap on the ass.

"And here I thought you were being a gentleman."

"Nope." His grabby hands slide beneath my miniskirt, flirt with my silky tap shorts. "These are something."

"Oh yeah?"

"They do things to me."

"What kind of things?"

"I'd rather show you." His fingers tease farther up my thigh, near the join.

Sweet Jesus on a tricycle, I'm ready for him to finger me in plain view of the kiddie train ride.

"Hold that thought."

His frustrated growl drowns out the splashing of his sure-footed stride through the water. "How much further, then?"

"Check it." The sandstone cliffs are luminous in the bright moonshine.

"I'd rather check you out, thanks." He settles me above the tidemark on the opposite shore, his hands still locked on my hips.

"Brushing up on your Shakespeare? I'm the sun to your moon?"

"Pretty damn close. I don't shine if you don't." His gruff accent is devoid of sarcasm. He confers on me these words the way some guys give flowers. Except anyone can go buy a bouquet, all it takes is a few bucks. Finding the exact perfect sentence to send a girl swooning takes hella-mad skills.

I scoop my hips against his. His rough denim brushes through the skimpy fabric of my skirt.

"Where to?" He won't stop staring at my mouth.

"This way." I take his hands and walk backward.

His gaze flickers over my shoulder. His jaw sets when he sees the cave. The cliffs along the San Lorenzo River are dotted with them, and during low tide they are dry. Since high school, I've day-dreamed about having my dirty way with a hot guy in one of them.

Time for the fantasy to become reality.

"Sure you don't prefer to go back to the room? Have a bed?"

"Positive. I want my wild man."

"Do you now?"

"Yes." Shit, my voice squeaks. I'm like a field mouse hot for a panther.

Those magnetic eyes hood as he gives me a slow, devious smile. His bare toes flex into the sand. His shorts end just below the knees. The diffuse light from the boardwalk cuts over his muscular, runner-honed legs. I rub my tongue along the top of my mouth fighting an urge to drop to my knees and bite his calf. After making me come yesterday, he flicked my switch. All systems are go. Holy crap, I want this guy so badly my jaw hurts. The BJ in the tub was only the beginning of my master plan.

"Why do you look like that?" His voice is deceptively soft, hypnotic.

"I feel so crazy, like I could eat you."

"If that's crazy, Captain, then I'm a goddamn lunatic."

We pitch ourselves into each other. His fingers snarl my hair while I push off his shoulders, hitch my legs around his waist, and rock my pelvis into his. He returns the grind, hard, against my silky undershorts.

"I've bloody starved for you." He tears his tongue from my tank top strap to the side of my neck, a place directly wired to my sex. His teeth graze my earlobe and I suck in a sharp breath. He's not gentle, but I don't want him to be.

I'm not a breakable, weak girl. I'm a woman who wants her man, in every way he can give it.

I'm vaguely aware we are on the move, that Bran gets us inside the cave. I don't know how he even sees where we're going because he's got me hoisted so that my boobs are smack in his face. He draws my nipples with hungry lips through my top's thin cotton. Oh my God. How does he do that? Make me feel all the feels and not even touch my bare skin?

He lifts me free of him and unzips my skirt. The ground's dry underfoot. Once I'm naked from the waist, he drops to the loose gravel and pulls me down, settling my thighs on either side of his head. He sucks me hard, right on the clit. Wait, what? He seriously wants me to ride his face? I love what he's doing, don't get me wrong, but I don't want to squish him.

"Talia." He rumbles the word like it's an order, as if he wants me to do this, to be the kind of girl who fucks her boyfriend's face. There's no way he can miss the way my belly trembles. My mind hesitates, but my body is straight up, *HELLS TO THE YEAH, HI-HO, SILVER.*

"Don't think," he whispers. "Feel." He slides his tongue along my sensitive skin, making his claim, until my eyes roll back to check on my brain. "You feel me, Talia?"

I unleash a soft, shivery moan. Another lick, a little harder. Jiminy Fucking Christmas.

"I asked you a question."

I manage a faltering nod.

"Can't hear you."

"Are you writing your name on me?"

He blows lightly on my skin. "Want me to?"

"Whatever it is you are doing——"

His tongue is across me in five different places. "That?"

"Jesus, yes. That. You can keep it up."

"Grind on me."

"I——I don't know."

"Do it."

"What if I break your nose?"

"The doctors will high-five me."

"What if I suffocate you?"

"I'll die happy."

"Bran…"

"Talia, if you knew how hot you look. You're blowing my mind here."

"Fine, but don't say I didn't warn you."

I sink my weight onto his mouth and do a self-conscious back-

and-forth roll. No way, this isn't going to work. I want to crawl off. Be safer. Less exposed.

Moonlight cuts through the sea fog, and my nipples contract from the chilled air. His fingers lock into the soft flesh in my ass. Fucking fuckity fuck, he devours me and I couldn't stop moving if I tried. That pace? That pressure? Pure sensation overrides the system.

I let my fingers get lost into his thick, glossy hair and pump hard, ride his clever lips until he takes me to a place past shame, past need. I fight for breath. It's undiluted taking, but in a way that's holy—a gift pulled straight from his soul to mine. More. More. When I fall apart he's already put me back together in a way I can barely explain.

I'm me, but a so much better version.

"That was…" I dismount, sit on the back of my heels, and watch as he undoes his flannel.

"The hottest thing ever?" He tugs too hard. A button ricochets off the wall. "You're sure you're okay with this? On the ground?"

"Fantasy cave sex with you? It's like Christmas combined with Mardi Gras."

He spreads his shirt across the bare earth. A second later his T-shirt follows. "Come here." He eases me down, kneels between my spread legs, and opens his shorts. A quick tug of khaki and there it is. The part of him that is so Bran and yet always somewhat of a surprise.

He digs out the foil and goes to tear it with his teeth.

"Ouch, don't do that." I snatch the condom wrapper from his hands. "Let me." He stays on his knees while I sit and remove the latex circle and set it against the head of his dick. "We haven't had to use one of these in a while."

He twitches.

"Do you mind?"

"A little."

"Really?"

"I mind that if you don't hurry I'm going to come all over your hand."

I hit the end of his shaft and pass my fingers down over his balls.

"Bloody hell!"

"That close?"

"You have no bloody idea." He lifts me on top of him. I'm so wet I don't even think he pushes. He's just there.

"Bran."

"I know."

"I held you at bay for so long."

"That's over." He fists his hands into my hair and tilts my head back. His lips fasten to the thin skin beneath my jaw. "This is now. Be here."

"I am."

I brace his shoulders and press until I get the grind exactly how I like it.

"There you go, sweetheart." His voice is a ragged rasp.

I tighten my legs around him, not wanting any space in our contact. All I can hear is our heavy breathing. I move faster, harder until sweat beads my brow like some sort of baptism.

"You own me." He doesn't take his gaze off me, from what I'm doing. "You fucking own me."

"We own each other."

My inhibitions disappear so fast I don't notice them leave. I ride him harder, faster. He hikes me closer, our bellies slam and I can barely move, except what little I manage sends out shivery tentacles to every corner of my body. Each little rub of friction is more intense than the last.

"I'm close." He sinks his teeth in my shoulder. "You're too much."

I brace his head between my hands as pulsing tingles build and build and build. It's like that roller coaster across the river, inching higher and you know you're going to fall, but can't wait. We gasp at the exact same time and hang on through the rush. Wherever this crazy ride takes us, we're going there together.

10

TALIA

I wander the Westside Farmers' Market with a huge smile on my face. Bran woke before dawn and took me in ways that are probably illegal in some states. He and Dad hit the water after breakfast while Jessie headed downtown to browse Bookshop Santa Cruz. The next few hours are my own. An old-timey band fills the air with fiddle music and washboard rhythms. My coffee is perfectly brewed and the morning is an ideal balance between retreating fog and emerging sun. This is the kind of weather where it's reasonable to wear a wool sweater and a short skirt, the kind of weather where magic seems possible.

It's good to be back home—better than I expected. I walk in my college graduation this afternoon. Things with Bran border on amazing. I rock my head back and let my eyes close.

Thanks, universe. I needed a day like today.

There's no snicker. No cosmic elbow nudge. Nothing warns me for what's coming next.

A ghost. My own personal demon.

Tanner. My dead sister's epic love.

The guy I lost my virginity to in a gigantic whisky-fueled mistake. The guy who left me passed out in my underwear on the cold sand. The guy who walks toward me like it's his job.

Okay, okay, okay. No need to panic. I'm wearing glasses and a slouchy hat—pretty incognito, right?

Shit and fuck. He's coming closer.

If I had access to a bucket of lamb's blood, I could swathe myself in the hopes he'd pass me by. What's close? Heirloom tomatoes? Dinosaur kale? Vegan baked goods? Crap, not going to cut it.

Tanner gives a stiff nod. I'm definitely in his sights. The last time our paths crossed was over a year ago near the skateboard ramp at Derby Park. He looked right through me. I figured that was our new normal. He pretends I don't exist and I pretend it doesn't hurt.

Should I glance away like I don't notice? Acknowledge? I end up doing both, an awkward head jerk. My chin collides with my shoulder. Super classy.

"Hey." Tanner pulls up short and addresses the ground between us.

How does he do that? Sound exactly the same? Like someone that I know. A guy who'd chowed sunflower butter sandwiches at my house every afternoon for eight years.

At least I'm wearing appropriate footwear. The fact is mildly heartening. The hey-I-never-spoke-to-you-after-taking-your-virginity conversation definitely requires combat boots.

Be cool, aloof, politely distant.

"Hi. Wow. So . . . how's it going, you?"

Falling all over yourself = NOT cool.

"I didn't know you were back in town." He rolls a pebble around with the toe of his old-school Adidas.

"I didn't know you would care." *SO NOT ALOOF.* I take a giant gulp of coffee.

He resets his trucker hat. His hair's shaggier. Loose waves hang over his ears. Pippa always liked it shorter, buzzed right to his skull.

"Been a while, Tea-bag."

His unexpected use of that old jokey nickname distracts me midswallow, flushes the bitter liquid down my air pipes. "Tea-bag" was the number one way he used to annoy me. It used to be kind of funny, before I actually performed the maneuver on him.

His stricken expression echoes my own thoughts.

You there, God? Go ahead and smite me. Please, I beg you, have mercy.

I choke, bend over hacking, because really, this situation needed to get just that little bit worse. He pats my back before we throw ourselves apart at the casual touch.

"Yeah," I gasp, wipe my mouth with the back of my hand, and reset my glasses in a gesture that I hope passes for dignified. "A while. I got sick."

"Sunny said you were in Africa."

My eyebrows squish together. "Since when do you talk to Sunny?"

He rolls his shoulders. "We, uh...hang out."

"You and Sunny? She never mentioned."

Sunny *hates* Tanner. Okay, maybe *hate* is a strong word, but she's always been curiously immune to his charms. "Golden Boy," she calls him behind his back, pretending to gag. She enjoys being contrary. Everyone else and their pet donkey loves this guy.

Still, is it weird she hasn't mentioned having any Tanner-related change of heart? Yeah, kind of. But I haven't exactly been a master communicator. Anyway, as much as I love the girl, she's a smidge flaky.

"You were sick?" He frowns.

"Oh, you know." I shrug and give an airy wave of the hand. "Malaria."

"Holy shit, Talia." This is the first time Tanner looks me straight on. Those wide baby blues used to give me all the flutters. He's like an altar boy, impossibly angelic, ripe for a little corruption. I crushed on him even though I knew it was wrong, that he was my sister's. They'd been together since middle school. I was so shady, wishing he'd realize that even though Pippa got all the looks, the charm, and brains...I was a diamond in the rough. All I needed was the right kind of polish and I'd shine.

Thou shalt not covet your sister's boyfriend. I broke the eleventh commandment. Then I doused it with cheap whisky and fucked it under the Santa Cruz Wharf.

But now?

My sketchy feelings toward Tanner are gone. The realization disorients me. He's still completely attractive, but that old, familiar yearning is gone. He's like a brother.

He shoves his hands deep into his jean pockets. Muscles cord in his forearms.

Okay, maybe more a cousin. A distant cousin.

"I came back to walk for graduation."

"Right on."

"Yes," I say, tasting the sweet truth. "It's pretty awesome. A long time coming."

"Your folks around?"

"Dad is, he's out for a surf with my um, with my boyfriend." I pass my coffee cup between my hands.

He whistles under his breath. "Your guy's going to be put through his paces. Swell's massive."

"He can hold his own."

"Good to hear. Your pop's gnarly."

"He's something."

The silence drags until I have no idea what to say next. "How about you? What are you up to?"

"Taking time out," he mumbles.

"From skating?"

He shrugs. "Life."

"Oh." We've established a thin, wavering connection, but it's no stronger than a spider strand, and there's a huge gulf between us. "Are *you* doing okay?"

"Touring, the scene, it got intense."

"You work hard." Tanner has a freakish gift. His mom took home videos of him popping ollies at three. Doing railslides by six. I mean, this is Santa Cruz, ground zero of skate culture, and he's a pro. Add the fact that he is an anti-hooligan, all honest smiles and self-deprecating kindness, and sponsors fall over themselves. He's a public relations wet dream, the looks plus the squeaky-clean role model.

He's perfect.

Just not perfect for me.

"So." I shift my weight. "I should probably head back, get ready for the big ceremony."

"Where are you staying?"

"Dream Inn." The same place where his mom cleaned rooms before Tanner made it big and bought her a place, set her up right—another part of his mythology.

A shaft of light cuts through the fog and his hair catches it, turns every shade from white-blond to honey wheat.

Sunny is right. He is such a golden boy.

"Good to see you."

"You too." I give his shoulder a playful punch. I want to touch him just once. Because once, I loved him. There. That's enough.

"Catch you later." His gaze drifts away.

"Take it easy." I turn and start to walk. Does he turn to watch me leave? I can't bear looking back. The sidewalk ahead is filled with cracks. It takes every ounce of self-control not to skitter around them. I push myself to West Cliff, the multi-use trail that hugs the coast. My heart remains compressed like it's double wrapped in elastic. I don't want to hold any thought too close. I toss each one to the crashing waves below and walk faster and faster.

Breathe, just breathe. Let it go.

Warm rays fall on the back of my neck. I pass Lighthouse Field, nearly at Steamer Lane where Dad and Bran are in the surf, when I hear my name.

"Talia!"

Tanner?

I pivot on one heel. He jumps off his board and runs toward me.

"Hey! What—" My words stifle because my face slams into his broad chest. He grabs my shoulders and hangs on tight. My glasses dig into my face. It's hard to breathe.

"Tanner?" I say. His name comes out more like "Tshmsmoffr."

He shudders.

Holy shit. He's crying?

I can stand a lot. Well, maybe not a lot, a lot. No way can I handle his tears. I brace my hands on his ribs and shove back a little. I don't want him this close.

"What happened—what we did—what I did—taking advantage…"

I take a deep breath. "It took two for that to happen."

"You were drunk." His eyes are wet, their expression hollow.

"You could barely walk. We were wasted."

He punches his upper thigh. "I shouldn't have let it get out of hand."

"But, Tanner, I wanted it, all of it. Everything."

"Me too, but I freaked."

"Yeah, well, I kinda noticed." I'd woken to the high tide pulling at my toes, a homeless man snoring a few feet away, and Tanner nowhere to be seen.

His gaze scours my face. What's written there?

"You deserved better."

"It sucked." I shrug. No sugarcoating the truth. "But nothing short of building a time machine will change the facts, and I'm no help there. I suck at physics."

He grinds his fists in his eye sockets so hard that I worry he's going to do damage.

"You're different," he says at last.

"Wow, a loaded statement."

"You seem more, I don't know, like your own person. Confident. That's cool."

I shrug. "Truth circle? I don't know who the hell I am."

But I'm starting to have a better idea.

"Hey." I extend my hand in lieu of a white flag. "Can we be cool again?"

"Come over here." He wraps me into a bear hug. My nerves get the best of me and I laugh, then he's laughing too, a low, deep rumble.

"Hey."

I wince at the familiar accent. What's Bran going to think finding me in Tanner's embrace? I turn slowly, and brace myself. His wetsuit is unzipped, the top hanging over his waist. It looks like someone took an eraser and rubbed away any emotion on his face. His stomach tells a different story. Each abdominal muscle stands out as he flexes, reining himself in.

Shit. He and I just found our way back together. What do I say? *This isn't what it looks like?* Totally lame. Instead, I cock my head to the guy fastened against me.

"Bran, this is Tanner. And uh, Tanner—this is Bran. My boyfriend."

"How's it going, man?" Tanner releases me and throws out a hand to execute a brotastic hand slap as per his usual friendly self.

The problem is that Bran doesn't do the whole outgoing thing. At least, not with people he doesn't know well, and especially not with guys who tackle hug his girlfriend.

There's an excruciating second where I'm 99 percent confident Bran will ignore the proffered hand or land a sucker punch.

"Wait, holy shit." Tanner peers closer. "I know you, dude! You're the guy from that show. I saw the commercial, you jumped off a boat to save the girl. That was badass."

Welp—that seals the deal—Tanner's getting a fist in the face. The only question remaining is when, and how hard.

Bran's arm flies out and I flinch.

"Hey, man. I'm all right, yourself?"

The moment shifts from scary to surreal. I've slept with a grand sum of two guys in my entire life and here they are, shaking hands, being cool with each other. Tanner quizzes Bran about his surf session and they trade knowing references about how things are going with my dad. I can't maintain focus.

Tanner adjusts the brim of his hat and glances to where his

board is kicked on the edge of the path. A gaggle of middle school kids cluster around it, stare at him, back to the board, at him again.

Unlike Bran, Tanner's used to attention. People in our neighborhood view his success as theirs, and he never lets it rattle him. He takes the adoration with the same easy stride he does everything with.

"Looks like you've got a fan club," I say.

Tanner raises a fist to the boys in greeting, and they sputter into nervous giggles. "I should probably go say hey. You sticking around long?"

"Nah. Only until tomorrow morning," I answer.

He takes a step away. "Well, take it easy. Don't be a stranger."

"You too."

"Ever think about moving back to town?"

I shrug. "Might be good to give the place a break."

"Sick of the patchouli already?"

"I should try something new."

"Do me a favor and tell Sunny hey when you talk to her again," he says with a suddenly bright smile.

"Will do." There's that weird feeling again. Not jealousy. Just so odd. The idea of them hanging out does not compute. "I wish she was around this weekend." *I have a few questions for that girl.*

Tanner's shrug could mean a thousand different things, but I have enough to worry about.

"See you around, T." Behind him, stretching out over the bay, is the Santa Cruz Wharf—the scene of our crime. We are so much better off as friends. I'm glad we have a chance of that becoming a possibility again.

"Good catch-up?" Bran asks when we've walked out of earshot.

"Hey, if you're not okay with what just went down..."

"I didn't say that."

"We ran into each other at the farmers' market. It was so awkward. Then he showed up here. He cried, Bran. Not a lot but it was—"

"I don't need to hear the details."

"Please—"

"No, I mean it." He stops, takes my hand, prowls restless fingers across my wrist. "You guys have history. You don't need to pretend it didn't happen. I might not want to hear all the particulars… wait, why are you smiling?"

"I'm proud of you."

"For what? Not losing my shit when the guy you used to love was all over you?" His words suggest a barely there smile.

"Yes. That."

He makes a deep noise in the back of his throat. "I almost lost the plot when he brought up the *Eco Warriors*—"

"I know, I know."

"It was all I could do," he mutters.

"Gold star restraint."

"That guy's your past?"

I squeeze his hand. "Ancient history."

"What I care about is your future." Bran pulls me close and fits his chin to the top of my head. "That's where I want to be."

11

TALIA

*W*e walk toward the hotel. I grin at Bran's bare feet. His exposed toes are everything cute. I can't shake the sense we head in a new, better direction. He didn't go all dropkick ninja on Tanner. Instead of masking insecurity with animosity, he managed to calm down. Even after the fact, he hasn't retreated into himself. He's here with me. He glances at my face, and his gaze softens. In public his countenance typically shifts between gruff and expressionless. Only when we're alone does he ever remove the defensive mask. For him to look at me like this—out where anyone can see— makes me ache with sweetness.

I lace my fingers tight around his. For too long he convinced himself he was unlovable, and lashed out, hurt before being hurt. In Africa, when he wrote and asked for another chance, it wasn't easy to muster the trust. I'm so grateful I believed in him. There's no guarantee that his abandonment fears, the ones that almost destroyed us in Tasmania, won't rear in the future, but I had hope, and now proof, that he's moving forward and trusts my love for him.

He squeezes my hand as if sensing my thoughts. Below us, in the bay, otters splash in the kelp beds. Playful pups bob while adults crack oysters' shells on their bellies. Ahead, a lone woman perches on a bench at the lookout, legs drawn up.

Barbed wire lances my heart. *Wait. No. It can't be.* Holy hell, what's up, today? First Tanner. Now *her?* The universe has a wacked sense of humor. I can almost hear the Fates cackling behind the ocean's dull roar.

"Tell me that's not who I think it is." I stumble, stunned, as if I've been Tasered.

Bran tightens his grip, steadies me. "That's not your mom staring at us."

"It's really her, isn't it?"

"Yeah." A grim finality infuses the word.

I'm dizzy, almost floating. Now and then I experience moments that feel fake, surreal, as if I watch a hazy movie of this thing that's supposed to be my life. The action isn't happening to me, but to another girl. I see myself but have no control over the situation. In the past, this disassociated sensation meant a panic attack loomed. Anxiety stirs in my depths like a viper in a pit. I could give in and let it slither to the surface, or fight for calm. My next breath is deep, from the diaphragm, as I roll back my shoulders.

Come on, come on, come on. Keep it together, girl.

Bran tugs me close—that contact—his touch—is always real. I slam back into myself. No time to raise the drawbridge or man the battlements. This moment is happening, full speed ahead.

I haven't seen Mom in a year. Not since she blamed me for killing Pippa. Okay, maybe not killing in a stabby ice pick way but through my OCD. If I hadn't returned home for yet another compulsive check on whether or not my hair straightener was still plugged in, I wouldn't have been late to my dad's birthday. My sister wouldn't have jumped in a car to fetch me. She wouldn't have been in the path of the neighborhood meth-head when he ran his truck through a stop sign.

My bad thing caused a worse thing.

We draw closer to Mom.

Scratch that. This woman abandoned me. She hasn't been a mother these past two years any more than I've been a daughter.

"What should I do?" I settle my free hand over my churning stomach. Blood roars in my ears.

"Want me to throw her off the cliff? I know a guy who knows a guy."

"Machiavelli much?"

"I'm on standby for whatever you need." His voice is low pitched, but steady. His chin is high and posture strong. "You can do this, Captain."

"Can I?" I lean into his strength, hoping to absorb a little self-possession.

He kisses the side of my hand. "I got your back, you know that, right?"

An image flies into my brain, of Bran standing there, bemused, holding my spinal cord. I choke on a nervous giggle, but the rigid tension remains.

His eyes soften in a silent plea. He wants to help but I don't know what to ask for. In so many ways, just the fact he's here is enough. Then we're there.

"This is a surprise." My voice is reedy, obviously nervous.

"Hello." Mom's formal. Polite. But her hands ball so tight the knuckles go bloodless.

How would she react if I cast a bland smile and kept walking?

Of course, I stop, because I can't resist self-torture. "What are you doing here?"

"You mailed a graduation invite." Mom is startlingly pretty. She lives in Hawaii so her highlights are au naturel. She's all defined cheekbones and wide-set eyes. Her hummingbird-boned hips are so narrow it seems impossible she was ever pregnant twice.

"No, I didn't actually." *Don't get up or anything.* God forbid she hugs me or demonstrates actual motherly affection.

I'm in a slouchy hat, wearing my glasses, dressed in the disheveled way she abhors. She doesn't wear makeup or blow out her hair, but her yummy-mummy hippie chic takes commitment. She's like Gwyneth Paltrow, looking effortless, but doing three hours of Pilates a day, surviving on mixed greens and wheatgrass shots.

"Oh." Her perfect posture wilts. "Your father must have sent it."

"I don't know. He's pretty busy."

"Yes, I imagine. His life is full."

How does she sound Zen? Her ex-husband started a new family. Whatever. She's probably loaded up on Xanax.

"Guess it must have been fun for him the first time round." I bite off the words and spit them at her.

She blinks twice. "He's an excellent father."

At least I lucked out with one half of the parental equation. My laugh is bitter, a little hysterical. I can't even pretend at self-control.

Bran rests a hand between my locked shoulder blades. He's so close I can feel his heart beating against the back of my ribs. I lean into his strong, steady rhythm. The cramping in my chest eases a little.

Mom shoots him a pained smile, but returns her gaze to me. Her nose wrinkles. "You look—"

"I know, I know." I wipe my hands on my holey-kneed jeans.

"No effort." How does this happen? I get in front of her and it's like boom—back to being the always-lacking daughter, consumed by the need for approval, and hiding the hurt behind self-deprecation. My mom is a perfectionist and I'm a walking mistake. We are genetically programmed to be at odds.

"I was going to say happy," she says softly.

I arch a brow. Seriously? We're really going to do this? Mom appears back in my life for graduation and decides to fly the peace flag? Make it all better? No way. This isn't a Lifetime movie. A knot forms in my throat. I need to strive for some shred of empathy; she's hurting, and hurt people often hurt people.

The guy behind me, giving me the courage to stand here, taught me that lesson. Maybe she's lonesome. Maybe she's guilty. Maybe she's grieving. The thing is, I'm not sure I'm ready to give her compassion, but I also don't want to carry around more painful baggage.

"I just arrived." She pauses. Takes a visible belly breath. "Parked the rental car a block away, took a walk by the house."

Our old home is at the end of the adjacent side street. No way I'd go look. Not yet. I'd rather tear out my toenails.

She fingers her amber necklace. "Looks nice. Different—they painted it blue."

Well, la-di-frigging-da. My tenuous grasp on inner calm breaks. What's next? A convo about how the Giants are doing? A little idle speculation on the weather? *Jesus Christ, Mom. How about, "I abandoned my family when you needed me most and that sucks."*

"It's peaceful," she murmurs. "There are flowers everywhere."

"Sounds like a cemetery. So…" I make a big show of glancing around. "You here by yourself? Not seeing any young, hairy-chested boyfriends. I heard you were at a meditation retreat while I was laid up in a South African hospital. That's your equivalent of a pickup bar these days, right?" I'm out of line, but fuck-a-rubber-duck, so is she.

Her thin lips mash together. "The retreat center had a strict no–cell phone policy."

"Funny, I've been in California for a month and never heard from you. Not one single phone call. Must have been one hell of a retreat." *I needed you, damn it.*

Bran slides his fingers up my spine, begins to knead the back of my neck. He keeps silent, but his touch tells me everything I need to hear. *You are loved, you are wanted, exactly as you are. Perfectly imperfect.*

She avoids eye contact, kicks off one sandal, and gouges her toes in the gravel. "I came to watch you walk for graduation. Also, I—I left Hawaii." Mom gives her necklace another twirl. "I got a job and am moving back to California."

"Come again?" She's returning to California? Joining the workforce? Since when did Mom ever do anything more strenuous than drive to the gym? She's the only child of wealthy parents. My dad doted on her.

"I found a position at a resort an hour and a half south of here, in Big Sur, as a yoga instructor."

"For real?"

She flashes a brief, shyly proud smile. "The owner is one of Grandpa's friends, and he was willing to overlook my inexperience. I recently completed my teacher certification. That retreat was my first gig."

I shove up my sweater sleeves, overheating.

"I know I've missed a lot," she whispers at last.

"Yep." My move to Australia. My fallout with Bran. My freaking cerebral malaria. The fact I don't know what to do with my life and wish I had a mommy who could make it better.

"Losing Pippa..." Her voice falters on my sister's name. "Having a child die young, gone forever without any reason..." Her chin dips to her chest as her shoulders slump. "You, you can't imagine what that's like."

"Especially when you're left with the one who's not your favorite."

Her head snaps up. This time she looks at me, really looks at me, and the pain in her eyes makes me sick to my stomach. Mom displaying humanity is overwhelming my circuit board. "Why would you say that?"

"Oh, come on, you always loved Pippa best." I hate the bitter taste of jealousy on my tongue. "She was like your Mini Me."

"Someday you'll have children of your own and see how that's impossible. I haven't been what you needed, what you ought to have had, but my heart broke in an instant. Utterly." A single tear runs down her cheek. Another chases in hot pursuit. The sight makes me a little dizzy.

"Why are you here?"

"When your father got through to me, about how sick you were, you were already flying to California. I didn't know if you'd want me there, or if I'd make it worse. Things haven't been easy between us in a long time, but the idea of losing you too..." She rubs her eyes. "It doesn't bear thinking about. I knew it was time to leave Hawaii. Begin to face my life, the consequences of my decisions."

I want to be angry—incandescent with self-righteous rage. Tell her I am making my own peace, no thanks to her. I could say it's

A Separate Peace, but she won't get the book reference. She doesn't read. Another sign that she may have incubated me in the womb, but if we were seated next to each other on an airplane, we'd politely ignore each other. We are not kindred spirits. We are not bosom buddies.

I don't owe her anything.

Except my whole life.

Maybe that's why there's no surprise when a crash of longing slams me. Despite everything, I want her love. Maybe I don't need it. Not in the way I would if I was a little girl. I'm furious but even still, God, I crave her forgiveness and approval so bad I can taste it.

It's a fight not to plop on that bench, rest my head in her lap, and ask her to rub my back the way she used to, and sing, "Mary, Mary, Quite Contrary." Even when I grew up and realized the lyrics were creepy, it still gives me a Pavlovian response of warmth and security.

Instead, I do none of those things. As much as I want to let go all my resentment, find Zen, empathy, compassion, I don't know how. Bitterness and resentment tangle around me like rumpled bedsheets, and the more I struggle to break free, the tighter their hold becomes.

We stare each other down, like marathon runners, ultra-marathon runners. The finish line should be in sight, somewhere ahead if we push, give it all we have. But I only have enough energy for myself, and the guy behind me.

I'm tapped. My bucket's empty. I want to try with Mom. I do. Just…not right now. "We're going to have dinner at Pizza My Heart after the graduation ceremony." Pepperoni and mozzarella is all I've got to offer.

"Your favorite restaurant."

"Want to join us?"

"Are you sure?" She gives me a hesitant smile, seems to understand that this isn't going to be a big run toward each other in slow-motion makeup, followed by a giggly sleepover where we braid each other's hair and catch up on secrets. "I don't want to impose. I only wanted to see your face, check if you were okay."

"I'm trying to be." *I'm trying so hard.* "Please, come." Why am I urging her? Mom and Jessie together at the same table? Dad's head is going to explode.

"I'm proud of you." She opens up her purse, and for a moment I'm terrified she's going to offer me money. She has access to her family's fortune, and since she and Dad divorced, she's not afraid of using cash as a replacement for basic human affection. She forgets, I've always been her cheap-ass kid. The one who didn't love to go shopping over the hill at Santana Row. Didn't buy cute stuff. Her money doesn't get me all excited.

"Mom, listen—"

"Here." She passes me a plain, white card stamped *Bee Stolfi, Yoga Therapist.* "That's my new number, if you'd ever like to talk."

"Thanks. Look, I…I got to go. I'll send you the details about dinner." I shove the card in my back pocket.

"I love you, Talia."

Maybe I should answer in kind, maybe I shouldn't take four or five fast steps, literally dragging Bran down the sidewalk. Then I release his grip and spin. "If you want to blame someone, why don't you ever blame the guy who hit her car, Mom?"

"I did."

"But you said—"

"Talia, honey, for a long time I blamed everyone. Yes, that

included you. And your dad for having a birthday. And me for making reservations at the restaurant rather than staying home to cook dinner. Everyone was to blame in my mind. Except you're right, only one person really is, a drug addict who decided to text and drive. And even then, what's the blame going to give me? Not your sister. Not peace. All it does is carry me further from you, and away from my best self."

I'm trapped in the doldrums, wanting to care, and not being able to muster the energy.

"The accident wasn't your fault." Her voice wavers. "Peanut, it was never your fault. I'm so sorry for ever making you feel that way."

This is too much. My legs are weak. I need to sit, have space to process, and that's not going to happen here on a sidewalk. "Mom, I can't…I have to go. I'll…I'll be in touch." I half run before tears overwhelm me.

Joggers and cyclists stare as I storm past, but there's nothing I can do but keep moving forward. "What was that?" I say to Bran when I can finally speak, over a block away. "I just acted like a douche canoe businessman. 'I'll be in touch.' Might as well have said 'I'll have my people call your people.'"

"Want to talk about what just happened?"

"Which part?" Holy crap. A lot went down the last hour. My plan this morning was simple: Walk to the farmers' market. Buy a scone and coffee. Maybe go wacky with a punnet of strawberries. Instead I ended up in a twisted haunting from Ghosts of Christmas Past.

He hovers beside me in full protective mode. "Let's get you back to the room."

"Please."

He takes my hand and doesn't say anything for the rest of the walk. He doesn't have to. It dawns on me. Bran gets it. The minute the hotel elevator doors shut, I face him. "How did you survive the after-anger limbo? When you and Adie broke up, the pregnancy, everything? You went numb. How did you come back from that place?"

"I met you."

I stiffen. What if something's wrong with me? I have Bran, but still feel like shit about my mom.

"After meeting you I wanted to be a better guy. I messed up a lot." His eyes darken, going a little haunted. "But I'm trying. The trying helps."

We exit on our floor and I follow him out. "So there's no magic. Just trying. More work."

More opportunities to mess up.

"Hey, now." Bran covers my mouth with his, slow, like we've got all day. I breathe him in, salt spray and sunscreen. Our tongues meet and we both shiver.

Okay, maybe there's magic.

The kiss deepens, turns fierce. I taste the sea, suck his lower lip while his hands explore my waist. My shirt hitches at my belly. The slide of my bare skin on his hard abdomen radiates through me with tremendous force. I don't know how he does it, gives me a way to channel all my feelings.

I unearth the room key card from my hip pocket and shove it into the lock. We fly forward, collapsing on the carpet. He somehow back-kicks the door while I unleash my emotional hurricane into the kiss. We're talking anger and lust, shame and hope, grief and most importantly, forgiveness. If I can forgive him, maybe I can forgive my mom.

Maybe I can forgive myself.

He strips off his wetsuit in a quick jerk, and reveals lean, naked muscles. I shimmy off my skinny jeans and kneel.

There's a sound of foil ripping. He removes my shirt from behind with quick, efficient tugs. "Better." He pops my bra off before my next breath. I don't know exactly how many he's removed in his life to perfect the move, but I swear he never fumbles. Every freaking time it makes me want to combust.

"I need to get back on birth control," I murmur huskily. "I can't stand barriers between us."

"Sounds like a plan, but for now this is part of the game."

"Put me in, coach." I wiggle against his erection as he sucks in a ragged breath.

He doesn't laugh at my dumb joke, too occupied with turning me around to face him and sucking my nipple into his mouth. My brain can't wrap itself around the incredible sensation. We kneel before each other and I rake my hands down his cut waist. "Can you go-go-gadget me to the bed?" I teasingly skim the length of his shaft, not touching him with anything approaching the pressure he needs.

"No." His finger strokes my inner thighs, drawing right up close before backing away. Apparently two can play at this game. "Fucking hell, sweetheart. Do you know, do you really have any idea, how beautiful you are?"

This is part of Bran's voodoo. When he looks at me with those eyes, I feel it, beautiful on a cellular level.

"God, just gorgeous." He sits back on his heels, taking his time to look his fill. That lazy, hooded gaze sends goose bumps prickling down the back of my arms. I'm positive my eyes mirror his same desire. The air is thick with it, pulsing and hot.

He rises in a fluid motion and pulls me with him. I'm just getting to my feet when he slams his lips on mine, his tongue sweet and deep. Our teeth knock, not in a way that hurts or is awkward, but is everything hard, and raw, and urgent. I yank his hair, thickened with salt water, urge him closer, as if I can break apart the arbitrary skin and bone separating our bodies.

Tomorrow we'll be in Bankside, at Jessie's house. No way is my guy squatting in the veranda alcove anymore, but shacking up in the nursery isn't going to cut it. We need to get moving.

But first, I need to get there. With Bran. Right now. We stand naked before each other. The sun pours through the window, makes his olive skin glow. He lifts me off my feet, hitches me against his pelvis, and thrusts us against the wall. My shoulder nicks the picture frame and it rattles in protest.

I lock my legs around his hips. He plunges to the hilt, and I'm full, tender, stretched and it's not enough. It's not nearly enough.

He braces his forearms under my knees, holds me open, completely exposed. I lean back, hands splayed on the wall as our gazes lock and he's just there and I'm just there. His face reflects the love that fills my heart to bursting and that's when I have it.

Enough.

12

BRAN

The field is crowded with graduates. In their flapping black robes they resemble a murder of crows. No way I'll spot Talia out there. Some people have messages spelled on the back of their caps in bright electrical tape. Things like *Go Kristi!* or *Slug Power.*

We wandered campus before the ceremony. Talia explained how American universities have mascots, a tradition she says started during the U.S. Civil War, when soldiers kept animals like dogs or eagles as regimental mascots. After the war, the tradition seeped into their inter-collegial competitions. When established, the University of California, Santa Cruz, wanted a response to all the bull-dogs and hawks out there. They settled on the humble banana slug.

"His only superpower is the ability to slime." Talia found me one, inching through the undergrowth, a brilliant yellow. It reached a redwood base and started to climb.

"He's got a way to go," I said.

"Adventure Slug."

"Reminds me of you."

"Wow." She knocked my chest.

"Hey now." I covered her hand, tugged her close until we stood hip to hip. "I meant it'll get where it wants to go eventually."

"Think so?"

She's going to take the world by storm. "Without a doubt."

Names start being announced from the podium, and I'm jerked to the present. Strangers file forward, grab their piece of paper, and pump victory thrusts. The audience whoops. Scott sits beside me. Space is tight and we are pressed together, knee to knee. He gives me a stiff nod just as Talia's name blasts from the speakers. She hikes her gown and walks up to the podium. I expect her to keep her head down. She gets shy in big crowds, seems uncomfortable with attention. Instead, she turns and gives the crowd a radiant smile that makes my heart swell halfway up my throat.

"Oh, Talia." I whisper under my breath. She waves furiously. I'm not sure she can see us or if she's caught in the moment.

I stand and clap anyway. Two rows up is Bee, her mom, arms wrapped tight around her middle like she's holding herself together.

Talia steps to the edge of the stage and flings her cap into the sky. I half expect it to sprout wings and soar.

After the ceremony, it takes a while to find her in the crowds. I let her dad go first, give the big hug and proud kiss on the cheek. Her mom hovers like she wants to get in there, but all she can do is offer a brittle smile and encouraging head bob. Right before Talia's smile falters, I swoop in and swing her around.

She rubs her nose against mine, laughing. "I did it!"

My answering kiss is the sort appropriate to bestow in front of parents. One that's not nearly enough to convey the bone-deep pride vibrating through my body.

"You did good, Captain." I want to say more, but I can't because those words aren't even born yet. "I love you."

She hugs me closer and kisses my eyelids, slow, one at a time. Each strikes me like the sweetest arrow. "Thank you," she whispers, resting a hand on my jaw. "Thank you for believing."

"Thank you for showing me how." This girl has ransomed my heart, and I never want it back.

We hit up Talia's favorite pizza joint. It's a crowded, family-style place with deep booths. Good thing there's blaring background music and noisy chatter. Our group is awkwardly silent. Somehow Scott ends up squished between Bee and Jessie. Talia and I sit across the scratched table.

"Wow, everything looks great!" Jessie examines the menu with forced cheer. "What do you recommend, Talia?"

"All the pizzas rock. I've probably had every single one at one point or another. We've been coming here since I was a kid." Talia's gaze shoots to her parents and the pronounced gap between them. "Dad and I like anchovies."

"Oh, Lord, no can do." Jessie makes a face.

"I'm with you." Bee leans around Scott. "Salt and fish flavors do not belong on a pizza."

"Worst invention since Smell-o-Vision," Jessie says wryly, and Bee's laugh appears genuine.

Scott's napkin is even more shredded than Talia's. Jessie and Bee are both blond; clearly that's his preference. I've got to say that Bee is better looking, but I prefer Jessie's laugh lines.

The orders get put in and by the time the pizza arrives, Jessie's got Bee drawn into a semi-comfortable conversation about different types of yoga, comparing hatha to vinyasa. I pretend to listen, playing footsie with Talia under the table. She relaxes a little and the napkins get a reprieve. Bee reveals herself to be adept at discussing topics other than herself. Her questions to Scott still hold a terse edge, those two are hardly mates, but Jessie's wide-mouth laughter and open features lend themselves to likeability.

Somehow everyone manages to eat without choking on tension.

Talia shovels in a second slice of pizza. "Mmmmm," she groans, eyes sliding shut with delight. She inhaled the first one. "I haven't eaten all day," she says to her mom. Defensiveness undercuts her speech. Talia thinks her mom is always judging her. Fucked-up thing is, from the little I've seen of their interactions, she's not wrong.

Bee stares at the tray for a few beats. "I think I'll have another one too." She selects a fat slice and bites off the tip. The extra cheese stretches, and a piece of pepperoni plops onto her white shirt. "Oh, rats." She looks at Talia and giggles.

Talia joins in after a second and hands over her ragged napkin. "Looks like we might be related after all."

The rest of the meal isn't exactly perfect, but the way I see it, it's a beginning. At the end of the day, that's all any of us needs, a place to start.

Bee checks her watch. "I better get on the road."

"She hates driving after dark," Scott says, to no one in particular.

Talia watches her mom stand, clutch her purse, and regard the table like it's a place where she wants to fit in, but doesn't quite belong. "Congratulations on graduating again, honey. I'm so very, very proud."

"That makes two of us." Scott's voice is gravelly with emotion.

Bee reaches down and pulls up a bag from under the table. The large one I watched her walk in with. "A graduation gift."

"Thank you." Talia takes the bundle with clear hesitation. She opens the wrapping paper carefully, along the seams. "My baby blanket?"

"I patched up the tears using fabric from your favorite old clothes, and your sister's." She points. "See, there's her old soccer jersey. Remember how she wore it that whole summer? And this one, here, from your First Communion dress."

"You sewed it for me. I felt like a princess." Talia sniffles and brushes her fingertips over the swatch of her sister's shirt. "Jesus, Mom."

"I have a lot more mending ahead of me. When you feel the time is right, please, call me. I promise to be there."

"I will," Talia replies without a trace of rancor. "And thanks for coming. It meant a lot."

Bee gives us all a last uncertain smile before heading out to the door.

"Well," Talia says to everyone and no one in particular. "That was weird. Good weird, but also just plain weird weird."

"You can tell she really cares about you," Jessie says, kneading her brow.

Scott's attention lasers on Jessie, who is increasingly white-cheeked. I don't think it's anything to do with the dinner company. She looks like she's about to be sick.

"Another headache. A normal, boring pregnancy thing," she mutters, before excusing herself to hobble to the bathroom.

Talia's phone vibrates on the table and she glances down. "Beth!"

Her friend lives somewhere in Silicon Valley, works for a big techie firm. All I know is that she hasn't been my number one fan. Neither has the other one, Sunny, who's currently not in town. While I'm sorry Talia's disappointed by her mysterious absence, I'm not exactly broken up.

"Hey girl," she says into the phone, beaming. "Hang on, I'm in a loud restaurant. I'll give you the lowdown but let me go outside." She covers the phone with one hand. "Do you mind if I have a quick chat? Beth is always so busy. It's been forever since we caught up."

"Knock yourself out," Scott replies right as I say, "Go for it."

She looks between us with a half smile. "Um, that was meant as a rhetorical question."

I slide out and make room for her to leave. "Yeah, I know."

Her dad drains half his soda in one giant gulp.

"That stuff will rot your guts." I point to his glass.

"Says who?"

"Have you ever seen what Coke can do to a battery?"

"No."

"Look it up. Shit's scary."

Scott grimaces. "I needed the caffeine. I was up half the night with Jessie."

"She still sick?"

"Yeah."

"Jesus, I'm sorry."

We sit in silence for a moment.

Scott consults his glass like it's a Magic 8 Ball. "How do you think it was for Talia today, seeing her mother?"

"Awkward."

"Bee...she didn't make things easy."

"Doesn't sound like it was an easy situation."

For a second Scott gives me a what-do-you-know-about-it look and then he relents. "No." Another sip. More ice crunching. "It wasn't."

"Talia's going to be okay, you know that, right?"

"She's my baby. Or she was until..." The muscles in his neck cord. "Aw, hell, she'll always be my little girl."

"She's special."

"She is." He raises his glass to me. "I came down on you hard."

"Nothing I didn't deserve."

Scott narrows his gaze. "She's got a big heart."

"And I mean to do right by it."

He grimaces and leans in, poking my chest from across the table. "If not, I've got a gun."

I choke on my water.

"Just kidding, hate the things. But hurt her again and I'll kick the everlasting—"

Jessie returns to the table a trifle pale, but composed. "What's this about kicking?"

"Talking about the baby," Scott says.

"Soccer," I respond.

"Next time you want to fib, coordinate your stories better, boys."

Talia returns wearing a puzzled expression. "So Beth wants to know if we could stop by her work tomorrow."

Scott shakes his head. "We need to get home. Jessie and I have to teach classes."

"I know, that's what I told her, but she said if Bran and I were dropped in Palo Alto, she'd arrange for a driver to take us back."

"A driver?" Scott says, incredulously. "Hell, I should have gone into computers instead of rocks."

"Don't say that," Jessie pipes in, flashing an adoring smile. "You're a rock star."

He cracks up at the stupid joke. Bloody hell, dude must have it bad.

"The guy who's the head of Zavtra, the start-up Beth works for." Talia gives me a hesitant look that I can't interpret. "Apparently, he wants to meet you."

"Me?" I sit straighter, startled. "What the fuck, er, pardon..." I shoot Scott and Jessie an apologetic glance. "What for?"

Talia twiddles her straw in her cup. "He thinks you're interesting."

"Sounds dodgy."

"He watched the *Eco Warriors* clip, all right? It's splattered all over social media. You're like some kind of an Internet celebrity. Beth said it's blown up bigger over the weekend. The YouTube clip has almost a million hits. There are Tumblr pages in your honor."

"What's a Tumblr?" I ask, lost.

"Beth talked a mile a minute and all I gathered is that her boss, who happens to be a billionaire, wants to meet up."

"No." I shake my head. "No way."

She hesitates, gives Scott and Jessie a furtive glance. She doesn't want them to witness a tiff. "I don't know what's going on, Bran. This is crazy. But I want to see my friend. She is chained to her desk over there."

"So make plans. Meet her in the city. I don't own your time. See her whenever. It would be good for you."

"She seemed urgent, like she didn't want to disappoint her boss. Like our presence would be this big favor."

"Bloody hell." I don't want to do this. "Fine. But I go for you. Not her."

Scott gives me an approving nod, like I'm doing the right thing by his little girl. I inwardly groan. Trapped by the brilliant smile Talia gives me.

"Thanks." She rests her hand over mine. "Just a quick visit. It's not going to change our lives or anything."

13
TALIA

D ad zips along Highway 17's hairpin turns. Bran's silent, but his index finger drums a staccato rhythm on the window. The ocean retreats as redwoods close in. The gloom eclipses the light. Jessie huddles in the passenger seat, hands clasped tight. The seat belt barely stretches over her swollen middle. Whoever's inside will be my brother or sister. I need to ramp up something approaching affection. It's a baby, not a betrayal.

But somehow, it is. This little spawn's not my sister. I shouldn't resent it for that fact. But I do and can't tell anyone. Not even Bran, although with him, I don't have to. He probably senses it, like he does all the worst parts about me.

He notices my side eye and musters a halfhearted smile, not really feeling the cheer. He dreads this stopover in Silicon Valley. He agreed to meet Beth's boss, Aleksander Zavtra, founder and CEO of Zavtra Tech as a favor. I'm grateful and guilty—a mixture that unsettles my stomach. This morning before breakfast, I engaged in a little Google fun while Bran and Dad snuck out for a last surf session.

Those two.

I wouldn't say they've achieved BFF 4eva status but they've embarked on a definite bromance. Bran's skills in the water, plus his devotion to me seem to have brought Dad around. My father says you can tell a lot about a person by how they surf. I hope he's halfway kidding because otherwise I'm tentative and flailing.

Oh, wait. Maybe he has a point.

While Dad and Bran indulged in their newfound love affair, I read what I could about Zavtra. He is young, a multimillionaire by twenty-two and at twenty-four is feted as a leader in a new generation of Silicon Valley wunderkinds. His company, Zavtra Tech, is in development on a social media site that's generating a ton of buzz and speculation. The new Facebook? Twitter? Anyone's guess. Besides being ridiculously wealthy, Zavtra is famously reclusive. He doesn't take part in a flashy lifestyle or do philanthropic activity.

He's a freaking Willy Wonka.

People would beg, borrow, and steal to have a sit-down with Aleksander Zavtra and yet my boyfriend acts like he's doing the guy a big favor. Bran's Charlie with the Golden Ticket and a chip on his shoulder.

Once we reach the South Bay, Dad sets the GPS to the address Beth provided. We reach Palo Alto and an office that is more steel than glass. Zavtra Tech is spelled on the side in massive glossy typeface. There's a huge parking lot, full of Audis, hybrids, and at least two Teslas even though it's the weekend.

This place is so Beth. So not me.

Or Bran.

Dad taps the brakes. "This is the right address."

"Looks like it," I say.

Bran and I climb out of the car. He pushes down his sunglasses. He's in faded jeans, a striped hoodie, and fitted gray shirt. Once we get inside he'll look like any other techie—minus the extra few million in the bank. Although Bran had a trust fund, he reneged it because he disagreed with how his family earned its money.

"We need to hit the road before traffic gets worse. Sure you'll have a ride home?" Dad gives the building a skeptical once-over. The 4Runner reflects in the one-way glass. Anyone could be staring back at us. Even Oompa-Loompas.

"Beth says it's no problem."

Bran grabs my hand. "Let's get this over with."

"I want the full report," Jessie pipes in, rubbing her belly. Seriously, she looks about to burst. How can she last another two months?

I wave as they drive away. "Shall we storm the battlements?"

"As you wish."

I fold my hands together, prop them against my cheek, and bat my eyes. "Are you my Westley? I always wanted a Westley."

"What's a Westley?"

"Even you have seen *The Princess Bride*."

"No."

I slap my forehead. "Inconceivable!"

"It's a movie, right?" He tilts his head and his hair hangs in his face.

I smooth back his tousled waves. "Like only the best one on the planet."

"We should watch it. I'm curious to see this Westley competition."

"As you wish," I say with a giggle.

He frowns, missing the joke, then freezes in place. "This place reminds me of Lockhart."

His family's company.

"Remember, it's only a meeting."

"Aleksander Zavtra doesn't invite people round without an agenda."

"You've heard of him, then?"

"You should do a better job of cleaning out your search engine history." His voice is low. Not accusatory, but tense.

Crap. I also had rechecked Bran's growing online fandom. "So you saw..."

"The shit people were posting about me?"

"The ladies love you."

"They don't know me."

"The interwebs are the Wild West. In another fifteen seconds, something else will grab their attention."

"There've been all these phone calls." He folds his arms, regards a plane soaring through the sky toward SFO with far too much interest.

"What do you mean?"

"I turned the damn thing off because strangers keep contacting me. I don't even know how they got my number. It's messed up."

"Girls?" I'm aghast.

"Worse, like television agents and shit."

"Television agents and shit, he says." I have to laugh, because this is bonkers. "What are you talking about?"

"Hollywood fucks. People who want to make a buck off my pound of flesh."

"Are you serious?"

I assume his arched eyebrow is a yes.

"How long has this been going on?"

"Since the promo clip aired. The one you watched."

"You haven't breathed a word."

"This was your big weekend, Talia. Graduation. Going back home. Us. I didn't want to distract you with this crap. At first, I figured the call was a fluke and let it ride. The next day there were more. The messages keep multiplying. Shit's like goddamn rabbits."

"Give me your phone."

His face hardens. "What?"

"Did you delete the messages?"

"Not yet."

"Can I check them out?"

A flush creeps up his jaw as he passes it over.

I listen to the voice mail, it takes minutes. By the end, my fingers press to my open mouth.

Bran's shoulders are practically in his ears. "If you laugh, I turn around and walk out of here, billionaire or no. I don't give a shit."

"Hey, hey, settle down." I wrap around him, slip my hands in his back pockets. "I know, I know you don't. But, holy hell, Bran. People want you to go on late-night shows and everything."

"Not happening."

"But think about it, you could get exposure for what's going on out there, the whale hunts. Help the Sea Alliance spread the word."

His gaze narrows, green eyes radiating an intense strength of will. "I said it's not happening."

"But—"

His hand on my hip slides to my waist. "They want a hero. That's not me."

"I disa—"

"Ms. Stolfi? Mr. Lockhart?" An Eastern European accent rumbles. I turn and look up, and up. A giant looms over the parking lot, swathed in an impeccably tailored suit, aviators, and black silk tie. His hair is buzzed close to his broad skull, and the head of a Chinese dragon is elaborately inked on the side of his neck. "Mr. Zavtra waits for you." He turns, not waiting for us to follow.

O-kay. This situation has left the station and we're officially on the way to crazy town.

"We're talking about your hero issues later," I mutter, trying to keep up with the giant's brisk pace.

Bran grimaces like I just suggested an in-depth chat about the benefits to drawing and quartering in medieval England.

Zavtra Tech looks more ominous and soulless the closer we approach. Sure, there's a lawn, and immaculately landscaped gardens, but the green space feels perfunctory, unnatural.

"Never forget," Bran fires back. "Knights might try their best, but sometimes, the dragon wins."

The security guard bypasses the impressive front entrance in favor of a nondescript side door. He swipes a key card and we're inside. I glare down the intricate tat on his bull-thick neck as we approach the chrome elevator.

"Not today," I answer.

14

BRAN

*T*alia and I stand on one side of the elevator. The Polish security guard—whom I fight the urge to refer to as Tiny—hulks in the opposite corner. Maybe if I taunt a little he'll pound me with one of those meat slab fists, put me out of commission. Might be better than the alternative. Who the hell knows this Zavtra wanker's angle?

Talia glances at me, worry stamped on her expression. She wants to disagree that I caused the accident. I'd love to give her everything she wants, but I can't wish away how things happened Down South. It was my fault. My inexperience nearly killed a woman and now idiots want me to pretend to be a superhero. The idea makes me want to spew my guts out.

We reach the top floor and Talia's friend, Beth, is there when the door opens, smoothing her sleek bob. She's beautiful in a predictable, well-groomed way, everything in place, boring as batshit. She engulfs Talia in a shrieking hug, the way girls do when they haven't seen each other in ages. Tiny and I stand to one side while they hold on tight and execute a twirl. He still wears his shades despite the absence of natural light. I take mine off and shove them in my hoodie pocket. I have enough fake celebrity in my life without needing to posture.

With all this media nightmare garbage, am I going to need to lawyer up? I owe Dad ten grand already. He insists on referring to it as an advance on my services, not a loan. I'm getting pressured to work for the foundation. There's a part of me that knows I've got sound ideas, that the start-up money Dad sank into the organization can be put to good use. But I've devoted over five years of my life resisting the Lockhart name, and everything it stands for. Environmental pillage. Legal but ill-gotten gains.

No. No lawyers. The last thing I want to do is draw on more family resources. I need to keep my head down, wait for the next celebrity to climb from a car without knickers and divert the attention. But bloody hell, Talia has a point. People are interested in me. What if I turn the tables and beat them at their own game? Could I manipulate the situation to make the public knowledgeable about the issues despite themselves?

"Bran?" Beth says, like she's said it before. "You listening?"

I blink. Everyone stares.

"What?"

"Z says you're to enter alone."

I take in the double black doors. "Who's Z?"

"Zavtra? Aleksander Zavtra?" She adds a silent *duh* to the end of the word. "Thank you, Katya, that will be all." She dismisses the gigantic man with a curt smile. He gives a silent nod, steps into the elevator. The doors shut and we're alone. The anteroom gleams white, with one wall a glass pane that looks out to a massive, open-plan office filled with people behind desks, scurrying around, chatting.

"That guy was huge," Talia murmurs to Beth. "Creepy."

"I know, right?" Beth shudders. "He is Z's bodyguard."

"This place has a weird vibe." Talia shakes her head. "I don't like it."

"Don't worry, Z's not scary." Beth's nervous laugh doesn't comfort. Neither does her surreptitious glance to the surveillance camera. She dips her chin down enough that her chin-length hair covers her features.

Whoever he is, the bloke's definitely a type A megalomaniac. Takes a special variety of wanker to flaunt his name on the side of the company building so large it's visible from rush hour traffic. I don't give a toss if the guy is a recluse and this is a big opportunity. The way I see it, he's a phony. The less he reveals himself, or talks to people, the more everyone will think he possesses profound deepness. No doubt it's the opposite.

Beth checks her watch. "We have another eighty-five seconds until you can go in."

"Are you bloody serious?"

"He said ten-thirty a.m. Z...well...he appreciates punctuality."

"Does he have OCD?" Talia asks with forced casualness. She keeps her condition secret from her friends with amazing acting skills. I prefer the real Talia, warts and all. I've had enough fake perfection in my life.

"No, I don't think so. He's...precise."

"What's up with the pauses?" I ask.

Beth examines an invisible wrinkle in her skirt and pretends not to hear. She carries baggage from this guy. The assistant's desk is empty.

"You work here?"

"No! I'm downstairs, in public relations, but filling in at the moment. The last assistant left abruptly."

"Zavtra has a lot of assistants?"

That earns me a sharp look from her.

I look up at the camera and stare down the lens. It watches us like a black, blank fish eye.

"He requested to meet you in person, Bran." Beth's breathy voice drops lower, husky with an odd intensity. "This is a big deal. Huge. He never meets anyone face-to-face."

"Why?" Talia pushes. "Is he deformed or something?"

Beth checks her watch. "All I did was watch the clip of Bran online." She notices my frown and gives me an apologetic face. "It got e-mailed around a couple days ago. The women here think you're way cute. Some of the guys too."

I snort.

"He doesn't like to talk about it." Talia pats my back.

Bloody oath I don't.

"Anyway, I told someone I knew who you were; I mean, we're at like one degree of separation, right?" There's a hairline scar next to Beth's eye. Is that from the accident? Talia said she was in the car when her sister crashed, but that she never speaks about the day, says she can't remember anything.

Beth's gaze shutters when she notices my examination. She's good at hiding her feelings. Takes one to know one. Talia's the opposite. Her face is a billboard. She tries to remain hidden, and to others it might work, but for me, I can read everything. I always could. I have the key to her code; it's what drew me in from the start.

How can people talk to her, even just walk past her, and not fall in love in an instant? She's a rainbow ending in a pot of leprechaun gold. How can't they see? How don't they know?

"Time." Beth strides toward the closed doors with clear relief at being able to execute the duty.

She knocks three times.

"I can just go in."

Beth holds a hand in warning. "Wait thirty seconds."

"Hey." Talia steps beside me. "Maybe I should come with."

Beth shakes her head. "Just Bran. He was very specific."

"What's he like?"

"He sounds definite." Beth twines her fingers through her hair, gives the camera another furtive glance. "It's time you go in."

"What do you mean sounds like?" I place my hand on the door.

"I've never seen him. He either messages or calls. Katya is the only one allowed in there on a regular basis. It's time. Go." Beth nudges my shoulder. "Oh, and Bran?"

"Yeah?"

"Good luck." The deep uncertainty behind her murmur sends the hair on the back of my neck skyward.

I push inside. My eyes don't have enough time to readjust before the door shuts.

The floor-to-ceiling windows are dark from light-canceling blinds. Instead, the office is lit from six mounted flat screens. Each one highlights my face, paused during the promo clip. Gives me the same slow-motion feeling I'd had in those first few seconds the accident unfolded.

The sound of slow, mocking applause. "Quite brave." The voice comes from behind me.

I spin around. "More like a bloody idiot."

"Brandon Lockhart." A guy slouches in the shadows against the far wall, dressed in the same style as his security guard. His face is obscured because he chose the darkest part of the room to lie in wait. A deliberate act. He misjudged his audience. My father hardened me against strong-armed intimidation tactics. "You captured the public's imagination." There's a vague Russian inflection in the growl he gives the consonants, also a hint of British poshness. "Eager to capitalize on your fifteen minutes?"

"Is that why I'm here?" I shove my hands in my hoodie and hold my ground.

"What do you think?"

"Mate, if I had the answer, would I ask?"

"You don't like talking in circles, do you, Lockhart?"

"No. Not particularly."

"Rather be out in all the California sunshine with your girlfriend?" There's a glimmer of amusement in his tone. He enjoys needling me.

"I'm not here to talk about her, that's for sure."

Zavtra raises his arm and there's a barely audible click. The same six flat screens switch to the anteroom. Beth brews Talia an espresso from a fancy coffee machine. Talia glances at the doors, the same ones to my back. Unease is plain on her face even as she tries to follow her friend's rapid-fire conversation.

"Pretty but average."

My unease distils to anger. Good. I'm better this way. "You like having a mouth?"

"Ah, there it is. The temper." Something about his haughty laugh, it's familiar but unclear—a shadow moving behind a frosted window.

"Do we know each other, mate?"

"Natalia Stolfi. Smart, not brilliant. No rare beauty. Nothing exceptional."

The screens flick off. "Why the attraction?"

Is this bloke for real? I lock my arms across my chest.

"I ask a simple question." He inclines his body toward me. I'm impressed by his presence despite the considerable space between us. He gives the impression that his every movement is one of careful consideration.

"Prepare for disappointment."

There's that bloody familiar laugh again. "Aren't you curious about why I am interested?"

"Not particularly, people are nosy fucks."

"A million dollars."

"I'm not following." I hate feeling like I'm missing out on some inside joke.

"A million dollars for you to tell me why you bother loving that girl. You do love her, correct?"

"Piss off."

"Two million."

"You'll pay me two million dollars to explain why I'm into my girlfriend?"

"I will."

"That's a shit ton of money."

"To some. So you agree?"

"No."

"You've refused your more than agreeable trust fund. With no job, or graduate program, what shall you do with your life? Go on another reality television program? I won't make the offer a third time. This is your last chance."

"Good, I'm sick of refusing."

"Very well." His voice is exactly the same, low, easy, deceptively friendly. "How is it? Knowing all that money is gone?"

"The same as two minutes ago." And it's true. Since stepping into this trippy environment, nothing seems real.

"You and I, Lockhart, we aren't so different."

"Sorry, mate. I can't agree with anything approaching confidence."

He starts to walk, staying close to the wall. "You don't remember me, do you?"

"No." *But I'm trying…*

"You even stand like a cocky motherfucker. Quite impressive. Always so self-possessed."

"You sound like a fan."

"Me, oh yes, you could say that. Maybe your first."

It's there, the memory swims below the surface, I grab it with both hands. "Bloody hell…Sander?" It can't be, but somehow…it is.

"Took you long enough."

"Dude, bloody hell. The theatrics, I should have known." I move to tackle him, but he steps behind his desk, not in a hurried motion, but enough that it's obvious he deflects the physical contact.

"Rather thought it would be obvious. You've lost your touch."

My old boarding school roommate has added a foot and a half of height, and fifty kilos in weight. No longer the skinny bespectacled kid who got the everlasting shit kicked out of him during Year Eight camp. His father's a Moscow-based oligarch who rose to power under Yeltsin with whispered ties to the Russian mafia. Rumors flew around that Sander's mother was a prostitute.

"Sander Dubrovksy. *You* are the famous Aleksander Zavtra." I can't hold back the laughter. "No shit. Hell, dude, it's been a while."

"Nine years." He smirks.

"What happened with school? You vanished."

"Many things." His cocky grin disappears. "Then I came here for study at Stanford. Silicon Valley presented itself and look, I'm a regular California dude, am I not?"

"Riiiiight." I check out his darkened lair. "Get out much?"

"I'm a busy man."

"So am I, Sander, but—"

"Z. It's Z now."

"You want me to call you Z?"

His face is expressionless. "I do."

"I . . . what the hell, man? What's up with the Stalinist surveillance? Is it true that you don't come out?"

"I go out."

"Beth said she's worked at your front desk for two weeks and hasn't seen you."

He waves his hand in an act of dismissal. "The eyes see what the eyes choose."

"You always were one for riddles."

"And you were always one of the few people I liked. With my little camera, I noticed that girl out there, Bethanny," he pronounces her name like it costs him effort. "She watched this video on her computer. Kept rewatching. I suppose I was curious."

"The watcher watching a watcher."

"And there you were on the screen, fucking Lockhart. I asked her who that was and she responded it was her friend's boyfriend. A simple matter to connect the pieces."

"Why didn't you just ring me?"

"People change." He sits in a fluid motion and steeples his fingers. "I wanted to see if you were still the same guy. The hero." He pronounces the word like it's a joke.

Which it is.

"Wrong guy, mate."

"Maybe to most. But you were a champion to me, when it counted." He tapped the side of his temple. "I don't forget debts."

Sander was a skinny kid with too many freckles, a big mouth, and a talent for poking people where it hurt. Kids at school camp were sick of his quick wit and took a hazing too far. I heard what happened in the canteen and found him when no one else could. It wasn't hard. No one took the time to think it through. Search parties were organized. The teachers assumed he'd fallen in a ravine, wandered into the woods.

No. Not Sander.

He was in the camp director's office preparing to unleash a computer virus designed to wipe out the financial records of the entire grammar school.

I calmed his ass down and the next year we roomed together. People didn't mess with me and so didn't bother with him. We were best friends, in our way. I didn't nose around with whatever he did on the computer, and he didn't ask me dumb questions. Neither of us ever discussed families. When Year Eleven came, he didn't show to school at the start of term. I never heard what happened to him, although I soon stopped wondering. That was the year that Adie Lind arrived from Denmark. I got distracted falling hard and fast in first love.

"You were a friend." He spins a pen between his fingers. "I haven't had many."

"Sander, Z, whatever, look—"

"You are as I remember. I'd like to make you an offer."

"If it's anything like the bullshit you just tried to pull with Talia—"

"No." He gives me a real smile and there he is, Sander—the wired, excitable kid too smart for his own good.

"Hang on." I glance back at the television screens. "If I said yes before, would you have given me two million?"

"Sure." He shrugs. "But I wouldn't have offered you a job."

15

TALIA

"Let me get this straight, Zavtra the Creepy is an old school chum?" I don't even bother to restrain my chuckle. We sit in the backseat of a giant, gas-guzzling SUV as Katya, the hulk of a security guard, returns us to Bankside as promised. "Why aren't I surprised?"

"Sander was an intense kid."

"Coming from you, that's saying something. Beth is fifty percent terrified of him and fifty percent in love with him. She says he sounds like sex. Is that true?"

"Not any sex I'd be looking for."

"What's he like?"

"I don't know, like himself except grown up."

I narrow my gaze with exaggerated menace. "Your descriptions are killing me, you know that, right?"

He rolls his eyes in response. "Don't tell me you have a Russian recluse fantasy too?"

"No, but come on, you have to admit, the whole thing is fascinating."

He shrugs. "He's dark. Tall. A lot bigger than he used to be."

"Big? Too many donuts and hours behind a computer?"

"More like he hires a SWAT team and kicks their ass in his spare time."

I tilt my head to the side. "So he's built, then?"

"I refuse to feed this obsession." He tickles my ribs to let me know he's joking, mostly.

"It's like you met the Easter Bunny or something."

"Easter Bilby."

"Come again?" My eyebrows squish together.

"In Australia, rabbits are feral pests, remember? Screw the Easter Bunny. We celebrate the Easter Bilby, a desert marsupial with long ears."

"That's pretty cute. So your old buddy, Z, is sort of like the Easter Bilby, except instead of chocolate eggs, he brings offers of gainful employment?"

"That's one way of looking at it."

I lean forward. "Tell me more about the position."

"It's heading development of citizen science applications."

"I have no idea what that means."

He settles back and fiddles with the door lock. "So these days a lot of people have smartphones, right?"

"Yeah, sure."

"They can be tools for automatic data collection, a way to involve the public in science in an entirely new way."

"Sorry, I'm guessing that's supercool, but I just snored off."

He rolls his eyes. "Think about it, smartphones can capture images, audio, and text—'stamp' the date, time, and geographic coordinates associated with an observation. It's low cost, with huge potential impact. There's scope for the general public measuring light pollution or local air quality. I mean, people could even track the energy usage in their homes. They already do with friends, books they've read, where they visit in a day, exercise—why not something with global implications? I don't think I'm ready to work for Dad's Lockhart Foundation yet. I'm open to doing some advising on the side, but want to do my own thing for a bit."

"But can you work in the United States?"

"Zavtra human resources can sort me a specialized visa no worries."

"This sounds kind of scarily perfect."

"Maybe." Uncertainty lingers in the back of the word.

"What's the hitch?"

He stares out the window a trifle too long. That's when I get it. He doesn't want to say yes to a job until I figure my own shit out.

"Wait, it's me, isn't it? I'm the holdup."

He shrugs. "I don't know what you want, where you want to go. You came to Australia for me, least I can do is return the favor."

"But I want you to be happy."

He reaches over and takes my hand. "And I want you to be happy."

"So we're in a happiness stalemate?" My laugh is more bitter than I prefer. "Well, speaking of the city. There is a job I've toyed with applying for there."

"Go on."

I shake my head. "It's stupid."

"You want to apply for a stupid job?"

"No, it's stupid to even apply. It's as a production assistant for a program on public radio. A *This Is Your Life* kind of show, where they do research on people's genealogies and unearth fascinating stuff. Kind of right up my alley."

"Sounds great."

"Except for the part where I'm so underqualified that it's not even funny."

"Are you joking? Don't sell yourself short; it sounds like you meet most of the requirements, and Friendly will give you a great recommendation. The dude loves you."

"Friendly? Professor Connors? I hate that nickname." My adviser from the University of Tasmania who oversaw my senior thesis. He liked me a lot, which is why Bran calls him friendly. Apparently it's weird in Bran World to be nice just for niceness's sake.

"That dude will sing your praises."

I unbuckle my seat belt, move to the middle seat, lock back in, and snuggle closer, unable to hide my unease about the public radio application. I don't want to get my hopes up. I need to try to live in the now, be present without stressing about what's to come. Except I want to build a life with the guy beside me. And that means making plans. What should I do?

I rest my head on his shoulder. Sometimes we have better conversations when we elect not to use words. Katya steers us expertly through traffic on I-80 and as we pass downtown Sacramento, the Sierras come into view, snowcapped, on the horizon.

"We could just screw the world and run away together," I say. "Hide out in the mountains."

He twirls his fingers into my hair, forming a loose knot. "You'd like that?"

"Doesn't it sound kind of perfect? Move to a little cabin. You can raise chickens and chop wood. I'll bake bread and finger knit. We can hide from the world."

"All I want is right here." His fingertips graze my scalp, and my heart gives a sideways thud, grasps his sweet offering, and hugs it close. We sit in silence. It's nice, having someone to be still with.

I lean into his head massage like a kitten being petted. "Do you ever think that our relationship is like a teeter-totter?"

He frowns, lost.

"You know what a teeter-totter is, right? Do they have those in Australia?"

"Yeah, of course." His tongue pokes against the inside of his cheek. "But I'm not following, Captain."

"This relationship, it's like we're constantly rocking, you know? Sometimes I'm doing well, so I'm the one who's up. And other times you're kicking ass and you're up."

"That's the worst metaphor ever. We're in this together." His tone is gruffer by the second.

"What are the chances of you and me making it work in a way where we both get what we want? Scoring two amazing jobs in the Bay Area? I'm not sure I want to get my hopes up." My pessimistic expression reflects in his shades. I don't like what I see. I stare out the window instead.

"No worries. I go where you go. You came to Australia and took a chance. This is me, taking a chance on you."

"No pressure. Anyway, this job, with your weirdo billionaire friend, is an amazing opportunity."

"Do you want to live in the city?"

"Yeah, sure. Yes. It would be great. But what if I can't make it?"

"What if you can?" He yanks off his sunglasses, his brows knit. "Bran—"

"Goddammit, Talia. Just accept you are amazing already." He yanks me close and shuts me up with a fierce kiss.

"I'll do the application," I whisper, breathless.

He picks a lock of my hair from my shoulder, rubs his fingers over the strands. "When is the deadline?"

I check my watch. "Um, three hours?"

"Today?"

"Yeah." I eye the traffic, grinding to a halt ahead. "We should be home pretty soon."

"Bloody hell, Captain."

We drive the rest of the way in silence while I dig my laptop out of the bag, and peck on the keyboard, taking window-watching breaks whenever carsickness twinges. When we get home the house is empty. Dad and Jessie must be out. I set up my laptop and dive into resume-writing panic mode while Bran hovers, bossing me over what bits to change until I kick him out of the room. "Go run a five K in sub-seven minutes. Don't come back until you burn off that nervous energy. It's making me hivey."

"Fine," he grumbles, tossing off his pants and picking up a pair of running shorts. I zone out for a moment admiring the indents in his muscular quads.

"See something you like, Captain?" He pauses, flexing his arms. That bicep—I want to lick it.

"Verra nooooice," I say in my awful imitation Australian accent. They always sneak an o into nice, just so the vowels don't get lonely. "Now shoo, let me be serious for a second."

"I'm serious as a bloody heart attack." He gives a curt gesture to his thickening dick bulge.

"Stop tempting me! This job is important to us."

"Okay," he says in a careful, noncommittal voice. He knows it's a big deal. Me putting myself out there again.

"If this doesn't work, I could be a barista or something."

"That what you want?"

"I suck at service jobs, would screw up everyone's order. Here's my point, I want this public radio gig, but if it doesn't work out, maybe I won't like explode from shame."

"Exactly." He plants a kiss on my forehead. "I'm proud of you for trying." He can't resist a naughty, handsy boob grab.

"Go you scoundrel, Mama needs to make the magic happen."

I hit send on the application at 4:57 p.m. Three minutes before the close of business deadline.

"You really like to live on the edge." Bran saunters in, hair wet from his after-run shower.

Hope hits me like a drug. I did it. I tried. I rallied. "Today has been totally crazy. My brain is zonked. Time for less thinking, more doing." I flash my best something-something smile.

He arches his brow as if he'll buy what I'm selling.

I swing my hips and stroll to the ancient dust-covered stereo propped against the far wall. It was mine and Pippa's from junior high. Apparently Dad thinks he is going to tinker around and get the CD player working to play lullabies. Lots of luck there but I'm pretty sure the radio works. Hopefully something is on that will accompany the striptease I have in mind.

Bran snickers at my awkward antics and that's fine, he's supposed to. Bonus points because his laugh is hot. I crank the volume. "I like my music the way I like my women—fast and wild." The DJ's voice drips with smarmy douchiness.

Bran rolls his eyes.

"Hold up, is this what I think it is?" The first chords from "Sweet Child o' Mine" kick in. I pump my fist. "Hells to the yeah."

"Turn it off—"

"Silence Axl? Not in this lifetime. Rock with me."

He folds his arms. "Never."

I imitate waving a magic wand. "The power of Guns N' Roses compels you."

He snorts despite himself. "You're a bona fide horror show, you know that, right?"

"Be my Slash, baby."

"No way in hell."

I do my best skeezy hip thrust. "Get up on this bed, show me what you're working with."

"Talia."

"Dude."

"Dude?"

I point at the bed. "This is our stage. Don't even pretend that you don't have a badass air-guitar solo inside you begging to be unleashed."

"Prepare for disappointment."

"Says the guy who danced to Justin Bieber with his nieces."

He smacks his forehead. "You swore never to speak of that."

"Come on, get over yourself."

"Bloody hell." He steps on the bed and begins to strum.

"Who are you, Art Garfunkel? Put your back into it."

"I'm not a performing monkey."

"Correct. You are Slash, and we are going to rage."

The chorus hits and I headbang, belting lyrics in a nasally high-pitched accent. Bran loosens up, rocks harder.

I jump up and down and flash him devil horns.

"This is crazy," he yells.

"Crazy awesome!"

I mosh thrust against his ribs and he play shoves back, and for a second all the bullshit stress about what we are doing with our lives is eclipsed by the world's best butt rock. We lean in together and belt the final stanza. The song finishes and my scissor-kick finale gains serious air. When I land, the old frame gives way and we spill to the floor in a dull thud.

"Ow!" I grab my elbow.

"We broke the bed." Bran rubs his forehead.

Once I start laughing, I can't stop. Bran joins in and we cackle in that good soul-clearing way that doesn't happen nearly enough.

"Oh, God." I wipe my eyes.

"Right." He pulls me on his lap, stares at me with intent. "I've got an idea."

I loop my arms around him. He smells so hot and soapy. "I'm listening."

"You applied for the job. They aren't going to call you tomorrow—"

"Remember, they may not call me at all."

"They will, trust me. But we have this grace period. No point sitting around stressing, checking your e-mail twenty times in an hour."

The guy knows me so well.

"I don't need to tell Sander anything yet. I put him off, said I wanted to talk things over with you. In the car you mentioned wanting to visit the mountains. Let's do it, take a road trip."

"Really?" Excitement bubbles in my belly. "A getaway sounds très romantic."

"That's me, Mr. Romance. But for real, I want to take you to Yosemite."

I ponder the suggestion. "Beautiful, but the Valley will be a zoo, it's almost Memorial Day."

"Yeah, no. I don't want to car camp with a thousand strangers."

"'Course you don't." This is Bran we're talking about. He'll probably suggest rappelling the nose of El Capitan.

"Tenaya Canyon." He pauses for dramatic effect.

I shake my head and shrug.

He looks a little crestfallen. "You haven't heard of it?"

"We were a beach family. I mean, I've been to Yosemite but not in ages."

"Tenaya Canyon is the Bermuda Triangle of the Sierras."

"Excuse me?"

"There is a legend the area was cursed by a Native American chief. Obviously that's a made-up story. Still, hiking the canyon is a mission, a real adventure. I think we can get by with a rope, and from what I read we may not even need it if we are careful."

I cock my head to the side because really, did homeboy sneak onto the medical marijuana app I've yet to delete from my phone? He's smoking something if he thinks my height-phobic ass is scaling a cursed canyon in the High Sierras.

He hugs me closer. "Now, Captain, I know what you're going to say—"

"Zero chance in hell?"

"I want you to consider—"

"No—"

He shuts me up with a kiss. "The idea that—"

"Nope—" I talk into his mouth.

"I'm a proficient climber and—"

I jam my fingers in my ears and chant, "Lalalalalalalalalalala-lalalalalala."

Eventually, I stop and there's silence. I open one eye and he stares at me, bemused.

"You've lost the plot."

"I happen to be overly attached to my intact spine."

"Me too." He walks his fingers down my vertebrae to the gap between my jeans and shirt. He takes his sweet time. I cannot guess how many seconds stretch until he brushes my bare skin in a tormenting caress. "I promise, nothing bad will happen. I'll keep you safe. You'll love it. I've seen photos of the place and it's staggering."

"Staggering is what I'll be if you drag my ass anywhere near a sheer cliff. Remember our hike in Tasmania? I panic attacked on a day hike populated by small children and the elderly."

"You made it through."

"Barely."

"You are braver than you know." His clever fingers circle to my stomach and tease my waistband.

I don't know what will happen or where things will end up with our future. He speaks like I'm capable of courage, and his kiss tastes like home. I want to fold his confidence against me like a secret poem. We're tangled in the rubble of a broken bed and crumpled blankets. The radio blasts Journey. Bran's three to four inches away from driving me into insanity. He's unleashed his hypnotizing voodoo. Makes me half believe I'm capable of this insane adventure—of anything.

"Let me take you there." His rumbling accent is an invisible rope encircling my girly parts. The pull is half pleasure shiver, half painful intensity. "Let's get you moving." He pops my top button and grinds my zipper down.

"Here or in the mountains?"

"Both." He brushes his lips over my ear with a featherlight

touch. Here we go, what always happens when his tongue slides over me, the disorienting sensation of being out of my body while fully inhabiting my skin. My nipples are button-hard, responding to the pressure of his chest as he settles against me.

"You talk like you want to take me on some sort of a spirit quest." My words are a gasp because his touch is lower. His fingers tremble a little. Incredibly, he wants me as badly as I want him.

"That's exactly right." He sets the perfect rhythm, exquisite, maddening circles. He doesn't have much room to maneuver, as my jeans are still tight to my hips, but sometimes micro-movements are all you need. Most of the world's beauty occurs, not in moments of avalanche, but in the tiny bump and grind of plate tectonics. People collide together, and the push is so slow, so gradual, you almost don't know anything's happening until, holy shit, holy shit, he's got me right there. Suddenly, everywhere mountains and I'm on one and oh yes, oh God, yes.

"So yes." His smile is wicked when I return, dazed, realizing I've half climbed him like a lust-crazed monkey. "You'll go?"

I let my body sink back to the floorboards. "This isn't fair." I slur my words a little. "I'm pleasure drunk."

"Come with me."

"I just did, didn't I?"

He wiggles my jeans to my ankles. "I don't want us ever to stop."

"Me neither," I say. Even though heights terrify me, I'm addicted to our edge-dancing. I'd rather be lost and with him, than ever play it safe.

"So, you'll do it?" He rolls a condom on.

"God help me but yes." I grab him by the root and he groans, his desire shoots through my fingers like a current. I let him enter me, but only an inch. "I'm not going to make it easy though, you know that, right?"

"I'm counting on it." He thrusts hard, breaking my grip. By the time he withdraws only to fill me again, I'm not sure if there's a difference between comings and goings, but I'm ready to get back in the scariest game of all.

Life.

16
BRAN

I make no bones about admiring Talia's ass as she bends to towel dry her hair. She's still pink-cheeked from our epic shag and subsequent shower. Stick a fork in me. I'm done, can't be bothered to budge from this sprawled-on-my-back position. One of the cats, Persimmon, sits in the doorway. Her orange tail twitches as she surveys the nursery. Blankets, sheets, jeans, shirts, and underwear are blasted in every direction. Bloody hell, it looks like a typhoon swept through here.

"Is she checking me out?" I ask Talia as the cat focuses her yellow-eyed gaze on me and starts purring.

"Huh?" Her phone buzzes, and she turns to hunt it down, finding it beneath a pillow.

"It's been ringing since you've been in the shower."

"Why didn't you answer it?"

"I hate the phone."

She rolls her eyes as the cat licks a paw. The purr intensifies, like there's a motor in there. I think she winks at me.

"Well, aren't you a pussy pervert," I mutter.

"Don't razz the cat!" The phone stops ringing, but whoever is on the other line immediately calls back for the fifth time. She pauses to tighten her towel around her chest before answering, as if whoever's calling might suspect she's naked. Damn. There goes my free peep show. She's a cheeky one, mocks my protesting groan with a sexy pelvic wiggle.

"Keep that up and I'm not responsible for my actions." Even though I'm knackered, I'd still go another round.

Talia pokes her tongue in my direction and extends a thigh through the towel slit in a showgirl move, flexing her pink-painted toes. She clearly wants to slay me. I'm rock hard before she hits answer and chirps, "Hello? This is Talia, Queen of Devilish Good Fun."

There's a beat where her face is still flushed with amusement, but her brows knit, eyes blank with panic. "Dad? Wait. Stop. I need you to slow down. What happened? Who is in trouble?" Her tone turns my belly to water.

I'm up, dressing in a flash as Talia nods. "Yes! Sorry, I'm still here. Don't worry about a thing. We're on it. See you at the hospital. She will be fine, promise."

She hangs up and throws on a shirt, fumbles for her pants. "It's Jessie," she says, doing the zip. "She phoned Dad freaking out after not being able to get through to me. He's on campus and her water broke when she was getting out of the car in the driveway. I'm calling an ambulance. Can you run outside? Keep her calm?"

I hear her real words. Do something. Fix this. Make everything better.

I tear from the room, take the stairs three at a time, and trip over the dogs snoozing on the living room rug. They tag after me onto the veranda, try to lunge from the side door. "Sit!" I order in a tone that sends Chester squealing into the safety of his den. Out on the driveway Jessie leans against her Toyota. Her head hangs between her legs, elbows braced on her knees. Her ponytail bobs as she struggles to breathe slow and even.

"Hey, Jessie." I jog closer. "That's the way, easy now. I'm here for you."

As if that's going to make a bit of bloody difference.

"Bran."

"Everything is okay." I kneel on the concrete. My voice is low, carefully modulated, a tone I'd use to address one of my nieces if she were hurt. Important to pretend at calm, not let on that I'm shitting myself. Reframe the situation to a stubbed toe. A skinned knee.

Jessie grapples for one of my hands with a guttural, animalistic sound. Her stomach heaves, moving like it's got a life of its own. Bloody hell, I guess it does. No point pretending this is anything other than serious. She's not full-term. Undiluted panic sluices through my limbs, makes me jittery as fuck. Another sob tears from her, one that's high, keening, and rips off the dungeon door in my heart. The one swathed in iron chains and shielded by a pile of heavy boulders. Guess those defenses weren't enough.

I got Adie, my girlfriend before Talia, pregnant. Our relationship was already in the death-rattle stage. She wanted to break up and lied about an abortion. Turns out she was fine with a baby. I was the unwanted one. The fetus had an abnormal heart and ended up stillborn. I don't talk about it. Never think about it. Except when I wake in the deepest part of the night, choking on shame and a sadness beyond the powers of language.

Jessie fumbles closer. She wipes her nose on my shoulder as her tears soak the side of my neck. There is a wet circle between her legs. Body fluids are everywhere. They don't gross me out, but I can't fix this. I'd do anything to make it better and don't have the first clue where to start. I warned Talia. I tried to tell her that I wasn't a hero. She didn't listen. She wouldn't believe me.

Jessie whimpers through the duration of her contraction, unable to speak until it passes. "Promise you won't let the baby die. Promise you won't let the baby die." She moans the phrase like a song on repeat. Each word is another bar to my own personal prison cell. I'm trapped in a waking nightmare.

"You'll be fine."

"Promise me." Jessie won't break her stare. She clings like I'm a bloody anchor rather than something next to useless. "I need your promise."

"I won't let anything bad happen." I'm fuck all qualified to make such an oath, but I'll be hung before adding to her fear with my own shit. I grip her hand between both of mine. Project myself like the bloody definition of self-assurance. "No way is this baby dying."

But mine did. My intestines coil like a tiger snake. Venom spreads through my abdomen. Panic roils my bile.

Don't get sick. Stay in the game. Be strong for her.

Jessie relaxes as if somehow my touch keeps away monsters. She doesn't know I draw trouble like a magnet.

"Hey, hey, you're fine. I've got you." I'm a fraud.

"I called 911." Talia flies from the house. "An ambulance has been dispatched."

I give her a curt nod, gritting my teeth while Jessie tears off my fingers as another contraction puts her on lockdown. Didn't she just have one? Are they supposed to be this close?

"Hurts." She arches her back. "It's coming. I can feel it."

"Grab my hand," I order. "Squeeze as bad as it hurts."

Ow. Maybe I shouldn't have said that. Still, the bone-crushing pain keeps me here, in the present. Away from the past and its demons.

Jessie's gaze is wild. She grunts, starts to bear down.

Shit. "No! No! Breathe. Don't push."

"I can't. I can't. I can't stop this." She clutches my hand so hard I lose feeling. "Want to push." Her eyes bulge. "Got to."

"Focus on muscle relaxation." I swipe her hair off her sweaty forehead.

"I'm going to lose it, aren't I?" Jessie whispers. "It's early. Too early." She yelps as another contraction bears down. They are coming around a minute apart.

"Didn't you and Dad do a pregnancy class?" Talia squats beside me. "Practice breathing techniques?"

Jessie shakes her head and collapses against the open door. "The first class starts tomorrow. I don't know what to do. I haven't even read that far in *What to Expect When You're Expecting*."

"Should I boil water?" I vaguely remember reading about someone doing this when a woman's in labor. Shit. Why? Sterilization? My field of vision contracts. The world blurs on the edges.

"Bran!" I jerk when Talia sets her hand on my lower back. "You're hyperventilating."

Jessie groans. Her face crumples when another contraction breaks. "Here we go again."

"You got this Jessie, you so got this," Talia says, turning away from me with a worried look. "Your body knows what to do."

Jessie moans in a way that's a cross between agreement and rebellion. I'm not even sure if it's a cry of pain or fear—most likely both. Her gaze locks on me like I'm that kid from the nursery tale, Hans Brinker, the one who saved the Netherlands by putting his finger in the dike. I need to hold back her fear. The same fear that's threatening to drown me. She looks too close. She'll see that I can't help. She'll know. I can't hide. "Talia, please."

Help me.

"Come on, Jessie. Pretend you're Rocky." Talia is in ramble mode. Is she humming "Eye of the Tiger"? Whatever. Better than anything I got. "You're getting the shit kicked out of you, but you're going to dominate the ring."

There's a high-pitched whine from an ambulance a few blocks away, coming closer by the second.

"Rocky, huh? How many hits do you think I can take?" Jessie fights for good humor. That's a positive sign, right?

"You got this. You so got this." Talia sounds calm. Believable. Her bright brown eyes radiate unshakable confidence. Hell, she's almost got me sold.

Jessie gives a weak nod. If the baby's head pops out, I wouldn't be shocked if Talia reached down and delivered it single-handedly. She's being a bloody champion.

Jessie transfers one of her hands from me to Talia, gripping us both. "You here for me, guys?" She stares at us like we're going to single-handedly deliver us through the valley of darkness.

"Remember," Talia says with a sage nod. "Your body knows what to do."

The ambulance speeds up the street. Talia rushes to the sidewalk and jumps up and down. This is no Kermit flail. She's gone full-scale Animal. She's getting shit sorted while I'm worse than useless.

The paramedics spring into action.

"Hey," Talia croons as they load her onto the gurney. "We're right here, and you're going to have a beautiful healthy baby."

"I'm going to need you to pant very gently, ma'am. Try not to push." A paramedic checks between her legs. When he steps back his gloves are bloodstained. I swallow another rush of bitterness. Is this what Adie went through?

"Her name is Jessie," Talia tells the bloke. "She's thirty-four weeks." Despite her phobia about blood, she remains unfazed.

"You're almost fully dilated," the paramedic tells Jessie.

I don't know exactly what that means, but from the way he says it, this can't be good news.

"This isn't happening." Tears course Jessie's drawn cheeks. "I can't do this."

"You're rocking it." Talia wipes Jessie's face, keeps the tears from puddling in her ears. "This little baby is so lucky. You are going to be the best mom. All kids love animals, and you run a menagerie. And Dad? He's like a rock ninja."

"Rock star." Jessie's attempt to laugh ends with a whimper. "Ouch, hurts."

They load her into the back of the ambulance, and we move to follow suit.

The paramedic holds up a hand. "Sorry, only room for one. The other has to follow behind."

We glance at the haphazardly parked Toyota.

"Maybe better if I drive?" Talia gives me a once-over. Do I look as ruined as I feel?

"Go with Jessie." I can barely manage to shake my head. "I'm fine."

"Bran…"

"She needs you."

Talia bites her lip. She looks like she wants to say something else.

"Later. We'll talk later."

"Okay." She forces a quick smile and rushes to the ambulance. The medics are getting Jessie sorted as Talia climbs in the back, talking a mile a minute. "Dad will be at the hospital when we get there. Remember, Davis is one of the best hospitals in the state. You and the baby are going to get top-of-the-line care. Everything is going to work out. This is what kids do, right? They cause all sorts of trouble. We make our parents' lives haywire. The little one is doing its job. Think of it as a considerate heads-up. You thought you were in control, but guess what, you're not. None of us are. What you need to do is fight. Fight for yourself. Fight for this baby. Fight like everything in the world depends on this."

All eyes train on Talia. She looks around and gives a self-conscious fist bump. "Go team!"

The doors slam and I jump into Jessie's sedan. The keys are still in the ignition. I reverse and follow the flashing lights. Try to remember to drive on the right side—fucking wrong side—of the road. It's all I can do to keep focus. My thoughts drift to a faraway birth. A silent, still little body.

Adie should have told me about the baby. She didn't because I made it too hard. I wouldn't have been able to change the outcome, but I could have been there, borne witness. I barely see the road as I drive.

The ambulance halts by the ER doors and I park in the nearest available spot. Scott's there, jumping out of his 4Runner. He sprints in my direction, darts in front of a car, ignoring the horn blast. His gaze is wild, unfocused. "Where is she?"

"Over there." I point to the ambulance where Jessie is being unloaded.

"Scott," she cries.

Talia flashes her dad a thumbs-up then turns back to Jessie. "You're a tiger, lady, got that?"

"Tiger," Jessie repeats with a weak smile.

The paramedics push her inside. Scott plows after in hot pursuit. After all the hectic adrenaline-pumping confusion, the sudden shift to silence is disorienting. The ambulance drives off slowly and Talia and I are alone, like nothing ever happened.

"Bran?" She settles a hand above my elbow, frowning at my flinch.

"It's cool. I'm fine." My voice is hoarse as if I've been screaming.

"You keep saying that."

"It's the truth."

"I'm almost scared to give you a hug. You're about three seconds from shattering."

She's not wrong. The life I helped create, one that died before it ever began, is an action that struck at my core, a rock on my soul's windshield. It left a divot. One I wanted to ignore because to deal with it, bloody hell, what a nuisance. Instead, I tried to tell myself maybe it would be okay. But as with any ding, the inevitable happens. One day you see it. The first crack. It's like a betrayal because you and the ding had an understanding. A truce. But it wasn't content. The crack grew, fractured, and spread destruction to all corners. That's the nature of an unchecked wound.

"It's stupid." I loathe myself. Shouldn't I be the strong one? I made Talia carry the weight of the whole situation in the driveway.

"Your feelings are far from dumb."

"I don't want to make this about what happened to me." I start walking, where? I have no idea.

"Bran, this is only you and me now. I'm listening. I'm an expert in panic attacks. You had one in the driveway."

"Doesn't matter." I double down on my pace.

"Hey! Stop. If you run there is no possible way that I'll catch you." She grabs my hand and steers me to the curb in an out-of-the-way section of the parking lot. We sit. "Want to hear a story?"

"No." I don't want to do anything except jackhammer my brain. I can't even wish away the memories, because I wasn't there. When death came to a life I created, I wasn't there to say good-bye. "I don't need stories."

"Too bad because I've got one. Once upon a time there was a boy who was ignored, who built walls around walls because he had to keep out the feeling that he didn't matter. That he didn't count. He was terrified that if he ever tried to open up and no one listened he'd feel worse. It was easier to give a hard face to the world. Shoot life the finger before getting one back."

I hunch down and grow still.

Talia practically crawls onto my lap. "You matter." She takes hold of my cheeks. Her hands are so soft, warm. "You matter so much. And what you feel, matters to me."

We lock in a stare that has its own kind of gravity. In this universe there is no oxygen, only this pressure that builds behind my eyes until I'm certain we can't withstand any more, and that's when it happens. I yank her forward, crush her into my chest, and shed harsh, ragged tears into her hair. I hid these shameful feelings, fought them tooth and nail with rage and self-loathing. My grief tears me open, and all the poison washes away under the torrent.

When I can finally speak, it's nothing but a hoarse mumble. "Sorry to be so weak."

"This is the bravest I've ever seen you." She settles my head on her lap. Her legs are bare, and I can smell a hint of her body lotion, vaguely sweet and comforting, like a vanilla slice. "I can't change what happened for you in the past, but I can hold on."

The sun has almost set. Across the street is a cheap motel. The sign light shines in a shaft over the broken asphalt. Everyone falls somewhere on this line of living and dying, walking over moments that are violet-fragile. An invisible clock hangs over us all, and we need to live as if it's not there, even as our hearts beat in time. Today, thousands of cogs have stopped, even as a thousand more begin.

Some people believe we choose this birth. This life. I don't know what I know and tonight, in the dark, that uncertainty suits me fine. Shadows tangle and in the stillness I breathe and she breathes and in this moment, us, breathing together is enough.

17

TALIA

After Pippa died I couldn't bring myself to look at a hospital for ages. I had to avert my eyes if we drove past. As if beholding one would magically pull me or a loved one into its cold, sterile orbit. The endless, plodding weeks in South Africa helped desensitize me to the places. I'd gotten to where I honestly believed my dread was diminished. *Hey, maybe hospitals aren't the worst places in the world,* I said to myself. I was wrong. I hadn't been nearly specific enough.

Children's hospitals are the worst places on earth.

"Ready for this?" Dad cracks me a smile, pops his knuckles in a way that only intensifies my nerves because it means he's masking a Stage-Five freak-out. We stand outside the Neo-natal Intensive Care Unit. "When life gives you lemons, Peanut, you and I, we make lemonade."

I can't even begin to guess what he's talking about.

When my sister was in the hospital, during those early weeks when hope seemed possible, Dad spouted off enough optimistic clichés to write a *Chicken Soup for When Your Daughter Is On Life Support*.

"Can't wait." My grin is so toothy I must resemble a rabid hyena.

There are signs posted all over the wall. One reminds us to wash our hands, which Dad and I both do, at the wide, stainless steel sink, for almost two minutes with the small sterile disposable brushes provided. The skin on my knuckles and palms is red, buffed and shined by the end. A nurse checks our identification bracelets.

Dad rings the buzzer to request access onto the unit. There's an answering click and he pulls open the door. "After you."

Visitors are limited so Bran cools his heels in the cafeteria. I hate leaving him alone, especially when the hurt from his past is bubbling so near the surface. He's never spoken of Adie's pregnancy, of the fact he almost became a father at twenty-two. Bran as a dad. The very notion is so foreign, utterly ludicrous, and yet, I know he'd be amazing. Someday. He wasn't ready for that much responsibility, and that knowledge clearly cripples him with guilt because at the end of the day, he never had to be. He never had to choose to do the right thing.

I'll get back to Bran as soon as I can, but first there's someone I need to meet.

A three-pound, fourteen-ounce baby without a name.

"He's right over here in Isolette fifteen." We follow the nurse through a space that is quiet, almost serene.

"Isolette?"

"Incubator," Dad murmurs. The room is full of them. Each has a tiny body nestled inside. I'm surprised how large it is in here. Classical music plays at a low volume. Two doctors in blue scrubs pass us with a nod and gentle smile. A few parents hover and coo by their little incubators. One mother is holding her baby skin to skin in a glider chair.

Where is number fifteen?

We stop. There, visible through the hard plastic shell, is my brother.

It's impossible to blink, or swallow. He's impossibly small. Skinny. He looks like a baby bird fallen from the nest. "Oh my God," I whisper, trying to register what I'm seeing.

"Isn't he something?" Dad's voice is thick with emotion.

"Yeah," I say, unable to take my eyes off him. "Hey, Sea-Monkey." His heart rate and breathing patterns are being carefully monitored. A feeding tube runs into his nose. Jessie's up in her room, pumping, trying to get her milk to come in.

"Oh, you overeager little buddy." I splay my fingers on the glass. "You're supposed to cook for another two months."

Why the big rush?

"Can I touch him?" I whisper.

"Go ahead." The nurse has kind eyes. "See the holes on the side. Unlatch the panel and put your hand through there. You'll want to gently lay your hand on him. Don't pat or stroke. His skin is sensitive. Too much stimulation would hurt, but the pressure will be comforting, remind him of the womb."

Jesus.

"That's cool. I'm fine with looking," I say. I mean, I could hurt him with a brush of my finger? The idea of holding a full-term newborn makes me a little dizzy. A preemie? Maybe I should take another step back, admire at a safer distance.

"Go on," Dad urges. "Let him know you're here. Big sister to the rescue."

I have to do this.

"To the rescue? Hmmmmm. That's a rather ambitious statement." I slide my hand through the incubator's circular opening. His whole hand is smaller than my pinkie finger. My skin hovers against his, featherlight. He twitches. Tiny features contract into a grimace.

"Oh no! I hurt him."

"Don't worry, I think that means he likes you," Dad says thickly.

"Mr. Stolfi?" A woman in scrubs approaches. "I'm Dr. Clement, your son's neonatologist. Do you have a moment to come up front? I'd like to go over your son's care plan with you."

"Sure thing. You good to hold down the fort, Peanut?" Dad starts to walk away, slow though, like it's an effort not to stay right here, with him.

"No problem, but Dad?"

"Yeah?"

"Have you thought of a name yet? It seems weird not to call him anything."

He grimaces. "Jessie and I can't reach an agreement. We thought we still had time to carry out The Great Name Debate."

Inspiration strikes with lightening clarity. "What about Wyatt?" Dad loves old westerns. He'd force Pippa and me to watch them when we were little, bought us cowgirl hats and sheriff badges.

"Wyatt?" Dad pulls up short. "Huh. Wyatt." You can tell he's trying it on.

"Yeah, like the kid's a crazy fighter, you know?" I pretend to fast draw two finger guns. "The NICU is his O.K. Corral."

"Wyatt." His face creases into the first honest smile I've seen since we've been here. "I like it. We'll have to run it past Jessie, but something makes me think it'll stick."

I offer a mock salute. "Happy to help, sir."

Dad walks to the nurses' desk up front where Dr. Clements is waiting. The nurse assigned to us fiddles with another incubator nearby. It's just me and my brother.

"Hey, Wyatt." I whisper because I'm not going to start out our relationship calling him bro. "It's me. Talia, your big sister. Like really big sister. Sorry about that. By the time you're my age, I'm going to be certifiably ancient. You can help me find my pills, chase kids off my lawn."

He doesn't stir, but I get the strange feeling he senses I'm there. He looks impossibly wise, like a miniature Buddha, serene with enlightenment. I wonder if he knows everything has changed. Can he sense he's not inside Jessie anymore? Does he have any thoughts, or is he like a goldfish, where every second is a fresh slate wiped clean?

"I had a sister. I guess you did, too, although you never met her. In fact, if she was still here, you wouldn't be here. That's a head trip, huh?" My floodgates open. Oh boy, cue the waterworks. "All I know is that if I can be half as cool to you as she was to me, we'll be off to a solid start. Just don't expect me to kick the soccer ball around or take you rock climbing. I'm really uncoordinated. But I hope you like to read, because you won't have a choice. We'll cover all the Dr. Seuss obviously, and once you're around five I'll introduce you to *Charlotte's Web* and *Farmer Boy*. You need to hang in there, and, I don't know, learn to breathe or whatever. And fatten up while you're at it." I wipe my nose on my sleeve. "You look like a little alien. I could take a picture of you and sell it to the *National*

Enquirer. You'd probably beat out Bat Boy. Hey, for Halloween you could be Bat Boy. I'll make you a costume. I mean, you're going to pretty much have to accept that I'm going to be dressing you up every chance I get."

"Peanut?" Dad's beside me. I didn't hear him walk up.

"Sorry." I knuckle dry my eyes. Dad's got enough to carry. His shoulders are broad, no doubt about that, but he's the kind of guy who'll volunteer to Sherpa everyone else's shit until he falls off the mountain. "How are you doing?"

"Fine. Good. Great."

Which means he's a catastrophe away from tearing his hair, running in circles, and screaming, *We're all gonna die.*

I'm not the only one in this family who fakes it.

"Hey, Dad, it's cool to be real, you know. I can handle it."

"What are you talking about?" His chuckle is pure bravado.

"All I'm saying is if you want to break down a little, I won't freak."

He smiles, but there's no missing the hint of a chin quiver.

"He's going to be okay, Dad, but it's normal to be overwhelmed. This was a hell of an ordeal." I open up my arms, unsure how he'll react, but I need to make this move. For too long everyone in this family has wandered through shitty situations using meaningless upbeat language to shine the way. Maybe if we all are honest, admit we're scared but doing the best we can, we'd be a little better for it.

Dad looks at my outstretched arms, clearly hesitating.

"Jesus, it's a hug. Dad, you just had a baby. You're a father again. That's crazy enough. But this little guy was overeager and now we're in a neonatal intensive care unit."

"You don't need to carry my burdens."

"You're not Frodo with the One Ring. Share the load." Since he's not moving, I go to him, hug him hard around the waist. My cheek rests against the bottom of his rib cage. Next to the baby, Dad looks like the Jolly Green Giant. For a second, he stiffens at my touch. Shit, this is a bad idea. After my time with Bran in the parking lot, I've gotten lulled into a false confidence at the power of touchy feely.

I can't even talk my Dad off a cliff. He'll probably have a breakdown, or a heart attack or both and—

"Oh, Peanut." His sigh is one dredged from that place everyone has, but that he tries to pretend away. A shudder ripples through his body, and he squeezes me a little tighter. "You're something special, kid."

Warmth blooms through my chest. "Love you, too, Daddy."

He plants a kiss on the top of my head.

"Remember, it's not weak to feel."

He clears his throat. "I'll try." He slings his arm around my shoulder and we stand, quiet, watching the littlest member of our family, the weakest one in body, continue to fight with a strength that somehow manages to carry the rest of us.

When I get back to the hospital waiting room, it's nearly empty at this early hour. Bran is nowhere in sight.

"Talia?" I jump a mile when he says my name behind me. He holds two coffees.

"Oh, perfect, you read my mind." I take a sip. The sob comes out of nowhere as I try to swallow. I cough, tears gush down my cheeks for the second time in twenty minutes. "I'm dehydrating myself over here. Soon I'll be like beef jerky or something."

"Hey, hey." Bran removes the cup from my grasp, sets it on the seat, and tucks me into his arms. "I got you, I'm here."

He doesn't say shhhhh, which I am grateful for because I don't want to shush. Maybe my tears will douse the bitterness corroding my stomach. "Why did he have to be in such a hurry to come out? What's so good about being out here? It's hard. He should have waited. He's so little. I could hold him in one hand."

He lets me cry out all the stress and when I've finished, there's a huge wet stain on the front of his shirt. I dab it with futile hands. "God, sorry. I tried to drown you."

"Not sorry. I've been lazy about laundry. The shirt needed a good wash."

"More hugs?" I ask.

He holds out his arms. "Always, Captain. Get over here." He holds me tight, and I settle my head in the gap under his jaw. The fit is perfect. "You were amazing last night. Helping Jessie get through that in the driveway."

"I don't know."

"Fact. Do not argue me on this point."

"Our family had a baby." I snuggle closer. Maybe this is the beginning of something new. The fresh start everyone needed. A weird sensation shoots down my back. A light tickle. But Bran's arms are on my shoulders.

My sister loved to give what she called tickle backs. She'd run her hands up and down my spine while I wiggled and flailed. It was her way to show affection even though it made me squeal. I turn around and the seat behind me is empty.

"What's up?" Bran asks.

"Looking for a ghost." He gives me a raised eyebrow and I grin. Sometimes goose bumps aren't scary. "Don't worry, I think it was a friendly one."

I have waited since Pippa died to feel her presence. By this point

I'd decided it was never going to happen. As I walk out of the hospital that night, my heart full, Bran holding my hand, I look up at the moon.

Maybe anything is possible.

———

After two days, Baby Wyatt—Jessie cosigned on my name suggestion—shows marked improvement on all fronts, from lung function to feeding. Jessie and Dad have a room at the nearby Ronald McDonald House to be on hand round the clock, and Bran and I help out with housesitting duty.

"What's this cat's problem?" Bran grumbles. Persimmon, the fat tabby, has crushed the Edward Abbey book Bran's reading. She settles her paws on his chest and purrs loudly.

I glance up and laugh. "She's no dummy. You're the cuddliest." We're reading on the bed. The one Bran spent the morning repairing after our Guns N' Roses jam fest. He sprawls out vertically and I rest horizontally, using his hip as a pillow. I'm reading over my resume. In thirty minutes, I have a phone interview.

Holy shit.

I mean, it's fantastic, obviously. My dream job might actually become a reality. But even good stress carries with it a level of overwhelming bodily sensations. When Bran suggested a quiet snuggle, I was game. He also fixed me the cup of chamomile tea with extra honey that's cooling on the nightstand.

"Have I told you I love you today?"

He smiles at me over the mountain of cat. "I thought your feelings were bigger than plain old love." He's got the relaxed, teasing tone he's been using more and more since the day Jessie had the baby last week. The day he faced one of his own personal nightmares.

"My brain is scrambling through all possible interview questions. 'I love you' has to suffice for the moment. It's like the little black dress of big feelings. Perfect for any occasion."

"Do your brains need more scrambling?" He rocks his pelvis against me.

"That would be a negative. I'm trying to be a grown-up."

"Grown-ups don't get ravaged by love slave boyfriends?"

"If you have your wicked way with me, not only will I be unable to answer questions with anything approaching logic, I won't be able to make a sound above a smug giggle."

"I'd hire you on the sole basis of that giggle."

"Some people might want me for my brain instead of my body."

"I'm an equal-opportunity Talia wanter."

"Aw, and you pretend to be anti-romance." The cat flicks me in the face with her tail. I catch a wad of hair in the mouth. "Gah! Careful, Persimmon."

"Cat loves me. She's my minion."

Persimmon narrows her yellow eyes at me with a clear challenge for me to bring it.

"Okay, ask me a question." I sit and tuck my hair behind my ears. "Do your worst with a sample interview question."

He frowns, thinking. "If you were stuck on a desert island and could only bring three things, what would they be and why?"

"Shut up, they wouldn't ask me that." I bring my knees to my chest and wrap my arms around. "Oh, God, what if they ask me that?" I bury my face in my jeans. I am shit at uncertainty. Any interview question could be lobbed with a *Surprise!* and explode all over me.

"Relax, Captain, I'm messing with you."

"But they could, right?"

"Sure." His grin is a trifle wicked. "They could also ask if you have a creative use for scissors."

"I do, actually. They're useful for stabbing smartass boyfriends in the heart."

He grabs my hand and pulls me from my pretzel contortion. "Stop trying to make me laugh! I am wallowing over here. Let me be a depressed hippo." I ignore the death stare Persimmon gives me.

Sorry, cat. He's mine. Get your own Australian.

"You'll do great, just be yourself."

"Ugh. That's quite possibly the worst advice I've ever received."

"Why do you want the job?" He rubs my back.

"Because I need external validation at all times?"

"Okay, there's a start. Go deeper." He slides his hand in my back pocket.

"Not so fast, mister." I summon my best inner schoolmarm.

"I'm resting my hand, it's tired."

I lift my head. "On my ass?"

"As good a place as any." He leans back in a lazy stretch. A glimpse of tan skin peeks beneath his ancient *Star Wars* T-shirt. Not a movie original. A silkscreen of Chewbacca beneath a palm tree. There's a hint of that V-line muscle, the one that makes smart girls stupid.

"Hoo, boy, you are so smooth." Hmmmmm. Maybe a quickie would relax me.

He brushes my mouth with a light kiss. "I haven't thanked you."

"You're welcome."

"You don't know what for."

"Existing isn't enough?" I walk my fingers up his hip toward the sensitive side along his lower abdomen.

"Cheeky." He doubles over.

"I try." My tickle strike is sudden. I love to see him laugh almost as much as I love those dimples.

"Thank you for being cool," he says when I relent. He half sits and wipes his eyes. "When Jessie was in labor, well, I'm not proud of how I reacted. Your understanding meant a lot."

"Have you ever thought about getting in touch with Adie? To check in or whatever?"

"She e-mailed last week." He says it simply. As if this fact isn't a thing.

"Out of the blue?" Um, that is a thing. It's like the thing of things.

He grimaces. "She saw the *Eco Warriors* clip like the rest of the fucking planet."

"What did she say?"

"Not much, just that she thought of me. Wanted an update, to know how I was. When the show would be on."

"What did you say back?"

"Nothing."

"Well, you know you have to, right?"

His sigh is begrudging. "I guess."

"Here's the deal. We face our fears, you and me. Whenever there is something we are nervous about, we must confront it. Support each other. Face the darkness."

"I know you'll kick ass in your interview."

"And I know it will be a great start to e-mail Adie. You were really upset. This might help."

"You won't mind?"

I search myself, but to my relief there are no lingering feelings of jealousy. "What did you tell me after seeing Tanner?"

"He was your past and I was your future."

"Exactly. Why should it be any different for me?"

"Okay, you have a deal." He checks his watch. "I should clear out and give you some space. Doubt you'll want an audience."

"Thanks." I'm grateful he understands I'm not kicking him out of here. I hold up my hand in a high-five gesture. "Here's to facing our fears!"

He glances from my hand to me. "Really?"

It sounds like it's a struggle for him not to roll his eyes and tell me the gesture is oh, so American.

"Really." He's with an American. We eat apple pie and we love to high-five. "Slip me some skin, dude."

"What to the ever, dude." He gives me the world's most reluctant high five, but hey it's a start. I can work with that. "I haven't forgotten about Yosemite either."

My molars grind against each other. "Our crazy-ass hike along the Cliffs of Insanity?"

His puzzled frown reminds me I still haven't forced him to watch *The Princess Bride*. "You mean Tenaya Canyon?"

"Yes, Bermuda Triangle of the Sierras. A canyon of curses. The place you think would make a lovely stroll."

"What were you just saying about facing fears?"

"Oh, crap. Okay." I hold up my hands like I'm under arrest. "You got me, Officer. I'm a life coach hypocrite, guilty as charged. Do as I say, not as I do. Yada yada yada."

"All I need is you."

"For what?"

"Bloody hell, Captain," he says with a chuckle. "If I were stuck on a desert island, you'd be entertainment enough." I don't miss the fact Bran reaches out and gives Persimmon a behind-the-ear scratch. He can front like he's a grumpy curmudgeon all he wants.

I know the truth. I tackle dive his abdomen, and involuntary laughter breaks out of him. My guy has a sensitive underbelly.

"Now go on, get." I plant a kiss on his cheek.

"Fine, but I'm taking the pussy with me." He scoops Persimmon, who regards me with a look of smug contempt. But cats always look like that. Maybe it's thinking about naps on a sunbeam couch cushion, hard to say. It could also be contemplating mass murder.

"Pervert."

He dips into a gallant bow. "You dig it."

"The sad thing is I really kind of do."

He shifts the cat's sizeable weight. "You know you've got this interview."

"I'm faking my confidence like you wouldn't believe. If I were an animal, I'd be a duck. Serene on the surface. Paddling like crazy beneath."

"What are you scared about? At the core?"

"Messing up. What if I say the wrong thing?" I run a hand through my hair, muss it up in the back. "Ruin everything."

"Do you know what makes you amazing?"

I throw up my hands. "Let me see…could it be my endless navel-gazing?"

Bran rocks on his heels and smiles, even though his eyes are dead serious. "The fact you feel the fear and do it anyway."

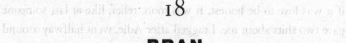

18

BRAN

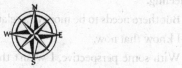

*T*alia's laugh is muffled upstairs, a good sign. I know she'll ace the interview. All she needs to do is be her amazing self. I understand why she wants me to reach out to Adie. I should have checked in with her ages ago. After our brief reconnection a year ago in Melbourne I got lost in Talia Time. Talia Time is a whole lot better than the shithouse guilt of Adie's memory. After Jessie and Wyatt, I had a harsh reminder that I need to patch some holes in my heart. So I sit on the living room couch, starting and stopping an e-mail.

~~Dear Adie~~ *too formal*

~~Hello Adie~~ *sounds like an evil villain who is about to say "So we meet again"*

~~What's up~~ *fucking douche*

That's when fate decides to kick me in the balls. Her name pops up on G-chat. The little green dot next to her name illuminates my screen like an unholy lighthouse beacon. From time to time I see her there. I'm always set to offline so it doesn't matter. She never knows I'm on, and I'm at the point where I barely notice her presence. Whatever love I ever bore her is long gone. I don't even know if it was love to be honest. It was more relief, like at last someone gave two shits about me. I tagged after Adie, went halfway around the world because she acted like I mattered, and I was addicted to the feeling.

But there needs to be more to a relationship than that.

I know that now.

With some perspective, I wasn't the right guy for her. I liked her, but I don't think I ever cared enough about who she actually was as a person. I appreciated her beauty, and her violin talent captivated me. She was my opposite. I coveted her bright cheer like dragon gold, but was less interested in who she was beneath the shine. We had so little in common and wanted different lives.

In a kind, just world, we'd have simply broken up. For a time, I'd have hurt, but I'd have moved on. Instead, we screwed up, skipped a condom, only once, but enough to be taught the hardest lesson in my goddamn life. I got her pregnant. Our disintegrating relationship crumbled to dust under the weight of this thing we'd done. I tried to give it a last shot, pile the rubble into something that could shelter us. I might have been the wanker who got her pregnant, but I wasn't going to abandon her. Or force a choice.

I was ready to step up and be there if that's what she wanted, because I know how bad it sucks to be an unwelcome kid. From the first second I heard, I made a conscious choice. I'd want this child. No matter whether or not I was pretty much a kid myself.

So I did.

I wanted it right until the day I came home to find Adie with someone else, exactly when she knew I'd arrive. Because she knew she had to hurt me that bad to make me leave.

I might not have taken the time to know her in the right way. But that girl understood enough about me.

When she said she'd aborted the baby without telling me, I didn't question. I was too angry. I ignored all the signs she was lying. Because she wanted the baby too.

After Adie hunted me down in Australia last year, I thought I'd reached some sort of peace. What I found was Talia, who brought me love and a calm I hadn't ever experienced. But I learned the hard way, when Jessie was in labor, that the wound of what happened hadn't fully healed. It had festered to the point where the ache was dull, low, throbbing, and I lived with it day in and day out. I grew used to it. Never even noticed. Or at least pretended I didn't.

I don't think I owe Adie a hell of a lot. But I owe her this, to check in. We made a bad choice together. Yes, she lied, but she also paid a higher price.

She's there. If I write to her, she'll see it straightaway. These aren't butterflies in my stomach. They are ants, marching through my guts on relentless tiny feet.

Shit. This was a bad idea.

Hi Adie,

Shit. "Been thinking about how I got you pregnant and the shit storm that followed" isn't really a great lead-in.

I recently experienced a situation that made me think about what happened between us, and to you. I want to say, for what it's worth, that I am sorry I wasn't there. That I wasn't able to help you more. I regret that I wasn't careful with you. I should never have slept with you without protection. I was a

bloody idiot and you paid the price. We weren't going to work
out, but during that time you meant a lot to me. And I'd hate
for you to think that I don't ever think about you, your pregnancy, or what followed. I do. I wish I could have done something to help. I'm ashamed I didn't. I hope you are well and
enjoying life. You deserve it. You deserve every good thing
that comes your way.

　　　　　　　　　　　　　　　　　　　　　　　Bran

I slam the computer shut as soon as I hit send, go for a long run.
When I get back, she's already responded.

Hello Bran,

　Good to hear from you. I expected an update about
your new television career. I admit, this message took me
by surprise. You don't owe me any explanation. I have never
blamed you. You aren't the only one who made mistakes. I
lied to you and that was wrong on every level. We were young
and stupid. It took me time, but I have found peace with what
happened and wish you the same. Thank you for writing.
Despite the angry words I said in the past, you're a good guy.
I'm glad you were my first.

　　　　　　　　　　　　　　　　　　　　　　　xxx A

I read her words again, *You're a good guy.*

I'm trying to be. I really am trying.

The exchange wasn't much. It was fuck all really, but I'm
lighter. The choking guilt releases its stranglehold. Quite possibly I
won't ever talk to Adie again. There's no reason. But I'm glad I did
this. I needed her to know that our shared history affected me. Last

year when she came to Melbourne, I don't think I ever gave her that. I was in too much shock. Now she knows. Now I can move on. The wound can heal.

There's only one thing to do with the past—learn from it.

———

Turns out Talia rocked her interview. She was the only one surprised. Within a week, the radio station invited her into the city for a face-to-face. She drove to San Francisco for the day. Scott and Jessie are still at the hospital with Wyatt. The little guy is strong, putting on the right amount of weight. He needs to learn to feed on his own before they let him come home. Meanwhile, I'm on pet patrol because there's no one else to feed the animals. The minute I head to the kitchen, a parade of dogs and cats follow me. I'm bloody Dr. Dolittle. There's distant scuffling from the veranda. Chester. Whatever is happening out there is straight-up *Island of Dr. Moreau.*

That horny furball is a mutant freak.

I've taken the dogs for a run and rubbed down the cats with more affection than I'd like to admit. What can I say, for having not grown up with animals, the whole pet ownership thing isn't half-bad. The idea of simple domesticity with Talia, our own place, the whole kit, sounds a bit like heaven.

My phone rings. I wonder how her interview went?

I check the number and it's unlisted. "Hello?"

"Mate."

I straighten at the Russian accent. "Sander? What's up?"

"Z."

"Right. Not gonna lie, that new name is going to take some getting used to."

"Work on it."

"Noted. So, you've called me. Obviously you want to discuss more than your name changes?"

"I do, Lockhart. I want your answer."

"About the job?" I fiddle with the living room blind. The street outside is empty. "I told you, I'm waiting for Talia."

"Patience isn't one of my virtues."

I prop the phone against my shoulder with my ear and shove my hands in my pockets. "Dude, I got to say, I'm excited about the offer, but it's not like Zavtra Tech is reliant on application development. That shit's hardly going to be a money earner."

"No."

"Why the rush?"

"I never rush."

I like Sander—Z—and appreciate his eccentricities, but sometimes the dude makes me want to punch a hole in drywall.

"Good. So I'll let you know as soon as Talia decides what she wants to do."

"You run your life based on what she wants?" He sounds incredulous.

"We make decisions together."

"How egalitarian." His smirk carries through the phone.

"Out of curiosity, do you ever unwind? Leave the office? Chase a little skirt around Stanford?"

"That would be no."

"Anyone special at work?" Je-sus, I sound like a talk show host or some shit. Still, Z needs to get laid more than most guys I've ever seen and he seemed keen on Beth.

"I want you at Zavtra Tech, Lockhart. Like I told you before, I don't have many people I can trust. You are a rare exception."

"I'm not sure if that's a curse or a compliment."

"Neither am I." Z gives his first genuine laugh. The one that reminds me of the late nights we'd spend talking shit in our boarding room.

It's not until I hang up I realize he's avoided the question.

My phone rings back immediately. Unlisted. Doesn't Z have a multimillion dollar company to run? Why is he playing mind games?

"Fucking hell, what now," I say into the phone.

"Brandon Lockhart, I presume?" The woman's brisk voice in unfamiliar. The accent Australian.

"Speaking."

"This is Janet Rogers, your father's personal assistant, and he's requested I put you through for a call."

"I'm guessing I don't get a yes or no in the matter."

"Popping you through now."

"Great, Janet." *Just bloody great.*

I've got an intense Russian breathing down my neck for me to make a move. Now Dad's in the mix?

"Spunk?" That's not Dad.

"Gabbles?" My older sister, Gaby.

"Hey, mate. You're alive. Long time no talk." Her laughter is pure passive-aggressive.

"Dad there?"

"Yeah, he's wrapping up another call on his mobile. We didn't expect to get through. You don't have the best track record at answering the phone."

"Well, you did."

"How's America?"

"American."

"Talia hasn't strangled you yet?"

I grit my teeth. "She finds me charming."

"Hah hah." Gaby means well, but she's as sensitive as sandpaper up the ass. I guess you had to get a bit rough around the edges to survive in our house. It wasn't exactly a place bursting with soft affection.

"How 'bout you, the girls?"

"We're good. They miss you."

"Jockey come around much?" Her wanker ex-husband was a former jockey who traded in horses to ride socialites all around town.

There's a pause. "He has scheduled visits."

"That good?"

Another pause, followed by a sigh. "No, but the girls need a father."

Do they? Do any of us?

"Brandon?" Dad joins the conversation in his typical impatient fashion, as if I'm the one who's kept him waiting.

"Hey."

"G'day. Good to hear your voice, mate."

"Yeah, well. It's been a bit, yeah?" Fucking hell, I'm mumbling like a kid.

"I reckon. Set to come home?"

"To Melbourne?" Good thing they can't see me recoil.

"He knows, Bran," Gaby cuts in. "He knows you're staying in California for now."

"But perhaps you'd consider returning for a short stint," Dad pushes back. "The iron is hot to ramp up some promotion for the foundation. What with the visibility from your upcoming show, the publicity is free advertising. I've put calls in with all our contacts—"

"Hold up. What are we talking about?"

"Told you he wouldn't be into it," Gaby says in her know-it-all tone.

"Into what?" I am in the dark and don't like it.

"The foundation is fielding loads of media requests about you. *The Age*, *The Australian*. Papers from London, Canada, and New Zealand. You made a splash. The board wants to take the opportunity to leverage—"

"No, no way. Not happening."

"Son." His voice has a bite, like what he wants to say is *bloody dickhead*. "I don't think you understand—"

"I understand that I've been made a spectacle. That people who have never met me believe I'm something I'm not. Or even worse, think I believe I'm hot shit. I can't stand for it, Dad. It's too much."

"This is a family foundation, Brandon. We're well resourced, but this could be an opportunity—"

"Dad, I don't know how to say this in a way that will make sense to you. So here's my best stab. No way in hell am I going to be getting in front of a camera and talking about the accident. I didn't do it with the plane, and I'm not doing it now."

"The woman you saved is calling you a hero," Gaby butts in.

I blink. "Justine?"

"The media found her in New Zealand. We got that story into *The Age* this morning. She says she owes her life to your quick thinking."

"Is this a sick joke?" *The Age* is the prominent paper in

Melbourne, one of the biggest in the country. It's not enough for America to think I'm a wanker. Now everyone at home will know too?

"People love a hero, baby brother." Gaby relishes things that make me uncomfortable. She's always loved playing up the big sister role, poking at me. At the end of the day, she has a good heart, but that's easy to forget when you're stuck on the blackberry bramble she's grown around herself.

We're a lot alike actually.

"Let's get you a ticket home," Dad says, like a dog unwilling to release a bone. "Doesn't need to be long. A month. Maybe three. This visibility comes at the perfect time—"

"I can't budge on this. Not without selling myself out. Sorry. But this is a hard no."

"You said you were going to help get things off the ground. This is a family endeavor."

"You're right, and I've been reading the reports you've sent. Sounds like you have things well in hand, and I'm happy to advise where I'm able to give input." The foundation has set up carbon-trading schemes in a host of developing countries, and is investing in the development of solar-powered generators and solar ovens in the attempt to curb deforestation in the more denuded areas. "I'm not ready to commit full-time to the foundation, but that door's still open at some point down the road."

"I want you on television, SBS, ABC, Channel Ten."

"No. No. Fuck no."

"And once the show airs, this will be big, Bran. Australians love an underdog," Gaby says.

"Look, I can say no in Japanese, Spanish, Portuguese, and French."

"Remember the loan I made," Dad snaps.

And in for the bloody strong arm. "You calling in debts?"

"If you'd never given up your trust fund——"

"Dad, while of course we want Bran's involvement, let's not——".

"Son, you're a Lockhart." Here we go, Bryce Blowhard is in the house. "You've been wiggling out of responsibility in this company, this family——"

"You have the ability to hire experts in any field," I snap. "I didn't even finish my honors. Why are your knickers in such a knot?"

"Family is family. You're my son."

"Yeah? Well, you spent the first eighteen years of my life ignoring me and the last five ashamed of me, pardon if I don't feel all warm and fucking fuzzy."

"Now see here——"

"Enough," Gaby cuts in. "Nothing good will come of this at the moment so let's leave it there."

"The money——"

"You want your ten grand? I'd tear it out of my guts if I could. Give you a pound of flesh." I rake my hand through my hair and take a deep breath. "I have my own life. I'm tearing my hair out to make it work here with Talia. I've got a solid job offer, and hopefully, so does she. If money is so damn important to you, and not my happiness, then I'll——"

"I'm closing down this phone call before gunshots are fired." Gaby is serious. She doesn't mind giving me shit, but she'll protect me if Dad comes down too hard. She always has.

"See here, Brandon——"

"Good-bye, Spunk. As much as this family bonding sesh has been everything heartwarming, it's a wrap."

The line goes dead. I chuck the phone before I know what I'm about. The resulting explosion detonates broken glass and wires all over the lounge's rug. Chester shrieks his alarm from the veranda. The dogs and cats draw in, half circle me like they want to play the role of helpful woodland animals. Christ. I destroyed the phone and put a hole in Jessie's wall.

I thought I was getting better. Dealing with my shit. Looks like the joke's on me.

19

TALIA

*B*ran's phone is turned off as per usual. I swallow my exasperation and try to focus on driving in rush hour traffic. Better to fiddle my fingers on the wheel and attempt to keep my attention on the car in front of me. I mean, I only did one of the bravest things in my life of late and he isn't answering so I can download. No problem. I didn't really want to chat with him about the fact that I was so nervous my lip actually quivered when I answered my first question. The one where they asked, "So, Natalia, tell us a little bit about yourself."

Somehow I coped. At first, yeah I faked it, but honestly, I think I did okay. I answered every question well and by the end, the panel was leaning forward, all their body language saying that they were interested. In the end, one of the women winked at me. Not like a pervy *Hey, pretty lady*, but a *You nailed it, Soul Sister*.

I turn off the exit near Jessie's place and turn up the music. Holy crap, it's Wilson Phillips, "Hold On." Straight up old-school early '90s cheese pop fills the 4Runner. I cut off the air conditioner, roll down the window, and let the early summer heat barrel into the car. At a stoplight, a woman in the sedan beside me stares. Oops. I'm belting out the lyrics at the top of my lungs.

I give a sheepish wave, which she actually returns with a fist bump. I'm still laughing when I pull into the house. Bran's never been a big one for phone conversation. With the odd call still coming in about the *Eco Warriors*, no big surprise he isn't hovering over the phone.

I go into the house and it smells weird, like fresh paint. Bran is in the kitchen washing his hands. "Hey."

"Hi."

"Why is there a patch on the wall in the living room?" I force a smile, but my insides are chilled. Is Bran punching walls while I'm gone? What the hell? Panic flares, makes it impossible to take a deep breath.

"My phone broke."

"On the wall?"

"Yeah."

I raise my brows. "Um, I'm going to assume it had assistance. It's not a Superphone, faster than the speed of light, right?"

He doesn't even crack a smile. "I lost it today, only for a second, but I didn't have control."

"What happened?"

"Shit with my dad." He waves his hand. "Not important. All I want to do is hear how you were a bloody sensation."

"I did kind of nail it." I throw my arms around him. "Although honestly, success in my world is refraining from panic vomiting. They said they'll let me know within a week."

"Oh, sweetheart, fantastic. I have a good feeling. You're going to get it."

"I may not have any nails left by then." I hold up one hand, the tips are ragged. "They'll be little chewed-off nubs."

He folds his hand over mine. "You'd still be hot."

"Wow." I jerk from his grip and waggle my fingers like a monster in an old-time horror flick. "You must really love me."

He moves so suddenly that I don't even know he's coming until I'm crushed against him. "You have no idea."

A throat clears. I turn to see Dad standing in the doorway.

"Hey," I say, adjusting my shirt. Even though nothing crazy was going on, I still have this uncomfortable sense of being busted. God, I can't wait for our own place.

"How were the animals?" Dad asks Bran.

"Walked, fed, watered, pet, scratched. I'm Old MacDonald."

Dad laughs. "Thanks for holding down the farm."

As they continue their easy chat, a sudden panic crawls up my chest, growing in confidence as it mounts. What's happening? Oh, no. Shit. I haven't had to deal with this in a while—a sneak panic attack. Anxiety, dread, uncertainty all of those terrible things that open the door for OCD to slink in, whisper it can make it better. I try to push back, knowing that it actually makes everything worse, but I'm like an addict. The rituals become the only thing that can help. OCD gives a false sense of security in an uncertain world.

Please calm down. Please calm down.

Even good stress in my world is dangerous. Anything that tips the balance has the potential to send me into a spiral.

"Talia?" Bran looks at me with concern.

"Yes." Do I seem normal? Is this how a normal person would stand? Engage? "How's Wyatt?" Yes. Good. Deflect. Deflect.

Dad falls on the couch with a heavy sigh. "He's doing great. He's coming home tomorrow."

"Oh, Dad, that's awesome." And it is. I mean it. Even from this disassociated state.

"Want us to clear out while you get yourselves sorted? I can clean up the nursery today and we can make ourselves scarce for a few days."

"Would that work? I don't want it to seem like I'm kicking you guys out."

"This one is waiting to hear back about that interview in the city," Bran says, jerking his head at me.

"How'd the interview go, Peanut?"

I force a smile that might look like a grimace. I need to get away. Have some space. I'm separating from my body, like I'm here in this reality, but also watching myself from this parallel one. A place that is two-dimensional. Makes it impossible to draw a breath. My pulse beats fast and heavy in my ears, like I'm chained to a ship's galley while some guard beats the inexorable drum. I have no choice but to stroke. Stroke. Stroke. Keep afloat. "Great! Hey, I need the bathroom. Back in a second."

Once I'm in the bathroom, I turn the tap on. The water's cold, and splashing it on my cheeks helps return a sense of normality. I can fight this storm. I have done it a thousand times. It's harder when it's quick, unexpected like what just happened, and after a long face-washing session and a few deep breaths, I'm still not 100 percent. But I'm better.

I open the door, ready to head to the kitchen and make a cup of tea. Instead, I run smack into Bran. "Oh, hey, all yours." I gesture to the bathroom.

"Let me guess. You don't want to talk about what happened?"

"I'm fine."

"That's exactly what a not-fine person would say."

"Look, I'm tired. I was up early. I've been amped today. With all the stuff going on, Wyatt, the interview, and everything. I'm bound to be a little wired."

"If we move to San Francisco, will you start therapy?"

"Okay, fine." I clip the words and move to step around him.

"Fuck fine." His eyes narrow as he grabs my waist. "I want a yes."

"You don't understand what it's like."

"You're right, I don't. But you don't understand what it's like for me. To stand by and watch you hurt. I'd rather double-fist pokers and shove them in my eyes."

"I'd cut off your hands before I let you hurt those pretty eyes."

He does a figure-eight twirl on my back. "Oh, Captain."

"You're right though."

"You're only just noticing this?"

"Arrogant much?" I lightly poke the ticklish place right above the sexy hard V muscle on his abdomen. My reward is a flash of dimple. "I want to work harder on getting better. It's time for therapy. You deserve my best and hell, I deserve my best too."

"Exactly."

"You're not worried to be stuck with a crazy girlfriend who has to go to a shrink to cope with life?"

"Talia, I'm not going to say this again, so listen hard."

I pretend to clean out my ears. Easier to make a joke than pretend I'm not intensely nervous about whatever he says next.

"I'm stuck on you, girl."

"Oh, you've given me a valentine." Easier to make another joke to pretend like my relief doesn't turn my bones to a quivering Jell-O mold.

"Come away with me."

"Where?"

"With Wyatt arriving home, Jessie and your dad will need space. We can't rent a flat until we're sure about our plans. Remember how you wanted to get to the mountains."

"Um, I'm pretty sure you were the one jonesing for the crazy hike." Still, the idea of Bran in backpacking mode, his cut legs flexing on the trail ahead, sounds like exactly what I need in my life.

"Let's do it. Go to Yosemite. I'll get the nursery cleaned up today. Help sort whatever is needed to get the baby comfortable. I'll talk to your dad about borrowing camp equipment."

"You sure? I mean, you seemed like you were having more family drama and—"

"Yes, I'm better after spending time outside. I'll think clearly. Calm down."

"This is true."

"Will you trust me to take care of you out there?"

"Yes. Will you trust me to take care of myself?"

"Absolutely."

20

BRAN

The next day we drive toward the mountains. The Sierra Nevadas are allegedly right in front of us. The same landscape that inspired John Muir to write that in "wildness lies the hope of the world." I guess we're royally screwed, because instead of wildflowers and grizzly bears, we're socked under a murky sky. The Central Valley is surrounded on three sides by mountain ranges. Air pollution settles in the bowl like a toxic soup.

Talia zones out the window. Scott gave us the 4Runner on loaner, eager for us to vacate the house. Jessie wants to whip Wyatt's nursery into proper order. I tighten my grip on the wheel. I've got plans for the next few days, big beautiful ones. Words that need saying. Questions that require answers. I want headspace, clarity, and sweeping, romantic vistas. Not smog.

"Waaaaaaait a second." Talia leans forward, squints. "Shit!" She flops back. "I saw it for a flash, a glimmer of mountain. Did you?"

"No, trying to concentrate. Driving on the wrong side of the road, remember?"

"Right."

"Huh?"

"Technically you are on the right side of the road so…" She gives me a rueful smile. "It's a bit tomatoes/tomahtoes, isn't it?" She pronounces her first word with a long *a* and the second with a short one. "It's seriously gross out there. Worst air quality I've seen in ages. We need a good rain to clear everything out."

"Might help if our species didn't ruin everything. I read about this landscape in Muir's naturalist books as a kid. The way he described the golden light in the Central Valley was fucking poetry. Fast-forward through the last hundred years and behold how the fingerprints of so-called progress have tarnished the landscape." Sunlight shunts through the haze, the same bleak yellow as the piss of a dying man.

She's quiet long enough to suggest that she fell asleep listening to my grandstanding. "You miss it? The Sea Alliance?"

"Yeah." No point sugarcoating. "I love being here, in California, Central Valley miasmas notwithstanding. But I do miss being Down South."

"What parts?"

"The purity. The animals. The wind. The emptiness. I hate that my time there has been compromised by sensationalism. I hate that I nabbed the spotlight away from what's important, the illegal whaling, the bloody reckless plundering of a fragile environment. It's like I did my best and—"

"It didn't work out the way you hoped." She touches my shoulder. "I so get that."

"I know you do, Captain."

"Hey! Will you look at that." She points. "Mountains." She's right. The sickly half-light relents at last. Up ahead, the dramatic ridgeline of the High Sierras is finally unmistakable.

"Tell me a story," she says, fidgeting with her chest strap. "Pass the time."

"You know all my stories."

"Do I?"

"Pretty much."

She grabs her lemonade out of the cup holder and takes a thoughtful sip. "I don't know how you lost your virginity."

I'm not even drinking and I choke.

"Ooooh." She perks. "This is going to be good. Should I pop popcorn?"

"Not much to say."

"I doubt that."

"Was over in less than a minute. I barely knew what happened."

"Well, hell." She takes another sip, a bead of condensation drips off the bottle, lands on her knee. "I'm in the mood for scintillating convo."

The drop shimmers on her skin like a diamond. I want to spread the wetness across her with my thumb. "This could get dangerous."

"The first time I ever masturbated, I thought of you."

My dick jolts. "Wait, what?"

"Oh, did that get your attention?" She's coy innocence personified. Not going to lie, her wide-eyed act is a turn-on. My body thrums.

"Hell yes it did."

She grins like the cat who got the cream. Impossible not to keep darting glances to the place where her tiny jean cutoffs rub her inner thighs. Today is over thirty degrees Celsius, or ninety-five Fahrenheit according to the car thermostat, but the fire boiling my blood has nothing to do with the outside temperature.

"You like the idea of me touching myself?"

"Do it." My words rasp as if I haven't had water in a week.

"Here?"

"Yes." My dick hurts with how badly I need this to happen. "Now."

"Holy Batman, this conversation veered in an unexpected direction." She laughs until she realizes I'm not. "You know I fail at being the center of attention. What about a little car head?"

"Put your mouth on me and I won't stay on the road. Fact."

"So requesting me to passenger seat masturbate is you being a responsible driver?"

"Yep." A responsible driver desperate to watch his girl get down and dirty. "But no pressure." I mean it. I'll drive with a hard-on for the next hour, but I'm not going to bully her into a one-girl wank show if she's not ready.

"You'd like to watch me?" She bites her lip as if she's actually considering this. "You're being serious?"

My heart accelerates. "As a heart attack."

"Can't decide if this is sexy or crazy."

"Only one way to find out."

She crosses and uncrosses her knees. "Okay."

"Really?"

She looks around self-consciously. "I mean, we'll see how it goes."

Speech is impossible. Want, lust, desire, whatever I'm feeling, grows in intensity, howls through my bones. There's a subtle metallic noise as she grinds down her zipper. Next comes the snap of elastic as she slides her fingers into her panties.

I'm about to explode like a bloody grenade.

"Want to hear what if feels like?"

I muster a single nod.

"Soft," she murmurs. "Slick."

I swallow hard. "Are you wet, then?" Screw grenades, this shit's nuclear.

"Yeah. Pretty wet."

Fuck me. "You have any idea how hot you look? All that sun in your hair?"

"My hand down my pants."

"Forget mountains, I could watch you do this all goddamn day."

She inches her fingers deeper into her panties. "Is this the part where I should make a joke about hard granite?"

"Touch your clit."

She lets loose a soft, feathery sigh, one that comes with a sharp hiss on the end. Her calves flex as her toes curl. She mashes her lips, and her next sound curls around my ears, a cross between an *oh* and an *ah*.

"Nice?"

"Un-huh." She quickens her pace, more uninhibited as her tension grows. Her noises deepen, almost as if she hurts. I get it. I ache all over. Her knees twitch. I want to lick the hollows behind them. She braces her shoulders against the seat. Her lower back arches out as her hips do a subtle back-and-forth rock. My sac pulls tight at her next moan.

She glances over, her eyes heavy-lidded. "This isn't going to cause a crash?"

"Bloody hell." I refocus on the road. Not watching isn't any less sexy. My senses are heightened. There is a quick slippery sound. My dick pulses in time to her rhythm. Her breath quickens.

"Good?"

"Oh, God." Her knees splay farther as she gets into it, works herself faster. A hot tangy smell undercuts the pine air freshener dangling from the rearview. I bite down on the inside of my lip. She slides her free hand under her lavender T-shirt. "Jealous?"

"Fucking A."

"Want me to stop? I can stop."

"Don't you dare."

"I—I think I could come like this."

"Counting on it, sweetheart." Sweat sheens my chest. My T-shirt sticks to my skin. If my dick gets more taut it's going to break. "What are you thinking about?"

"You."

"More."

"Your mouth on me. Down there. Kissing."

Fuck. "Where?"

"You know where."

"'Course I do, but I want to hear you to say it."

"My . . . my God, what? My pussy?"

"I can get down with pussy."

"Don't make me laugh." Her giggles are more than slightly strangled.

"Less talking, Captain. More fingering."

"Almost there." The husky note to her voice is the sexiest bloody thing I've ever heard. No matter how much stupid shit I've done in my life, I've done something right to earn this girl. She makes me feel things I never knew I was capable of. My heart was a geode. Plain. Gray. Cold. Hard. She drove her sweet blade into my center until I cracked and discovered a hidden beauty.

She gasps. Her legs take on their own bucking motion. Each micro-movement hits me like a double-overhead, sucks me into a relentless undertow. I barely have time to come up for air. Outlook is good that I'm going to come in my boxers without laying a single finger on myself. I've never done such a thing even at my most green, adolescent horny apex. Even though I'm expecting it, her cry recoils through me like a shot.

"Well, golly gee whillickers," she mutters, lazy, slow, like she's chewing saltwater taffy. I check the mirror. No one's behind me. A turnout is right ahead. I veer off the road, far up on the shoulder. We jounce over gravel until I brake hard.

"What the—"

I'm out of my seat and halfway over the console before she can finish the question. Her mouth tastes like lemonade. When she lifts her hand to touch the side of my face, I grab her wrist and bite the fleshy rise of her palm. Not enough to make it hurt, but with enough pressure that she sucks in a surprise hiss.

"Talia." She raggedly inhales when I suck in a finger, enjoying the salty taste on her skin before flicking my tongue in the crease between her fingers. "There was a time when I believed wanting you would break me."

"And now?" Her pupils are huge, unfocused.

"Your love is what makes me."

She grabs hold of my erection through my shorts. Her touch is a magnet, pulls blood from all my extremities. "Your turn?"

I don't have a choice. I never did. Not with her.

"This won't take long."

She works my belt loose and when she palms me, I can't hold on. It's too much. I collide against my seat. Throw my arms around the back of the headrest and hang on. It's that or burst from my skin.

She crawls onto her knees, doesn't stop pumping, but at this angle she gets a better grip. "Won't take long" was an exaggeration. If I last another minute it will be the most control I've ever executed in my entire life.

"I love seeing you like this," she whispers.

"How's that?" I open one eye. Her shorts are still open and reveal a glimpse of her white cotton panties. Jesus. Fuck. Not much longer.

"Wanting me."

"I always wanted you. From the first second I saw you on Lygon Street. I wanted."

"Can't say the same."

I flinch, but she keeps her grip firm. "You wore a koala head, remember? If I had wanted you straight off that would have been creepy. My fascination didn't start until you walked into that dodgy pub."

"After that you were all I thought about."

"You drove me crazy." Each stroke is magic.

"Good, because I was half-mad." Heat scorches my lower belly, my quads, I pump against her, riding the build. "I still am where you're concerned."

Her thumb brushes my tip, spreads the moisture beading there over my sensitive underside. Can't process. Can't think. The rush, it's too much. She sweeps a light caress over my balls. Here we bloody go. "Fuck, Talia." I explode right as her teeth lock on my flexed bicep. It hurts and is incredible and holy shit…

When my brain resumes function she's cleaning her hands

with a wet wipe. "Why don't we road trip every day?" I ask, scrubbing my face.

"We're pretty dang good at it." She giggles.

There's another sound. Quiet. Almost nothing. But not nothing.

I throw open the driver's side door. Shit. A nail protrudes from the driver's side wheel. Air hisses.

"Your dad has a spare, right?"

21

TALIA

*J*f anyone asked me five minutes ago what was the hottest thing I'd ever seen in my twenty-two years spinning around the sun, my answer would have been unequivocal. Jerking off Bran while he allowed himself to be completely bare to me in all his aching vulnerability. I did bite him. Because I love him so much it set my teeth on edge and drove out something animalistic within me.

What a difference three hundred seconds makes. Because here is Bran, shirtless, changing a tire while I watch his lean muscles bunch and flex while I sit cross-legged beneath the shade of the scrappiest tree this side of the Mississippi. I could be badass and get in there and change it. My dad insisted I learn how when I got my license. But there's a deep pleasure in watching a guy be manly. I take another swig of lemonade. I rest my head against the bark, pick up a piece of loose gravel, and roll it between my fingers.

For once I don't require a worry stone. It's not only the recent orgasms making me feel relaxed. It's everything. A month ago, I feared I'd lost myself in a wrong direction, but I found my way back to myself. Fear is part of living, and for me, I'll probably always be more anxious than most. Despite the recent panic attack, I have this rare feeling, cocooned around me. Maybe, just maybe, everything will be okay.

"This is as secure as I'm going to get it," Bran says. There's a greasy handprint on his lower belly. I want to place my hand over the outline.

We get inside and I breathe deep. "It smells like—"

"Sex."

I grimace. "We'll need to air it out before coming home."

"We'll have to buy one of our own."

"A shared car." The idea gives my heart a happy little tug. "God, it seems so official."

"Owning a vehicle together?"

"Yes, it's one of those things, you know. Like grown-up couple things."

"What kind do you want?" He wipes a hand over his forehead. We're winding into the foothills.

"Don't know. I'm not that big on cars."

"Maybe a VW van."

"Ooooh, that idea has serious legs, like a camper."

He arches a brow. "Instant bed action might come in handy."

I raise him a wink. "This is true."

Mariposa is ahead, a big enough mountain town to support a mechanic. It's getting late so we'll probably have to overnight there. No point risking a drive into the Sierra high country on an ancient spare. We hit the city limits. There's an auto shop connected to a gas station. Bran hops out and talks to the guy inside. He returns with a resigned look. "The shop will open first thing. He gave me the address for a cheap motel around the corner."

"What can go wrong?"

We park in front of an uninspired, single-story motel. The name on the sign, Vagabond's Rest, is marred by graffiti. Some genius sprayed a thick black line through letters so it reads, VAG REST.

"Classy joint." Bran gets out of the car.

"Looks cheap." I join him on the sidewalk. "Anyway, it's only for a night."

We open the door to the lobby, and a Christmas bell jingles. "Hoo wee, what has the cat dragged in?" The woman behind the counter must be pushing the wrong side of seventy. Her hair is tinted an orange better suited to jack-o'-lanterns, but when compared to the alarming purple lipstick, seems muted and tasteful.

"You kiddos on your honeymoon?" She peers over turquoise bifocals.

"Car problems." Bran whips out a credit card. He gives the plastic a long look before handing it over. I know what it costs him, spending the loan his dad gave him. He must be champing to earn his own cash. Zavtra is eccentric, but obviously brilliant. Got to say, I am pretty confident about Bran holding his own against any guy in the forceful personality department. Besides, I can always tickle him if he unleashes too much of the intense kraken. I know exactly how sensitive that underbelly is.

"Where do you recommend grabbing dinner?" I ask. Car trips and an amped-up sex drive have given me one hell of an appetite.

"The diner is popular."

"Diner." Bran perks. "Those actually exist?"

The motel lady shoots him a strange look. "Son, I can't understand a word that came out of your mouth."

"Australian." I pet his head, like that's explanation enough.

She nods, as if it really is.

I stifle a yelp when Bran pinches my ass.

We stroll hand in hand to the diner. "Why are you so excited about diner fare?"

"Seems like being in a movie."

"You don't have diners back home?"

"You've been there. Ever seen one?"

"I don't routinely seek them out."

We reach the building and it's all retro stainless steel, red vinyl booths, white Formica tables, and black-checkered tiles. Real deal though, not a tourist trap.

"What to order, what to order?" Bran studies the deep-fried menu. "Club sandwich? Tuna melt?"

"You sound positively gleeful."

He snorts. "Diner food is one American tradition I can get behind. Except for ketchup; it should be tomato sauce. And your fries suck compared to our chips."

"You are such a snob."

"Guilty on all charges."

"Can't go wrong with a chocolate malt. I'm nabbing one of those bad boys." I point to the glass case bursting with thick slices of homemade pies. "Blueberry. With vanilla ice cream."

"For dinner?"

"There is no judgment in a diner. That's the rule."

"Noted."

"Where do you source your tuna?" Bran asks when the waitress arrives to take our order.

"Chicken?" She stares, baffled, over the top of her pad.

"Tuna," he repeats.

"Sorry, what?" The waitress raises her voice like he speaks a foreign language.

"Tuna." Bran grips the table in an effort to maintain patience.

I bite my top lip, but the gesture does nothing to prevent an escaping giggle. Bran throws a *ch* sound in front of some words. Tuna comes out *choona*.

"He's asking where your tuna comes from," I say.

"A can?" The waitress frowns, snapping her gum in impatience. The diner is filling up. She doesn't want to decipher.

"A malt," Bran mutters. "I'll take a chocolate malt, garden salad, and chips."

"Fries," I amend before the he said/she said gong show starts again.

When the food arrives we clink glasses—my coffee mug to Bran's milkshake tin.

"So this is my equivalent to a last meal." I cover my mouth to make my massive pie bite appear slightly less greedy.

Bran leans over and dabs the corner of my mouth with his napkin. "Tomorrow will be epic."

I grimace. "It will be something."

"Look, I won't get you into anything you can't handle."

"Why are you pushing me so hard on this?"

"Because you're afraid you can't, but I know you can. Have faith." He waves a fry at me.

"Careful, tiger. If your magic wand splatters ketchup on my a la mode we'll have words."

"I'd prefer to settle our differences horizontally."

I waggle my brows and continue to dollop ice cream on the crust. I have to agree with him.

"What are you doing?" He nudges my ankle. "Little mess maker."

"I prefer the term *delicious disaster*." I hike my foot to rest on his inner thigh, tickle my toes against his dick.

His eyes widen, mouth fastened to the straw. He looks almost boyish—ripe for corruption. I place the spoon in my mouth and polish it slowly clean.

"You're trouble." His voice holds more than a trace of gravel. The memory of him, bared to me, in the car earlier sparks behind my eye. Okay, perhaps not so boyish.

"Trouble's my middle name." I clear my throat and his knowing look sends heat to my cheeks. I spoon more ice cream and he leans forward, licks it before I have time to squeak in protest. "Didn't your mother teach you table manners?"

His gaze shutters. "Apparently not."

Ice cracks under this conversation. I'm not backing away, but need to choose my words carefully. "Hey now, you can't avoid your family stuff forever."

He cracks his neck. "It's tempting to try."

"Don't give your past that much power."

"I can't be what they want." For a second I see it. That little boy. The one who ached to be loved.

"Which is?"

"My dad. He's been talking to the media about me. All the *Eco Warriors* crap. He wanted me to come home. Do interviews. Be a lap dog. He doesn't get that's not me. Someday, sure, I'll probably step up and take a more active role in the Lockhart Foundation, but I need more time to be my own person. Not sure that's good enough for Dad though. He wants a fictional son, not the one he has."

Ahhh, a dawning knowledge settles on me. "This is how your phone found its way to being broken, isn't it?"

"Yeah. I lost my temper. Not proud of that fact." He picks up his straw wrapper and tears it in half. "Why would he go to the papers about me? Never mind, I already know the answer. To gain exposure for the foundation, but not everything is for sale. I'm not a commodity."

"Are you sure that's the situation?"

"He spoke to reporters."

"What if he was bragging?"

"Why?" He looks so baffled that I jump out of my booth, walk around the table, scoot beside him, and wrap him in a hug.

"Because you"—I kiss the tip of his scrunched-up nose—"are amazing."

"Hmmmph."

"I'm serious. I understand that *Eco Warriors* show is going to be your worst nightmare, but you don't see yourself the way everyone else does."

"I'm not a—"

"You are a hero, Brandon Lockhart, and I'll tell anyone who disagrees to call their seconds."

"You'd duel for me?"

"Any dawn, anytime. Although realistically I'd probably be a terrible shot, so if you value my life, you'll accept the facts."

He grimaces.

"Curious, this little double standard of yours. I'm supposed to take on face value every last compliment you dole my direction. Regardless of if they feel uncomfortable or untrue."

"Because I'm right," he says.

"Then don't disrespect my intelligence. If I say you are a hero, that means you're a motherfucking hero." I mock slam my fist to the Formica, and the people at the table beside us jump.

"Okay, okay." Bran's shoulders convulse. "Bloody hell, Captain. No need to Hulk out."

"Don't make me angry."

"Pie does things to you."

"You have no idea." I grab the bill. "Now let's pay up and get out of here."

He looks around. "I seem to have mislaid my cape."

"Jokes are the first step to acceptance."

He stands and grabs me right before I walk to the cash register. "Thanks for believing in me."

"Likewise."

"I'm being serious now."

I brace his face and meet his eyes. His gaze is full of gratitude, and a relief that makes my throat thicken. "So am I," I whisper huskily. "So am I."

His lips brush mine, and I'd trade all the blueberry pies in the world for this moment of sweetness.

———

The motel is cheap, which is good. It also doesn't have functional plumbing, which is bad. Especially when you need to clean off after car self-love and after-diner, un-air-conditioned monkey sex. "I'll go see the lady." I drop my towel, and Bran sits up from the center of the bed. I shake my head at his latest and greatest erection.

"You can't be serious?" I pull my head through my T-shirt. "You can go again?"

He shrugs.

"I'm sorry, this…"—I wave my hands over my nether regions—"is on R and R."

"You make me sound like a war zone."

"I understand that in romance novels people go at it again and again. But in real life, after two back-to-back sessions, I need a break."

"Fine." He flops back against the pillow. "I'd rather lose the battle and win the war."

"Get some rest, G.I. Joe."

He salutes me, his eyes already closed.

I'm still snickering when I push the door open into the motel lobby. A little Christmas bell tinkles my presence.

The woman looks up from cards splayed on her desk. "I know."

I halt midstep. "You do?"

"We called the plumber, but no promises."

"Oh, okay." I start to backtrack calculating how many wet wipes are in the truck. If we start backpacking tomorrow, I really would prefer to start in the green as far as personal hygiene goes.

"Not so fast." The lady purses her purple lips, and crooks a finger at me.

"Um, okay." I creep cautiously forward.

"Pick one."

I look down. "Tarot?" My friend Sunny's grandmother is really into it.

"Go on."

I hesitate, but feel the need to be polite. "Okay." I pull a card and hand it over.

"Interesting."

"What?"

"Very interesting. You chose death."

My vision contracts. "Excuse me?"

She flips the card to face me. No mistaking the skull. "You selected the death card."

"No." I fight the urge to double over.

"You did." She waves it like I'm a dunce. "That means—"

"I'm good. I'm good. Thank you. Good night." I throw myself out the door while the receptionist is still hollering for me to wait.

Bran is asleep when I let myself in. I can't wash. I don't want to turn on the television and wake him. Shit. Shit. I am freaking out. All my good feelings from the afternoon have been smote down with one stupid card.

Death? I don't believe in tarot, but really? Really? Drawing the death card on the eve of this scary hike? When my preemie baby brother is just home from the hospital? My dad is carrying all kinds of stress? What are the odds? Bran looks so peaceful in the dark, his breathing easy, his arms thrown over his head in abandon.

What if it's him?

No. I physically stamp my foot, get my phone from my purse, and shut myself in the bathroom.

"Peanut?" Dad answers after two rings.

"Everything okay?" I keep my voice light, casual.

"Yeah, great. Jessie's here, she says hi. Wyatt is nursing."

"So he's doing well?"

"Fantastic. He's packing on the weight. A chowhound."

I close my eyes. "That's excellent."

"Aren't you in the park?"

"We got a flat, had to spend the night in Mariposa. We'll hike in tomorrow."

"All right, stay safe."

"Always do. And Dad...I love you. A lot."

"Talia? What's going on?"

"Nothing. Honest. But I don't think I tell you that enough."

"I love you too." His voice deepens with emotion.

"Bye." I click off the phone. One down.

I text Mom. How are you doing?

The phone buzzes. She answers. Clearly alive.

Busy. Moved into my own place. You'll have to come visit.

Will do. Talk soon.

Love you.

I rub my thumb over her words before replying. You too.

I creep back into the room and Bran stirs. "Get over here, cuddles." He opens his arms.

I nestle in and run my hand over his back muscles. He's so warm. So alive. Impossible he'll ever be anything besides this vital force.

"I dreamed I lost you." He murmurs into my hair.

My blood freezes. "Yeah."

"Kept looking, couldn't find you."

Bran, Dad, Wyatt, Mom, Jessie—everyone accounted for.

So maybe the card meant me.

Bran falls asleep again, hard and fast, as is his way. I watch every minute on the clock radio tick past until around 3:56 a.m. when my eyelids finally win out against my sense of impending doom and close.

22

BRAN

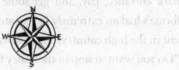

*T*he next morning Talia is off. Her eyes are dim, with purple bruises ringing underneath.

"Sleep badly?"

"Don't ask." She dresses in silence and walks to the door. "Will you deal with the receptionist? I can't face her this morning."

"Aw, she wasn't that bad."

"You're right, she was worse." Talia's out, the door slamming behind.

I go in to pay up, but the old woman is nowhere to be seen. A man, probably her husband, is there with a wiry beard down his barrel chest, bald on top. He gives us a good discount on account of the plumbing problems.

I fill our thermos with lobby coffee and head back out to the truck, and hand it over to Talia. "Maybe this will help."

"Doubtful." She takes a small sip, grimaces, and hands it back.

I know from experience that if a bad mood strikes, there's nothing for it but time. I get the car to the mechanic, have the wheel patched, and soon we're on our way to Yosemite again. We follow the narrow road tracing the landscape's contours, through a valley scarred with the evidence of past forest fires and rockslides.

"See, Captain," I say, smiling when we pass the national park sign. "We got there eventually."

She nods, forces her lips up, but her heart's not in it. We reach the park entrance, pay, and get some tips on current conditions. California's had an extremely dry winter so the snow is almost non-existent in the high country, our destination.

"Do you want to stop in the valley first?" I ask.

"Up to you."

I grip the wheel tighter; looks like she's committed to keeping this bad attitude. Bloody hell. I want this hike to be special. I'm counting on it. "My idea is to take us up Tioga Road, into the high country. We lost a day with the car, so we won't be able to poke around Tuolumne Meadows as much as I'd like. I wanted to check out the Pacific Crest Trail, but think we'll need to save that for a later trip."

"Whatever suits, this is your rodeo."

"You make it sound like a death sentence."

"Why do you say it like that?" She snaps.

"Whoa, whoa, whoa." I slow, pull off on the shoulder. "You okay?"

Her nod is curt.

"You're sending lots of mixed signals here."

"I'm fine."

"Uh, isn't that girl-speak for everything is wrong?"

Finally, a giggle. "It's nothing. I'm nervous and stupid and superstitious."

"Superstitious?"

"On second thought, I will have that coffee." She grabs the thermos. "Caffeine withdrawal is a bitch."

I get the nagging sense that's not the whole story, but she'll share when she's ready. If I try to squeeze the truth out, she'll go limper than a wrung-out rag.

"Okay, we'll go straight to the Tenaya Canyon trailhead. This time of year, the waterfalls are supposed to be raging, but drought conditions means that things aren't as they normally are. This is the driest year in the state's record." The ranger mentioned there might be a weather system moving in, a 20 percent chance of rain. Enough I'm glad we scored wet-weather gear from Scott and Jessie, but not enough that I'm worried about using it.

We drive up Tioga Road, and there's a turnout where we can look into the valley. I park at an empty spot and we climb out. There's a tourist snapping pictures on the far end. Otherwise it's just us.

"Whoa." Talia settles a hand on my back.

"Yeah." Because what else do you say? I've seen pictures of this valley since I was a kid, read countless rock climbing mags featuring these very granite walls. The beauty catches in my throat. It's humbling to be here, in their midst, and glimpse what Muir was on about. Yeah, maybe central California's valley has lost its wildflowers and grizzly bears, but there is still magic in the world.

"This. This is what I was looking for," I say.

"Me too," she whispers.

The other bloke leaves and the road behind us is quiet. It's a Wednesday, so not a lot of day-tripper traffic going into the high country. We stand in silence and watch the distant Bridalveil Fall pour over the cliff.

"It's weird, isn't it, seeing pictures of a place and then seeing it in person?" Talia says after a while. A red-tailed hawk swoops past with a scream as if agreeing with her assertion.

"How do you mean?"

"It's like I can know something is there, see it in a million pictures, but it's not right. It's like we have the exact idea of what it's supposed to be, how it's supposed to look, then—you realize, everything you thought you knew—"

"Doesn't even come close," I murmur.

She turns and catches my gaze, a slight flush creeping over her cheeks.

"That's how it feels," I whisper, "looking at you."

She blinks and the lovely sunrise color deepens, spreads down her neck. "I'm the most ordinary person ever."

"Says who?"

"My reflection in the mirror every single morning."

"Tell me what you see."

Her lips pull south in an embarrassed frown. "Just an average girl. Not a hag face or anything, but not a knockout. The kind of person you'd pass on the street and never notice. Just the usual. Nothing special."

I stare at her until she squeezes her eyes half-shut like my gaze hurts. "Do you know what I see, when I look at you?"

"Nope. I've voodooed you, obviously. I don't want you to overthink. The illusion might vanish upon reflection."

I settle my hands on her face so she can't look anywhere else. "You don't think I see you?"

Her eyes widen, pupils dilating until my heart sails through the blackness, into the boundless unknown, with no thought for the vanishing shore. "I'd been searching and searching until I saw you, and I didn't even know it."

"Searching for a girlfriend?"

"A girlfriend? A fucking girlfriend, Talia? Is that what you think you are to me?"

"I..." Her gaze flicks between my eyes and my mouth.

"You're home." She shakes from an invisible wind as I taste her mouth. When she returns the kiss, it's as if her lips brush over secret stones, rattling my insides with unsettled longing, noiseless promise. "I don't have the right words to explain my heart, but there's something infinite at work here. My love is as deep as the roots of these mountains."

She parts her lips and stares a long moment. "Um, I think you have pretty good words."

"You deserve better ones."

"Jesus." She throws her arms around my neck and buries her face into my shoulder. "Thank you."

"What for?"

She draws her head up and gives me a soft kiss. "Being born."

Talia turns back and climbs into the 4Runner. I stare out over the scoured rock. Once this place was blanketed beneath a glacier. I've been to the Antarctic and seen the vast ice sheets. What will happen if they melt further? People don't want to think about the hard stuff. We need to fight for what's left, because someday, maybe I'll have kids with this girl behind me. When I look into their faces, no way will I say, *Sorry I couldn't give you a better world. I was too busy watching TV or Googling stupid shit.*

I jump in the truck and start the ignition. "Kids."

Talia gives me a weird look.

"Want one?"

She startles. "Like this second?"

"No. In the long term."

"I'm not sure," she says carefully, as if each word is heavier than the next. "Do you?"

"Sure, someday."

"I'm afraid to mess one up," she says with a forced laugh. "I didn't exactly have a top role model."

"You'd love them at least."

"Your parents must love you."

I shrug. "I guess. If we ever have a kid, I'm going to do better."

"You will." She squeezes my leg. "God though. I can't imagine you with a little girl."

"Why not?"

"Because she'll grow up and get boyfriends."

"We'll make your dad proud, convert to Catholicism."

"You want a nun for a daughter?"

I shoot her a grin. "Right now I do."

"Maybe you'll spare some sympathy for my dad, then."

"Jesus. You're right." I shiver as the realization hits me. "I'm lucky he didn't murder me while I slept."

"That's why he tortured you with Chester."

"Fucking Chester."

"Still, it's cute to watch you get protective over theoretical children. What spurred all this?"

"Don't know. I just think about us, in the future. In life."

"Yeah." She fiddles with her seat belt. A nervous tic. Shit. Probably thinks I'm about to throw out another not-a-marriage sales pitch. The proposal I gave her last year as a way to keep her in Australia. Keep her with me. It was a mistake. One I've regretted a hundred times over. I only have one chance to do right by her on this.

"Look at that." A lake comes into view, bluer than the sky if that's possible.

"Tenaya Lake."

"This place is unreal."

"It means we're almost there." She looks at the map. "The trailhead is just up ahead."

"You ready for adventure?"

"We who are about to die salute you."

"Gallows humor, I like it."

"Then I'm your gal."

We park and unload. I put all the heavy stuff in my pack, leave Talia with her clothes, her sleeping bag and our snacks. I have the tent, stove, and the majority of the drinking water.

"I'll hold on to the map if that's cool," she says, tucking it into the drink pouch on the side of the bag.

"Okay, but do me a favor and put it in the top pocket. Zip it tight. We'll need that. Navigation might be tricky at a few points."

"I can barely read a compass."

I puff out my chest. "Stick with me, little lady."

She wanders around, spreading out all her stuff, before packing it back up.

"You are delaying."

"You're right." She throws stuff in the backpack, tosses it on, and tightens the waist strap. "I love you."

"You're not saying that in case they're your last words, are you?"

She flinches. "Why do you say that?"

"You seem worried, but look around. You've got a great day. Great scenery. A great guide."

"That's quite the advertisement."

I bend to tighten my boots. "I've been waiting for this for a long time."

She gives me a weird look. "Um, okay, but we only floated the idea like a little while ago."

"Yeah, well, you know. A lot's happened." I check my own pack. Make sure I've got everything I need. I look up and she gives me an uncertain smile. She's nervous, but only about the hike. She has no idea.

I wipe my palms on my pants. "Let's get going."

She pats the bonnet of the truck. "See you on the flip side, old buddy."

Our route will take us down a steep grade into the main valley. We should spit out right beneath Half Dome. The mountain is visible at the mouth of the canyon, far below our viewpoint in one of the highest parts of the park. Once we reach the end a shuttle will return us back here where we started.

She pulls out her phone. "Quick picture." She poses beside me, tilts her head against my shoulder. "Success. Neither of us blinked. I can't believe it." She peers at the screen. "Hey, we even have one bar of cell phone reception."

"That's depressing."

"No way. I'm glad for service."

"Got to make a bunch of calls, do you?"

"No, but if I go ass over teakettle off a cliff, you can call for help."

"But you'll have the phone."

"Shit, you're right, and yours is broken. Crap, here, better you carry it."

"Settle down, Captain."

"No, really. Please."

"Hold your own phone."

"It would make me feel way better." She is pleading. "I wreck stuff. I can't be trusted."

"Fine." I want to get going more than I want to argue, be on the trail before she starts to panic. Sure, there will be some challenges ahead, but I know she's up for it; we both are.

23

TALIA

*B*ran keeps us moving past the areas of greatest exposure. He holds my hand more times than I'm proud to admit, but he doesn't seem to mind. It's midweek so the place is quiet. We break for lunch on a wide, flat rock. A woman appears from around the corner, the first person we've seen since starting our hike.

"Hello." She waves. Her accent is French. Turns out she's Swiss and hiked up from the valley.

"How is it?" Bran asks.

She shrugs. "You've got rope. That's good. A few parts are tricky, but in this weather." She shrugs. "No problem. I'd hate to do it in low visibility though. Easy to get turned around."

"Weather looks fine."

She takes a long swig from her drink bottle, wanders to the edge, and looks out. She's the kind of badass woman that I'd love to be. The kind of girl maybe Bran deserves. But he's smiling at me, not her.

"What?" I murmur.

"You're doing well."

I roll my eyes.

"Hey, you are doing something that scares you."

"Don't like heights?" The hiker glances back before checking her watch.

"Not so much."

She frowns. "It gets more exposed."

My heart's dull thud reverberates to the soles of my boots. "Really?"

She nods. "But like I said, good weather. You'll do fine."

I take a bite out of my apple as she leaves, and choke. My throat is too dry.

"Don't worry about her," Bran says, patting my back.

I cough. "She thought it was a challenge. Did you see her? She was half mountain goat."

"Remember, one foot at a time, and breathe."

"I'm an anxious freak, remember?"

"What's the story you want to tell about yourself?" he asks.

"That I'm brave. Confident. Strong. Up to facing challenges and pushing through. If I get knocked on my ass I know when to keep going, or when to try another direction."

He tucks a loose lock of hair behind my ear. "That's a sight better than anxious freak."

"That fact still undercuts everything I do."

He stares at me, expression unreadable.

No more doom and gloom. "I did make a decision."

"Okay." He's hesitant.

"Whatever happens with the radio job gig, I want to move to the city, to San Francis—"

"We don't have to—"

"I know you feel like you want me to make a decision based on myself, but really? That's not how we should operate. In this case, you've got an awesome opportunity, a way to launch a career away from your family. Maybe someday you'll help with the foundation's work, but if you're not ready, why not go with Zavtra? Squillionaires offering dream jobs don't happen every day."

He shrugs. "I want you to feel like you have your own things going on."

"I'll figure my stuff out. There's a million people in the city. Someone will want to hire me."

"They will."

"And I'm going to begin therapy. I promise this time. Before, I was scared." My voice breaks, regret cuts me deep. So much time wasted rocking in corners, squandering the good moments.

Bran clutches me to him, holds me hard enough that fear can't blow me away. Life might carry on but we're traveling the road together. "Talia—"

"It's like I thought therapy would be an admission that I'm crazy, but that's the wrong way to look at it. I want to be my best self, Bran. For you. For me." The world distills to his mouth hovering on mine, and every time he breathes I can feel it, fuck, I can taste it, like the first sweet wind of spring after a long, barren winter.

"Captain." His voice is gruff. "You are one of the sanest people I know."

"That's not speaking highly for your circle of friends."

"I'm not retracing steps with you." He kisses each of my cheeks. "You're amazing. Deal with it." He glances over my shoulder and frowns.

"What?" I turn and my heart feels heavy. There's a cloud. A big, fat, purple cloud.

"Weather report said twenty percent chance of rain."

"Guess the odds aren't ever in our favor."

"Maybe it's a one-off."

"Yeah. Maybe."

The card with the skeleton flashes in my head. The old woman's raspy voice. *Death*.

"Let's get a move on. We'll put up camp in a few more hours."

We scramble down rocks as the trail disappears; soon our pace slows as we pick our way from cairn to cairn, loose rock piles that previous hikers have built to help define the route. Clouds come in fast and the temperature drops. It's not a question of if rain will fall. It's a matter of when.

We hit the first section that requires ropes and harnesses. Bran sets up a belay, gets me down with minimal fuss. He talks less and that makes me scared. What if he's nervous? We look around. There are three different options to move forward. "Which way?"

"You've got the map, correct?"

"Yeah, right here." I strip off my backpack and kneel, opening the zip. Nothing. "Weird. I must have stuck it inside instead." I unclasp the locks. Within two minutes I have emptied the contents of my backpack. It's not there. Shit.

I thrust my hand through my hair. "I must have set it down when I repacked at the last second."

"I don't remember seeing it left out."

"Me neither." Something Bran said once niggles my subconscious. "Didn't you say this place was cursed? Isn't Tenaya Canyon the Bermuda Triangle of the Sierras?"

"Just a legend."

"Well, maybe that legend took our map."

Death, she said, her voice a rasp.

"Uh, I think your distraction lost the map."

"This isn't my fault." I'm half yelling.

He doesn't say anything.

"Okay, this is my fault."

"Just an accident. Nothing for it now." His voice is tight. His fingers lock into a fist. "What's done is done. Okay, let's see." He looks around us with a grim expression. "I'm going to have to scout. See if I can pick up the right trail."

Rain starts to sprinkle. The granite underfoot is polished smooth from the glacier. Once it gets wet, this place is going to be as slippery as an ice rink.

"I'll go with you."

"No, I don't know what to expect. This is a safe place. You can sit tight."

"Okay. I can do that." Try not to cause any more problems.

"We'll be right." His face softens. "This is all part of the adventure, right?"

"Totally." We're bug-fucked and it's all my fault.

"It might take a bit, but I'll return soon as I get my bearings." Bran gives me an absentminded kiss on the cheek and disappears down the middle rise. I wait. And wait. The drizzle stops, but the wind begins to bite as surrounding granite absorbs the cooling temperature. After twenty minutes I get up and pace. How long is this going to take? After an hour I tiptoe toward the edge, cup my hands to my mouth. "Bran?"

Bran? Bran? Bran? Bran?

My echo bounces around me, mocking.

I inch forward. I'm not going to go far, obviously. Don't want to get lost in the rocky labyrinth alone. I peer down the rise Bran scrambled. No sign of him. In the far-off distance, a glint of metal catches my eye. There is a rusted engine. Part of a prop. A plane crashed here. Some time ago from the look of the rust.

Curse. Death.

Stop it!

"Bran?" I yell. Still no answer. I don't get it though. This was clearly the wrong way. The burned-out plane rests on a small ledge. There is no other place to go. Bran couldn't have gone down what looks to be a cliff edge, but I would have seen him if he came back up.

Unless he fell.

Panic grabs me with two cold fists, right in the gut. Okay. This has happened before. I remember being in Tasmania and freaking out that Bran had been swept off rocks near a stormy beach. He'd been perfectly fine. I'll wait as per the plan. He's got to come back. I'm sure he's fine. Everything's fine.

I look at the rock cracks overhead, so tempting to count them, zone out into a headspace of order, but no. I jerk my gaze away. Not going there, got to focus on healthier coping mechanisms.

Four hours later it's almost completely dark. Rain returns, a smattering of sprinkles dot the rocks. No one has come by. Bran hasn't returned. I can't go back to the car, because I don't have rope. I can't go forward because I don't know where to go.

Everything's fine, I say, my teeth chattering. *Everything's fine. Everything's fine.*

The phrase has grown more meaningless the longer I say it. I keep repeating the words, but it's like something sinister. Everything sounds like, *You are fucked. You should have listened to the old woman. You had a choice. You knew this didn't feel right. Intuition kept poking and you ignored it. Look what's happened. You should do something.*

I promised to sit still. I promised to wait. I trust Bran. I promised.

Are you going to sit here until the end of time? It's almost dark. Stop being a coward and find your man.

I don't know what to do. I'm scared, but less for myself than Bran. Is he okay? I put a bunch of rocks together in the shape of an arrow to point the direction of my planned route. This is pretty much the worst orienteering ever. I am not some sort of supergirl. I'm scared shitless. But I'll do this. I've got to find Bran.

I strap on my headlamp, and the light is laughably weak. Still, it's enough to see right in front of me. I won't be stupid. I won't go far. But I can't stay still any longer. If I go a little ways, maybe he'll see my light. Maybe he's not far. The ground tilts to a precarious degree and soon my quads are burning.

"Bran!"

Bran! Bran! Bran! Bran!

Nothing.

My weak light bounces off the rocks. Please. Please let him be safe. The temperature is falling fast. A misty chill gets under my thermal layer. I start to scramble back, but my foot slips. The drizzle turns to harder rain. I stop to throw on my jacket and waterproof pants. I can't get back up the rock. Not without seriously risking a huge accident. I inch lower. Within ten minutes the pitch is so steep that I'm on my ass, scooting in slow inches. The pants don't stop the cold. My butt is numb. At least there is one part of me that isn't hurting. My stomach might never untie from this knot. My face is wet with tears and rain.

What have I done? First, Pippa. Now Bran.

I ruin everything.

I throw back my head and unleash a scream. The void snatches it and nothing answers.

Then comes a rumble, followed by a boom. The unexpected thunder sends me hurdling belly down. The universe is laughing at me.

I wrap my hands over my head, can't stop whimpering.

No. Get up. Keep going. I keep a pace banana slugs would jeer at. Whatever. Time is what I don't lack. All I have is this endless night. Alone. Crawling in a canyon. Unable to find the person who matters to me more than anyone.

My headlamp flickers. Dims. The batteries are going out. Oh, no. Oh, hell no.

There's an overhang ahead, against the mountain, away from the edge. I scoot over and it's out of the wind. The ground is dry. I strip off my rain jacket and pants, teeth chattering hard enough they might break. My fingers are numb, so it takes me three tries to open the zipper on my backpack. I fumble out the sleeping bag and mat. I unroll the Therm-a-Rest and it fills with air. Bran has the tent.

"Please let him be safe," I say. To no one. To God. To Pippa.

Maybe she listens.

If not, I'd rather be the crazy girl talking to herself than sit in silence with my own thoughts. I turtle my head into the sleeping bag. My nose and cheeks burn as heat returns.

"Hey, Pip," I whisper. "I don't know if you're there, but if you are, I need you to help me cut a deal. Don't let the death card be for Bran. Please. Have whoever it is who does these things take me instead. It's my fault. I was careless. I got distracted and forgot the map. I'm so lost, Pip. I don't know where I am. I don't know what I'm doing. Every time I think I've figured my way out, it's the wrong direction."

Thunder booms again. The universe is continuing to mock, or rumbling in agreement.

"I'm sorry, Pippa. For what I did, with Tanner. You know that, but I needed to say it. And not just because I'm terrified. You were my best friend. You were everything. I'm what's leftover and it sucks. I thought having Tanner would give me some of what made you. But instead it took you from me." I wipe my nose, crying in earnest now. "I saw him recently. He looks good. I think we're cool now, but you and me…how about us?"

My hours in fight or flight have sent my adrenal system into a crash. Exhaustion hooks into my brain and begins to drag me down.

Here.

Pippa's voice carries on the wind. Goose bumps break across my belly. Maybe it's a dream. Maybe this canyon really is some Bermuda Triangle portal.

Nothing else is said, but a sensation settles over me, a feeling of being held. Not a lover's embrace but a sister's. "I told you I'd live for both of us and I try," I whisper. "I try my best, but I wreck everything."

Warmth spreads through my belly, slow and comforting like I've consumed a bowl of soup.

"I love Bran, Pippa. I love him. It's not a crush or puppy lust. Like this is it. I'm done for." I go quiet because those words have another meaning. "If that card was right, if death is in my future. Please. Let it be me who is done for. Me for him, okay? Promise? Everyone loves you. You must have great connections up there. Me for him, got that? Me for him."

The thunder comes again. Fainter. Enough that I convince myself it is begrudging assent from the powers that be. I shove my head out of the bag, push myself to the edge of the overhang. Rain hits my face. "You hear that? Me for him!"

My echo drowns in the torrent.

I retreat back, grab my water, and take a sip. The swallow pulls the lump in my throat. The ache spreads through my neck. "If we make it out of this, I promise to stop letting the bad stuff define me. At the end of the day, that's not what matters. I don't want to look down anymore. I want to keep my head up, keep an eye on what's to come. Because there are good things out there, and sometimes they happen when you least expect it. One day, you're sleepwalking through life, and the next you meet someone who wakes you up. A person who makes you want to try to dig in for your best self. That's Bran. He's so close to being the guy he's been fighting to become. He deserves a shot, because holy crap, he is amazing, someone who will do amazing things. The world needs more people like him. Heroes."

I fall asleep, cocooned in the down sleeping bag, mumbling to my dead sister. "Me for him. Me for him. Me for him."

24
BRAN

y forearms scream in protest on the final rise. I allow myself a respite and settle my forehead against the granite. I'm stuck on yet another cliff, the third one, and by far the trickiest to navigate. "You are a bloody idiot," I mutter to myself. I hate that I left Talia alone. After she discovered she'd lost the map, there was no easy way back to the car. Moving forward seemed a safer option, and in trying to find a way out, I selected one of three possible routes. I chose unwisely and just like the guy in *Indiana Jones and the Last Crusade*, I paid a harsh penalty. The route took me down a near vertical ridgeline. At one point I stumbled across a large bone, bleached and weathered by the elements. Hopefully from a deer and not some poor lost bastard. I passed the wreckage of a long-ago plane crash and reached a ledge. Below I spotted what looked like a cairn, hundreds of meters in the distance. The way down was too crazy for Talia to manage. I figured I'd down-climb, get to the trail, and retrace my steps back up to her. Should have been easy.

Except for the part where I messed up. Halfway down the

climb I realized that while I could make it, it was going to be fucking slow going. I had to throw off my backpack. It dropped with a sickening thud. A reminder of what would happen if I lost a foothold. I'd gotten myself into a situation that could turn deadly with one false move. I tried not to think about mountain lions prowling the canyon, or falling, breaking an ankle then crossing paths with a big bloody bear. People think Australian animals are scary, but shit, imagine five hundred kilos of fur eating off your face. No way. Give me a bloody snake any day of the week.

Sure, I've climbed a bit, but mostly on the You Yangs, hills outside of Melbourne, short routes on relatively small granite outcrops. This is a whole new game, but I try to remind myself the principles are the same—handhold to handhold, foothold to foothold. Took forever, but I made it through the worst before the rain fell. By dark, I was crouched on a ledge, legs quivering from nerves and exhaustion and grateful as hell for my rain gear. Night settled in, a dark without the mercy of the moon, and through the long hours one word pulsed in time to my heart.

Talia.

Talia.

Talia.

Dawn's light is muted by the thick clouds. Did she stay still through the long night? "Please, hold tight, sweetheart," I murmur. She won't be able to go back the way we came, not without ropes. And I hope to God she doesn't go forward, looking for me. Fear pours on my doubts, like petrol to a slow-burning fire. The resulting blaze sears my lungs.

What if she gets into trouble and I'm not there?

What happened in Antarctica, with Justine and the crane, I almost caused a disaster. What if my luck's run out? No. Shit.

Fuck. Talia's okay. She has to be okay. I need to shake these charred thoughts off like ash. Sweat breaks over my body. I can't afford damp hands, got to slow down my heart and settle myself. It takes a few deep breaths before my fingers stop trembling. I press my forehead against the rock.

"I'm coming back to you," I whisper to Talia, my lips against the earth. "Wait for me. Wait for me."

It's time to focus. I've got climbing experience, but without rock chalk and proper shoes, it's a trick. My foot slips on a hold. My hiking boots don't have the right grip. I balance on one foot, precarious as fuck, and get off one boot, then the other. My bare feet settle onto the stone and I feel hope return to my bones. Taking it old school, I can do this. She's just ahead. She's going to be less than enthusiastic about how we have to get down, but we'll manage.

"Please let her be there." I say the words aloud. To whom? I don't know. Whoever's listening.

I yank myself over the top and . . . nothing. A chill races through my veins, turning my vital organs to ice. "Shit." I quicken my pace up the trail. Fucking hell, I even have the cell phone. She's been out here all night. Anything could have happened. A fall. An animal. Hypothermia. No. Stop. I got her into danger and I'll bloody well get her out. Each time I turn a corner I hold my breath, *maybe this time*, and her continued absence settles over me like a mantle of lead. The harder it crushes, the faster I hike, near at a run as much as the terrain allows. I trip on a loose rock and skitter back as it bounces off the ledge, plummets into air. Talia's terrified of heights, gets vertigo looking out a second-story window. I wanted to take her out here to get her out of her head, show her fear can be conquered, as long as we're together.

Together doesn't include leaving her alone. Fear sinks its roots into my gut, all thorns and no blossom. "Talia," I yell, turning the next corner, rising fear making it hard to swallow. "Tal—oof." Something hits me hard in the ribs. I drop to my knees, but am tackled to the ground. Warm, soft curves press up against me.

"You—"

That's as far as I get before she cuts me off with a hard kiss. A pointy rock gouges the back of my skull. Her hair falls around us like a curtain.

"G'day," I whisper.

"You don't look like a ghost." Talia splays her hands across my chest.

"I don't suppose I do."

"You aren't dead." Her voice quavers on the last word.

"Not unless this is heaven." I wind her tresses around my hand and drag her close. Her lips are soft and taste like salt. Guilt hacks into my belly like a spade. "I should never have left you."

Tears glisten from the edges of her eyelashes. "I should never have let you go."

"We need to stick together," I whisper, meaning each word more than she can know.

"Always."

I lace my fingers with hers and plant a kiss on her forehead. "Me and you."

"You and me." She takes a deep breath through her nose. "Are you sure you're okay? Did you eat? Were you cold? Was it dangerous?"

"I am now. A little. Yes. Yeah."

She runs her hands down my arms. "I'll never be able to stop touching you. I was so scared."

"I need to ask you something," I whisper against her skin. Can she feel my heart pick up speed?

"No."

"No?"

She shakes her head. "Tell me all the things, but only after you prove that you are real. Love me. Please. Just love me."

I jerk when she skims my shaft through my shorts. My body registers the action before my tapped out brain does. "I don't have any protection. My bag is below."

"I do." She scrambles to standing and helps me up. "Jesus. Your fingers."

"I had to climb."

"Bran!" She presses my hands to her heart. "God, these look so sore."

I cup her breasts and groan at the rich, heavy weight against my palms. "This makes them feel better."

"Come." She takes gentle hold of my hand and pulls me toward a deep rocky overhang. There is her backpack and sleeping bag. "See, I made a little camp."

Pride grips me. "You did good, Captain. Exactly what you should have done. I'm so bloody proud of you." Emotion roughs up my voice. "Thank you for staying alive. Fucking hell, knowing you were up here, alone." My hold on her turns more like a clutch.

"Well, I wasn't that brave. I almost died from at least five different heart attacks." She kisses the side of my neck, smoothing my hair. "I had to trust you'd come back."

"I'm so sorry, you were left alone in the dark."

"Not so alone," she whispers. Her dark brown eyes hold mine, calm and steady—full of faith.

I start to ask, but she tugs my shirt up my waist. I fist it over my head and discard it on the rocky ground. The cool dawn air licks my skin, and I roll my bunched shoulders. She pulls off her own tank top, exposes her pink sports bra. Behind her are nothing but mountains. Getting naked outdoors, something about the action is primal, as if millennia of instinct coalesce, generations of ancestors who coupled under the sky. I step forward and her stomach hollows from the deep breath. She dreamily raises her arms as I pull her bra free. Her breasts, unbound, hang sweet. I dip, dragging my lower lip over the soft swell.

"Bran." Her voice is ragged. I cover her nipple with the flat of my tongue. It hardens into an adorable button that I flick, enjoying every hiss of breath she utters in response.

"Don't want this one to feel lonely." I move to the other side and repeat the action.

Her laugh is slow, woozy. When she rocks her head back, that lovely arch of her neck demands my full attention. I hunt out the sensitive spot beneath her ear, and hold her hips steady as her legs give way. I dip her backward. "I got you."

"I know." Her eyes close.

I turn my head and rest my cheek for a moment on the place above her heart. The vital pulse grounds me. I ease her down onto the sleeping bag and crawl on top of her.

"Am I squishing you?"

She tugs me closer. "The exact perfect amount."

"You slept here?"

"I wouldn't really call it sleep." She rests a hand on my cheek. "I worried."

"Bloody oath." I shake my head, not wanting to relive those hours. "So did I."

"Were you in danger?"

I think back to the cliff face. "A little."

"A little, like the amount for normal people? Or for you?"

I nuzzle her cheek. "All I thought about was getting back to you."

She hauls herself on to her elbows, rubs her nose against mine. "My job was easy. Wait and trust."

"That sounds hard."

"It was," she says, quietly. "I almost couldn't do it."

"I don't deserve your trust. Maybe this hike was a stupid idea."

"I might have expressed the same sentiment, in slightly stronger terms, about a million and twenty-five times last night."

I cup the back of her head. "I'm so, so sorry."

"You know what? Someday this will be something we laugh about."

"Will we?"

She smiles. "Yeah. I think we really will."

It's short work to get naked, grab a condom from her bag, but once we're ready, all I want is slow. Her breathy moan washes over me like a sweet wave. I want to float in this space forever.

"I like that sound, sweetheart." I cover her with every square inch of my body.

She makes it again. "That one?"

"Those little sighs do things to me." I grind my hips slow against hers. She returns the pressure. Her hair spreads around her like a wild golden river, bursting the banks. I trace the dip in her waist, the swell of her hips. Our breath comes faster. I'm not inside. But the friction starts a slow build. Her breasts press against my chest and it's impossible to restrain a shudder. I take a deep breath. She smells of earth, sunscreen, and her shampoo—tangerine and basil.

She slides her hand to the sides of my lower belly. "I adore these muscles." She opens her legs another inch.

I'm incapable of coherent speech. She's so wet that my dick slides in of its own accord. I hold back, rock shallow, teasing us both.

She clasps my ass. "In me."

"Talia." I'm there. A wave strike. A burning moon. Kiss by kiss we go deeper into infinity. Two bodies, a single sweetness. Our cries bounce off stone. My every touch is a question, and she gives all the answers.

—

"You really are a man of many skills," Talia says, watching intently as I finish boiling the water on the camp stove for coffee.

"I'm just practical."

"A hot breakfast will help us face the day?"

"Keeping you well caffeinated is my top priority."

She giggles, reaching as I hand her a mug. "I love how well you know me."

We're packed and ready to go, but I wanted to make our reunion last a little longer. We've shared so many moments, special seconds that bordered on perfect. Here, sitting beside her, hip to hip, as we quietly watch the morning sun cast shadows on the canyon walls, and sip coffee is another for the list.

After breakfast, it's a short hike back to where I'd only just come from. Talia stands on the edge of the cliff, her hand locked in mine. Below is a turquoise pool. My bag is off to one side. So are my boots.

"You climbed this cliff barefoot?"

"Yeah." *And a few before that.*

"And this is the only way down?"

I read about this section online before we left. "We could use ropes, but the jump is easier. The on-foot route through this section isn't passable because of the rain; there's a temporary waterfall in effect over the path."

"Cliff jumping? I'm not sure if I can really do this."

I read about this pool in the trail guide. "It's plenty deep enough. We'll go at the exact same time."

"Oh, Bran." She covers her eyes.

"Talia, Talia, Talia." I turn her to face me, rest my forehead against hers. "Last night, it was all I could think. Your name. Talia. It's my own personal mantra. The three sexiest syllables in the English language."

She attempts a smile. "You're not so bad yourself, Mr. Lockhart."

My heart swells until nothing is left inside me but love, unbeaten and bright. I'm ready for what this decision will cost me; the price is everything, my entire life. Now. This is the moment. My backpack is below, but screw it, I'm doing it. "Like that name?" I kiss the fragile skin at the corner of her eye.

"Lockhart? Yes, sure, I love it."

"I want you to have it." I wait a beat to let my words sink in. "Last year, I asked you to marry me, but not the right way."

She goes utterly still. I swear she doesn't even blink. My face reflects in her dilated pupils.

"Talia Stolfi." I swallow. I brace her face between my hands. My muscles tremble, not from strain, but stunning fervor. "I don't want a not-a-marriage with you. I need the real deal. Me. You. This. Forever. I love you more than anything on this entire bloody planet. You are the best person I know."

She blinks. Her face, the one I can read as easily as a book, is closed.

My mouth dries. "I love you. I want you to be my wife. I have a ring. It's down there in my pack. I was going to do this properly last night. Make it romantic. But I don't think that's me. I don't have those moves. All I can do is swear that my love for you is the realest, best part of myself."

"You have a ring?" she whispers.

"Yeah. I've had it a long time. I bought it last year when we were in Melbourne. I've always known I would ask you the right way. Fuck. And now I've gone and asked in exactly the wrong way."

"Yes."

"I'm sorry. I should have waited."

"No!" She grips my shoulders.

"You won't?"

"I will."

Is she starting to cry? "Talia, I haven't slept all night. You are driving me mad."

"No, you shouldn't have waited." She threads her fingers through my hair. "Yes, I will marry you. And fair warning"—she pulls in a way that hurts but feels bloody incredible—"I am going to spend the rest of my life driving you crazy."

"You're serious?"

"Oh, prepare yourself. You'll be begging for mercy."

"I mean, yes. You'll do this?"

"Marry you. For real? Without every possible disclaimer?" Her smile, I defy any precious stone to outshine her face in this moment.

"No disclaimers. I want a one hundred percent honest straight-up forever with you." I crush my mouth against hers in a searing kiss that settles into a softness filled with the promise of our future together. I know I'll hold on to this moment, like I'll hold on to her, forever.

"I can't believe you bought a ring." She nips my bottom lip.

"Not just a ring. A Killiecrankie diamond," I whisper.

"What's that?"

"It's a type of topaz, found on one of Tasmania's islands. Beautiful and real, just like you."

Her gasp is a laugh and a cry. "I'd love to see it."

"You will. Once you jump."

"Do you see my legs?"

"I do." The poor things are trembling. I bracket her waist in my hands, rock her against me until we're belly to belly. "You can do this, Captain. You are braver than you know."

"If I stand here any longer, I'm going to pass out and fall in."

"That doesn't count. It needs to be an active choice."

"A leap of faith?"

I nod and squeeze her closer. "That's it, exactly."

She bites the inside of her cheek. "We should do it before I change my mind."

"One." I step back and take her hand.

"Two," she shouts.

"Three!" We call together, and jump.

25

TALIA

ogwood trees burst into perfect white blossoms, back-dropped by four-hundred-foot waterfalls. We're driving out of Yosemite, and I wouldn't be surprised if a unicorn emerged from the forest. The fairyland setting perfectly matches my bright mood.

"Don't you just love how it catches the light?" I wave my ring under Bran's nose. It's low-key and lovely. I'm powerless to stop admiring it.

"You showed me five minutes ago. And ten minutes before that." He playfully nips the tip of my finger while keeping his eyes on the road ahead.

"Look again. This time it's extra pretty."

"Not as pretty as you." He takes hold of my hand, rests it against the hard muscle above his knee.

"Aw, you're the sweetest."

"Don't tell."

"The secret is mine." I mime zipping my lips.

A digital beep sounds, and my nerve endings fire to life. Service in the national park has been patchy. We've been out of range the whole drive back down.

"Think we have cell reception yet?" Bran plays a cool cucumber well, but won't win any Oscars for this purposefully dumb act.

"Um, pretty sure that's what the noise was." I reach over into his pocket. "What if the radio station called?"

"Only one way to find out."

Thud. Thud. Thud. My heart pounds in my ears as I check the messages. One from Sunny. Another from Beth. Nothing major, just the usual check-in. They want updates on Wyatt, and to see how I'm doing. They are going to seriously flip when I tell them we got engaged. The last message begins. "Hello, this is Diana Foster from NPR. We were very impressed with your interview last week and would like to offer you the program assistant position." She keeps talking, but it's impossible for me to hear over my shrieking.

"You did it." Bran's hand squeeze reveals he never doubted me. Not even for a second.

"Yes." The reality hollows my bones, makes me feel featherlight. "Holy crap, I really did it."

"We're moving to San Francisco, baby."

"Oh, God." I start laughing.

"What?"

"You're going to turn into an even bigger hipster."

He bristles. "I'm not a fucking hipster."

"Only a little." I strain the belt and kiss his cheek. "But you're my fucking hipster."

The sign announcing Mariposa is just ahead.

"Hey." I trace an idle pattern over his knuckles with my thumb. "Think we can stop at that motel?"

"Forget something?"

I clear my throat. "Yeah."

He turns down a side street and parks beneath the Vag Inn sign. "Back in a sec." I jump out and inhale a deep breath, let the pine and dry grass scents root me in the present. This is kind of silly, but I need to do this, go talk to the tarot woman, tell her she was wrong with that stupid death card.

When I open the door into the motel lobby, the Christmas bell tied above the door jingles.

"Coming!" The familiar smoker-gravel voice announces from behind the beaded curtain. The old woman appears. She's dyed her hair from jack-o'-lantern orange to a red that would pass unnoticed in a crime scene. "Well, look who the cat dragged in."

"Yes, yeah, hello. I stayed here a few nights ago?"

"Oh, I remember. You drew death and scrammed."

"No. I didn't."

The woman plops into her office chair and leans back with a heavy sigh. "I'm seventy-nine and my mind don't always work like it should, but when it comes to the cards, I never forget."

"I mean, yes. I did draw death. But it was a mistake."

"The cards are never wrong."

"They are." Crap, I don't want to raise my voice at the elderly. "Sorry. I mean, there was an error, ma'am."

"You weren't ready to listen."

"Listen?"

She points to the rattan chair. "Pull that over and take a seat."

I glance out the door. "Um, my boyfriend is waiting outside."

"It does men good to wait on a woman. Now, come on, dearie, I don't bite. Hard." She smiles, revealing a thick glob of lipstick on her front tooth.

LIA RILEY

256

"Oh, no!" I mimic brushing my teeth. "You have something stuck there."

She plucks a pocket mirror off a pile of receipts and grimaces at her reflection. "Aw, hell and a hot dog." She grabs a tissue from the Kleenex box, wipes, and then swipes her tongue over, polishing her front tooth. "There. Now, where were we?"

"Death. Or rather, not death."

"Definitely death. Ah-ah." She holds up a finger to silence me. "There's one privilege of age. I talk. You listen."

"Okay." I curl my toes with impatience.

"Death," she says, her tone dramatic. "Death is an ending, yes?"

I nod, uncertain.

"But it's also a beginning. That's what the card told you. Time to clear away the old and welcome the new. Change is scary, but this time it will have a positive, cleansing, transformative force in your life. Are you following me?"

"Yeah, I think so." I clear my throat. "Yes, I am."

"What I'm saying has relevant application?" She cocks her head, her eyes bright.

I twist the ring on my finger and nod.

"The death card teaches it's time to move forward. Rebirth."

"So not doom and destruction."

She explodes with a sound somewhere between an asthmatic donkey bray and belly laugh. "Heavens no. I tried to tell you that last time, but you ran away."

"I've done that a lot." I smile ruefully. "Mostly from myself."

She gives me a long, cryptic look. "You can run and run but you'll never escape you."

"I'm excited for what's ahead." I'm not perfect, never have been and never will be, but that doesn't mean my life can't be incredible.

"Good." She gives a brisk nod. "Because change comes. Ready or not."

"Are you sure I'm doing this right?" Wyatt wiggles in my arms as I clutch him to my chest.

Jessie laughs. "You're doing great. Maybe not so tight though."

"Oh, right. He probably needs to breathe and stuff."

"Isn't he something?" Dad beams at me clutching my kid brother, like it's the coolest thing he's seen in a long time.

"He's cute. Way cuter than a newborn should be." I mean it. He's all delightful yawns and loveable smiles. "I guess it figures though. I mean genetically. Babies need to be cute so that you can cope with all the work, right?"

"There's a lot of that." Jessie flops on the couch and rests her head on Dad's shoulder. "I'm pooped."

"Does he always move this much?" Bran asks.

"Always," Jessie and Dad answer in unison.

Wyatt kicks his foot and barely misses my nose. "He'll have a great future career in interpretive dance."

"So you're heading into the city to apartment shop tomorrow?" Jessie asks.

"Yep." Bran takes my hand, interlaces our fingers. We both accepted our jobs. All we need is a place to live.

Dad gives us a thumbs-up. He took the news about our engagement really well. We don't have plans to get married yet, but it'll come. I just want to enjoy this moment. No rush.

"Want to hold him?" I ask Bran.

He shifts his weight. "I don't know."

"Go on. He'll gyrate for your pleasure."

"Whoa, whoa, whoa," he says as I pass him over.

"Just support his neck and you'll be all good," Dad says. "I'm going to start dinner." He rises to his feet and Jessie stands, too, bumping his hip with hers.

"I'll help. Or at least uncork the wine." She giggles as he gives her a quick tickle.

My heart is full seeing him so content.

"Okay. Okay. I got this," Bran mutters, more to himself than to me.

Wyatt stretches out his two tiny fists, yawns, and drops off to sleep.

"You are a Baby Whisperer." I'm giggling more from the cuteness overload than anything.

"If your position doesn't pan out in Silicon Valley, you can always be my manny," Jessie says over her shoulder before disappearing after Dad into the kitchen.

My phone buzzes. It's a text from my mom. She sent an out-of-focus picture of the sunset along the coast. We don't talk much, but sharing the odd photo has been a good start, a gentle way to begin repairing everything that was broken. Bran sits back on the couch, cuddling my baby brother. Persimmon purrs against his leg. He notes my smile. "What?" His voice is soft. His dimples put in an appearance.

I shrug and reach to smooth the unruly hair on the back of his head. Sometimes happiness doesn't require any words. Sometimes happiness just is.

Behind him on the wall is a framed poster of the Golden Gate Bridge with Alcatraz in the foreground. For far too long my life was an island prison. I peered through steel bars at the world's bustling vibrancy, believing everyone had the answer except me. I was trapped, screaming, locked in solitary confinement.

And I escaped.

There were sharks in the water but I fended them off, hauled myself to shore, sobbing and gasping. I made the prison. So I have to be the one who dismantles it brick by brick, refashioning my life into something new. Build my own version of a castle in the clouds.

Bran glances over and it's a spectacular sight, this new smile of his. He used to hold back, like if he grinned too wide, he'd break, or give too much away and needed to conserve himself. Lately, things are different. Now he smiles with his whole self and every time I see it, I know.

My own grin feels permanent. We're going to make it. Wyatt doesn't stir when Bran sets him gently in the bouncer on the floor between us.

"You're pretty amazing with him," I say, unable to hold back a swoon when Bran tickles my brother's chubby cheek.

"You're the amazing one," he murmurs, and leans in, keeping our gazes connected.

"Am I?" I tilt my face. His breath ignites my skin before our lips brush. We kiss, and kiss again, sweet, soft, but with enough intensity to induce shivers. Our foreheads graze and breaths mix.

"Talia," he whispers, feeding me my own name like it's something rare and delicious. "Thank you for saying yes to me."

"Thank you for asking." I tease my tongue into his mouth, nothing much, just a flirtatious promise of later. Because we can do this tonight. Tomorrow. All next week. I'm saying yes to it, to everything, every day with Bran.

He peppers kisses up my cheek until I'm utterly helpless yet stronger than I've ever been.

Guess it turns out that I am a lot of things.

I'm the girl who will always miss her dead sister. I'm the older sibling to Wyatt, the world's sweetest baby boy. I'm a daughter of two fallible humans. I'm a person who took her life back from fear. I've become a woman, and I love a guy who is finally a man.

I turned my world upside down for love. There were times when the journey was hard, intense, even downright terrifying. But guess what? The road will always leave the dark wood if you stick it out and go the distance. And the moment you step into the light is better than any poor imagining.

But here's the catch.

You'll never believe such beauty exists—not really—not unless you have the guts to brave life, go off the map, and find your own way there.

The End